**Adventure House
Presents**

FAR EAST ADVENTURE STORIES

February 1931

This reprint edition is a facsmile edition. Variations in print
and quality are mostly attributable to the rough woodpulp
original this reprint edition is based on.

ISBN: 1-59798-071-4

**Published by Adventure House
914 Laredo Road
Silver Spring, Md 20901
www.adventurehouse.com
sales@adventurehouse.com**

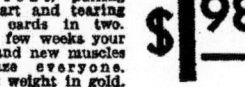

A Frank Appeal:

This is an earnest request for the readers' co-operation. In fact it is so earnest that it is almost a prayer. The publishers of FAR EAST Adventure Stories need assistance and need it immediately. For five months now we have put out a fiction magazine that is worthy of being classed with the best on the newsstands. And for four months the newsstand circulation has been gaining steadily—but not fast enough to keep the wolf from the door unless the satisfied readers put their shoulders to the wheel and help us with this issue, help us to gain more newsstand sales.

We have tried to put out a magazine that would be creditable and a leader in its class. That we have succeeded in doing that, we are most certain, judging at least by the volume of letters that has come in to our offices; and the comments of persons who are supposed to know just what a good men's fiction magazine is.

But with all that, our newsstand sale has not been large enough to enable us to carry on much longer, unless you readers get busy and help us to sell this present issue. The task is really very simple and will put a burden on none of you, but the results will be astounding—if carried out.

All that we ask is that each one of you readers, who have bought and enjoyed the past and present issues, take it upon yourselves, individually and collectively, to see that one other person who has never before bought FAR EAST Adventure Stories does so now. If each one of you will do that, FAR EAST Adventure Stories will become an immediate success from a newsstand sales standpoint—as it is now from a literary and good reading standpoint.

The publishers, in return for your hearty co-operation, will then strive even harder to make FAR EAST Adventure Stories absolutely the best magazine in its class.

But, unless you do? Well, like the Arabs, the publishers will have to take down their tents and steal away silently in the night with the knowledge in their minds, that they ran a good race but lost.

Will you readers who have enjoyed FAR EAST Adventure Stories thus far let us lose?

Our future is in your hands. And whether you respond to this frank appeal or not, we thank you for your interest of the past.

THE PUBLISHERS

W. R. Bamber, President

H. C. Langer, Vice-President

A. F. Feldman, Secretary

(*Coming Up Announcement on Page* 152)

Action Adventure East of Suez

FAR EAST
Adventure Stories

VOLUME TWO   FEBRUARY, 1931   NUMBER 2

CONTENTS

Manuscripts for FAR EAST Adventure Stories should be submitted to Fiction Publishers, Inc.,
158 West Tenth St., New York City.

PRINTED BY WILLIAM GREEN, A CORPORATION, NEW YORK, U. S. A.

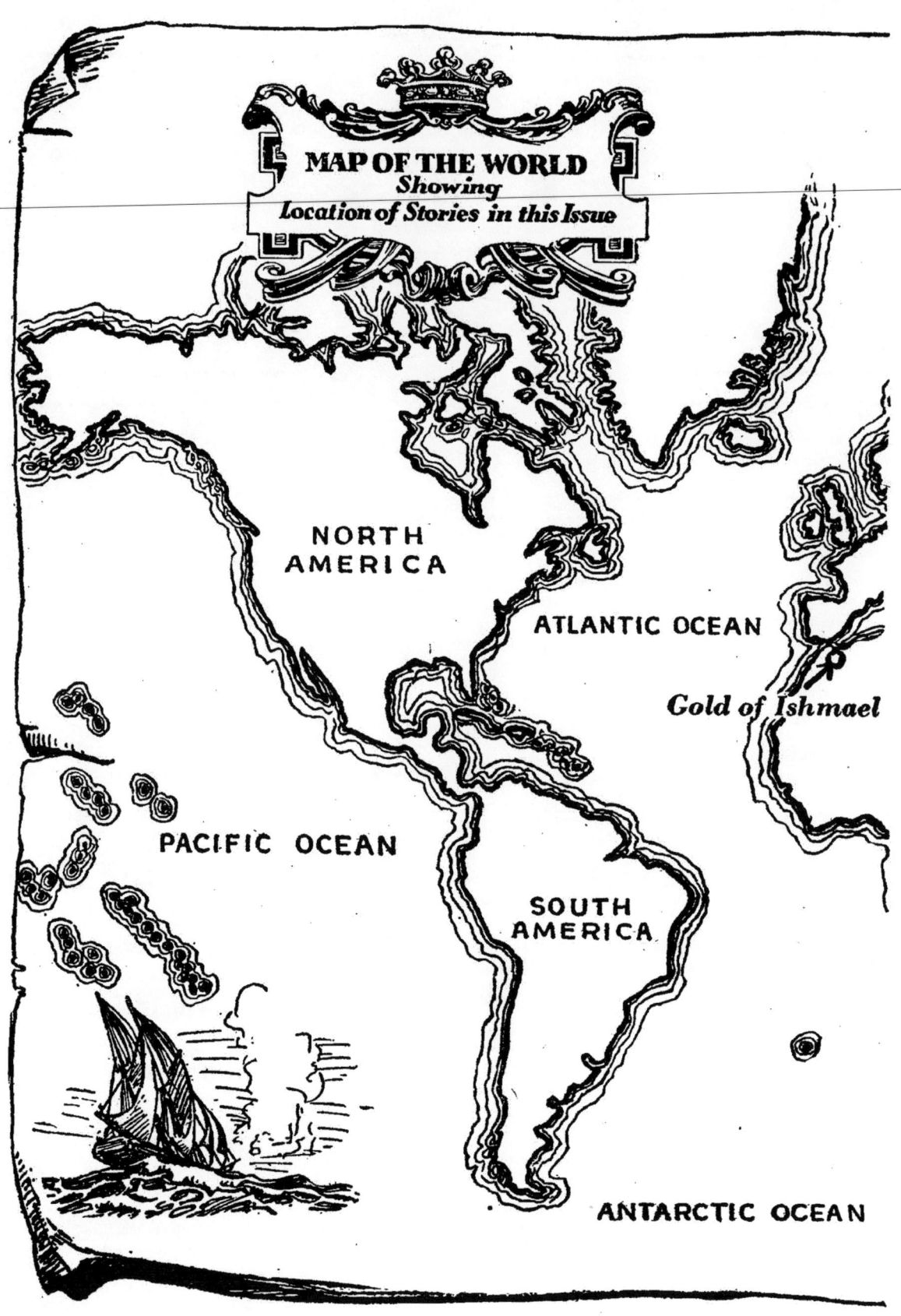

MAP OF THE WORLD
Showing
Location of Stories in this Issue

NORTH AMERICA

ATLANTIC OCEAN

Gold of Ishmael

PACIFIC OCEAN

SOUTH AMERICA

ANTARCTIC OCEAN

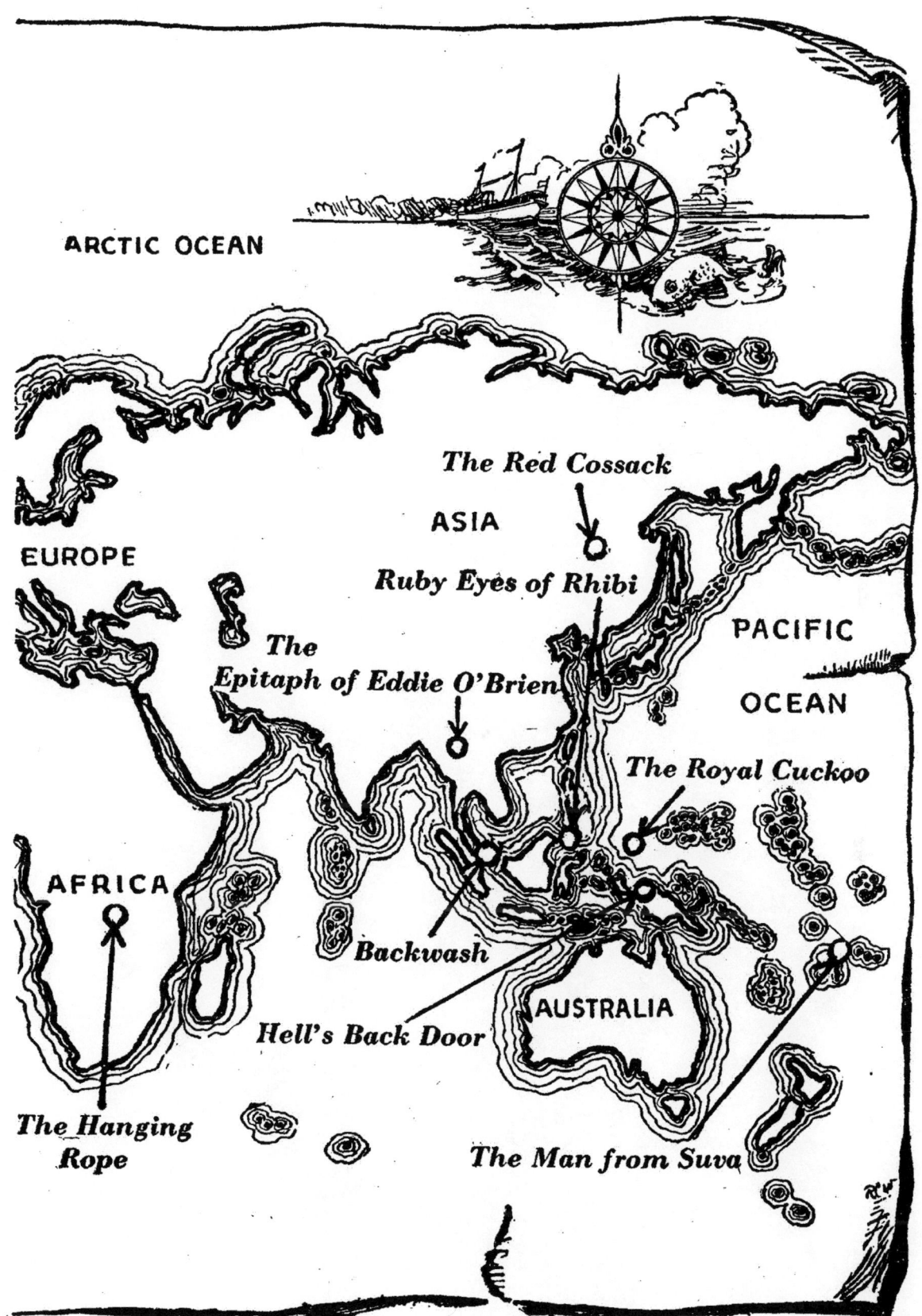

ARCTIC OCEAN

The Red Cossack

ASIA

Ruby Eyes of Rhibi

EUROPE

PACIFIC

The
Epitaph of Eddie O'Brien

OCEAN

The Royal Cuckoo

AFRICA

Backwash

Hell's Back Door

AUSTRALIA

The Hanging
Rope

The Man from Suva

GOLD OF

Part one of a new serial novel of Morrocan
intrigue which hails the return of
that amazing character
John Solomon

ISHMAEL By

H. BEDFORD-JONES

Chapter One

ENTER JOHN SOLOMON

 IT CERTAINLY is funny how you run into people. Here I was in Morocco— I had come down from Algiers across the whole country—and flattered myself that I did not know a soul in all Casablanca. I walked around the corner from the hotel, and went to a cafe to get a drink, and there was Tom Keyes sitting at a table as large as life.

"My gosh! It's Hank Smith or I'm a Dutchman!" he cried, and we shook hands. "What on earth are you doing here? I thought you were back in Chicago or somewhere writing newspaper stories and uplifting the human race. Heard you got married last year. Where's the wife?"

"Divorced," I said, just to let him have the news straight. "She turned out to be a paranoiac, tried to have me locked up for lunacy, raised hell generally. I divorced her, got a commission to do some stories on Algiers and Morocco, and here I am, a sadder and wiser man, free as a bird and ready to paint the town red. Let's have a drink."

"Let's have six," said Keyes. "Got ten thousand francs on you? Or can you raise it?"

"Can't raise passage home until I cable," I said. "I've got the equivalent of forty dollars in African money. Ten thousand francs! Gosh, no!

Why aren't you selling automobiles in Denver?"

"Because I'm selling 'em here. Invested my life's savings in the North Africa agency, see? And, Hank— listen! Don't ever take on anything in foreign parts. I've been here a year, and what they do to you when you're not looking is a crime—"

Come to find out, Tom Keyes was down on his luck, but he was not whining about it. He did not look ruined and he did not act ruined, and as a matter of fact he was not ruined —he was just three hours ahead of it. At five that same afternoon he would be sitting in jail, unless his unpaid bills were met. There was not the least chance of their being met, and jail in Morocco is not operated as a philanthropy. It is meant to be unpleasant, and it succeeds.

Keyes looked cheerful enough—he always did. He had a wide-eyed way of looking at the world which inspired confidence; dark hair, gray eyes, a hearty laugh, medium build. All in all, a sensible, solid sort. Not at all like me. I stand six foot one stripped, am long and lean and skinny, with a broken nose that was never set right and a habit of frankness which may be refreshing but does not make the wrong sort of people like me. A heart of gold, you understand, but nevertheless a general air of cussedness, as I have been informed at various times; if you want to believe my late unlamented better half, Hank Smith is an undiluted brute. Suit yourself.

We tried to figure things out, while before us surged all the astonishing life of the Place de France. Here in

Casablanca, the chief port of Morocco, met the old life and the new, at right angles—shuffling Arabs, trim French officers, Jews with flowing robes and black caps, horses, autos, trucks going to and from the rocks, large and small autobusses. Across from us rose the old walls of the native quarter or medina, in sharp contrast to the newly opened branch of a great Paris department store. And Arabs everywhere, hitching their awkward jellabs up over one shoulder, white Arabs, black Arabs and all the colors in between flowing past us.

Raising the money was out of the question for me, my account being already overdrawn. Hank Smith seldom has any money; my philosophy is that wealth is good for only one thing—to make you comfortable. I was comfortable enough, and broke. I plied Keyes with all sorts of suggestions, but he had overlooked no bets. He was through, done for.

So there we sat. At a pinch, I might help; I could go to the consulate, show my papers, and have him cable for the money on the plea that I was the one in debt. It would mean losing my job, but that was better than letting Tom Keyes go to jail.

Of course, the two of us were conspicuous enough, since American business men always stand out with sharp distinction from tourists or Frenchmen. Thus, if anybody were looking for Tom Keyes, even a stranger, and knew about where to find him, there was nothing at all odd in his coming straight to us. And come he did.

 A QUEER little man came up to the table, with an apologetic air, and took the third chair.

"I don't suppose, sir, as 'ow you 'ave a match?" he said to Keyes. "This danged pipe won't keep a-going, and a good match is werry 'ard to find in foreign parts, as the old gent said when 'e buried 'is third. Thank 'ee, sir—"

Keyes handed over a box of matches. I took a second look at the speaker.

He was a pudgy little old man with gray hair, a blank and expressionless face—not unlike the faces of Arabs, in that it had no lines or wrinkles—and very wide and blank eyes of sky blue. He was carelessly dressed, smoked a vile old clay pipe, and wore a black Basque beret, though he was obviously no Frenchman. I put him down as engineer or assistant chief on some ship in harbor.

"I was told, sir," he said, when he had his pipe alight, "as 'ow I'd find a gent name o' Keyes a-sitting 'ere. I don't suppose by any chance one of you is 'im?"

When those mild blue eyes met mine, I received a slight sense of shock. They seemed to go clear into my brain, as it were. Their blank appearance was deceptive.

"Why, yes, I'm Keyes," said Tom. "The office told you I'd be here, eh?"

The pudgy little man nodded, and I noticed that he seemed to be looking me over with a good deal of interest.

"Yes sir, just like that. I've saved up a bit o' tin, Mr. Keyes, and I am thinking of putting me money into the automobile business. I ain't as young as I was once, and I 'ave a business of me own in Paris, but me 'eart went back on me, so to speak. Go to Morocco, the doctor says, and set in the sun and do nothing, all winter. But a man 'as got to be doing of something, as the old gent said when 'e kissed the 'ousemaid."

Keyes was obviously astonished by this information. I kicked his ankle under the table, but he only gave me a look.

"I suppose my cue is to sell you my agency and duck," he rejoined. "But that's not my style. Don't put any money into cars; the new tariff will smash you. My business is wrecked and I'm broke. On top of everything else, my car was a new model, and on every blasted one sold the valves have stuck and half of 'em have burned up and there's been hell to pay all around. So you and I won't do any business. That is," he added, with an ironic smile, "unless you want to lend me ten thousand francs on no security, to be repaid God knows when!"

"Well, I might do worse'n that," said our friend calmly. Keyes jerked up his head.

"Don't be a fool. I need the loan to keep out of jail, but I wasn't speaking seriously—"

"There's nothing like a good serious talk, sir, says I." With which, the pudgy little man produced a wallet and drew out a sheaf of crisp yellow-and-lavender French bank notes. "There's fifteen thousand francs. If so be as you can use it, sir, you're mortal welcome."

Keyes sat there blinking. Our unknown friend turned his blue eyes on me.

"And where do you come in, sir?" he asked bluntly.

"Me?" I said, recovering from the shock. "I'm looking for a loan, too. Twenty thousand or so. Of course, I have no security; a newspaper man never has security. And I haven't any settled business, and I'm liable to skip out and blow in my money at Monte Carlo. But a loan of twenty thousand would just suit. I've no actual need for the coin, but it gives you a wonderful feeling to have that much money in your pocket all at once."

"Hm!" said our expressionless visitor. "You ain't in love, I 'opes?"

"Love?" I said "Love? Listen: I wouldn't fall in love with the Queen of Sheba herself! I fell for one dame and she was cuckoo. She robbed me of everything I had, fought with everybody I knew, tried to put me in

the bughouse, and is headed that way herself. I shook her off legally, and when I take on any more—well, Hank Smith lays off the females, that's all!"

"But there's a mortal lot o' temptation in this wicked world, as the old gent said when 'e 'ired the pretty 'ousemaid." With this observation, our friend dipped into his wallet again. He laid twenty thousand-franc notes on the table and shoved them at me. I felt my eyes bulge.

"There you are, Mr. Smith, and just to even it up, there's five thousand more for Mr. Keyes," he said calmly, and beckoned the hovering waiter to order a bock.

 I WAS past speech. My request had been a joke, naturally. I could only conclude that the old chap was a trifle balmy and needed a guardian. Keyes got rid of his shell-shocked look, and then laid his money down like a man.

"This can't go on," he said. "Lord knows I need it, but it looks to me as though you had worse need of a keeper. I don't know you. You never met us before. You can't haul out forty thousand francs and turn it over to absolute strangers—you simply can't! And I'm damned if I'll take advantage of an old man. Take your money and beat it, and look out for confidence men; that's my advice to you. This isn't business."

"Well, sir, I 'ave me own way of doing business." Our friend chuckled wheezily, and sampled his bock appreciatively. "You two gents may be werry bad risks, but I ain't often mistook in a man, if I do say it meself as shouldn't. Suppose you put up that 'ere money. If so be as you don't want it as a loan, then take it as advance payment, so to speak. A bit o' business 'as come up, and not being as young as I was once, I'd be werry glad indeed to 'ave two spry young gents to 'elp me out. There ain't nothing like a 'elping 'and, as the old gent said when 'e took 'is third."

"Oh!" said Keyes, and pocketed the money. "So that's the ticket, eh? All right. I'm in for the game, whatever it is. What do you want to do —kidnap the sultan's wife?"

"Not me, sir," and our friend gave me a look. "And Mr. Smith—'ow about 'im?"

Keyes gave me a grin. "Count him in—eh, Hank?.

"All right." I pocketed my own sheaf of notes. "I'd go to jail for twenty thousand francs any day. Only, I draw the line at getting married."

Our visitor chuckled. He produced a knife and a plug of very black tobacco, which he began to whittle into his palm.

"I don't suppose, sir," he said to Keyes, with his confoundedly apologetic air, "as 'ow you've been and picked up any Arabic?"

"Yes," and Tom nodded. "I was fool enough to think I might make good at this game, and I plunged. I can handle the language fairly well, and I've been all over the damned country—regular high-power salesman stuff, getting acquainted everywhere and so forth."

"Then, sir, you know as these 'ere Moors are a werry poor lot o' cattle?"

"Nothing of the sort," said Tom flatly. "They're not Moors, but Arabs, and want to be so called, rightly or wrongly. And the general run is pretty good. I've got some real friends among them, let me tell you."

The other chuckled in his wheezy way, though his blank eyes showed no mirth.

"You'll do, Mr. Keyes, you'll do," he said, pressing the tobacco into his clay pipe. "I was in the ship chandlery business meself at Port Said for some years, and picked up a bit

of the lingo, and I 'ave a few friends among the Arabs me own self. Do you know what this 'ere is?"

He leaned forward. On the table-top he drew a triangle with forefinger and spilled beer. He then drew a second triangle across the first, forming the rough design of a star with six points. I knew what it was, and so did Keyes, who responded.

"Of course; that's the sultan's emblem, or royal symbol. The natives call it the Seal of Solomon. It's used a good deal in magic and divination and so forth."

The other nodded solemnly at us, and held a match to his pipe.

"Werry good. Me name is Solomon, gents—John Solomon, just like that, only me friends make it John— and werry 'appy I am to meet you both. If so be as you could 'elp out for a matter of a fortnight or more with this 'ere business of mine—"

"Sure, glad to do it!" I exclaimed, as he paused. I had begun to like the little old man, and not for his money either. "Look here, Mr. Solomon, I don't really need this loan. Suppose you take it back. I was joking about it—"

"Don't never give back nothing, sir. You be just as 'ard-boiled as a woman lookin' for alimony," and he chuckled. "No, you keep it, Mr. Smith. You may 'ave need of it, says I. And what about that 'elping of me out?"

"Oh, Hank and I are old friends, and we'll hang together, if it's a 'anging job," said Tom, with a laugh. "Go on, feller. You've hired two men, and you don't know yet how good they are."

"I ain't so sure but what I do," and the mild blue eyes twinkled for an instant. "This 'ere errand is over at Fez, but it may not end there. It's one o' them things that ain't to be foreseen, as the old gent said when 'e buried 'is second. Suppose you go and pay up them bills, Mr. Keyes, then the both of you come along and join me at the Excelsior, right 'ere at the corner. Come straight up to me room—number four-twenty, it is."

"Right." Keyes glanced at his watch, then rose. "I don't know how to thank you, Mr. Solomon—"

"Make it John, sir."

"John, then. You've pulled me out of a mighty bad hole—"

"I 'opes, sir, as 'ow you and Mr. Smith may pull me out of a 'ole likewise. And if I was you gents, I wouldn't do no talking about 'aving met me. There's a mortal lot of things that ain't to be talked about, as the old gent said when 'e fired the 'ousekeeper."

 WE SHOOK hands with our new friend and headed off up the street. When we got to the next corner by the consulate, I looked at Tom, and he looked at me, and we came to a stop.

"Is it real?" he said.

"Yeah. It really happened, feller. He's a queer little bird, but I like him."

"Fair enough; and we're hooked." Keyes laughed. "Personally, I don't give a hoot! Do you?"

"Not a tinker's hoot," I returned. "Hold on! I just thought of something."

"What?"

"I only asked him for twenty thousand. What if I'd asked for fifty thousand?"

"I dunno, Hank. He had more where that came from. What you going to do with that twenty thousand, anyhow?"

"Save it for him."

"All right. Let's get another drink to celebrate, and then go see if the *huissier* is waiting to take me to jail."

The huissier was there, ahead of time, too, and he passed some observations on the cash reserves of American millionaires, and went away

with his money. Tom fired his stenographer and called in a furniture dealer who was waiting for the attachment to be lifted, and sold off his office junk. Promptly at five o'clock we locked up the office, turned in the key, and had another drink on our way back to the Hotel Excelsior. The spanking new hotel across the alley was not yet open for occupancy. To be frank about it, I rather expected to get to John Solomon's room and find that his friends had located him and had him under lock and key.

I need not have worried, however.

We got by the magnificently attired dragoman at the hotel door—Tom said he had lived for some years in America—and without stopping at the desk, crossed on to the stairs. The elevator was not working, which was to be expected, and we made our way up past the various floors—the walls were covered with matting—to what the French called the fourth. It was really the fifth. Four-twenty proved to be one of the high front rooms overlooking the Place de France, with the city walls and gates opposite. Bidden to enter, we came in to find Solomon sitting over the telephone. He waved a hand at us.

"Sit down, gents, sit down—I 'ave long distance on the wire, and a werry stiff job it is in this danged country—yes, 'ello! Allo, allo, dang it—yes, this is 'im—is this the Dar Jamai? Oh, it's Miss Pontois, is it? All right, miss, this is John Solomon, and werry 'appy I am to 'ear your voice. I'm a-sending over two gents to see you—"

He broke off and listened, then he chuckled wheezily.

"Yes, miss, but it can't be done. Cause why, I'm in Morocco for me 'ealth and I'm all alone except for these 'ere gents, just like that. Wacation it is, miss—what is it I don't understand? Well, miss, werry sorry I am to say it, but I 'ave to take care of me 'ealth, just like that, for the next fortnight or so. You're—what? Is that the truth, miss? Look 'ere, Miss Pontois, your father 'e was a werry good friend o' mine, and I ain't a-going back on you—"

He broke off, and I was astonished to see sweat gathering on his forehead. He turned from the instrument and spoke in an aside.

"Can you reach Fez by tomorrow morning in a good car?"

"You bet," said Keyes.

"All right, miss, you leave it to me," said Solomon, and somehow there was a new tone in his voice—a vibrant, metallic quality that thrilled me. "You sit tight, Miss, and don't trust nobody. Mr. Keyes and Mr. Smith will be there in the morning, and there ain't nothing to worry about. Worry ain't going to 'elp matters, as the old gent said when 'e found the 'ousemaid a-crying into 'er apron. You're safe at the Jamai palace—it's a good 'otel and well watched over. Yes, miss. I'll see to that. Goodby."

He laid the instrument in its rack and mopped the sweat from his face.

"Dang it!" he said mildly. "Dang it!"

"Agreed," I said. "Dang it three times, if you like. What's it all about, John!"

He got out his clay pipe, and made no response until he had shredded some of his cut plug and stuffed the pipe. Keyes grinned at him.

"John, I'll present you with a new meerschaum if you'll let me take that clay pipe over into the Arab quarters and deposit it there. It'll kill off the natives like flies."

Solomon grunted, then lighted his pipe and leaned back in his chair.

"This 'ere is serious, gents," he declared. "I've just 'eard that the daughter of an old friend o' mine is in trouble up at Fez. I've got to lend 'er a hand; cause why, what is a friend for except to be lendin' of a

'and, just like that? Where can you gents get a good car?"

"Well," said Keyes, "I know where there's a good Hispano for rent, and I know where there's a good flivver. Which?"

Solomon waved his pipe. "Dang it! Money ain't no object. Rent the 'Ispano for a month and tell 'em to see me in the morning about it. Take it and go to Fez and see Miss Pontois."

"What's it all about?" I demanded.

"Dang it, I don't know!" exclaimed Solomon with a trace of irritation. "She's been and called me this morning, and again just now. Says as 'ow she's in trouble and afraid of 'er life and so on. She's unearthed some danged mystery and wouldn't talk. It's got something to do with a gent name Maillot."

 KEYES, WHO had been sitting on the table, swung off it.

"Maillot? Captain Alfred Maillot?" he said.

"Ever 'ear tell of 'im?" asked Solomon, the blue eyes giving him a sharp glance.

"Lord, yes!" Keyes looked savage. "He's the damndest rotter in Morocco. Made a fortune after the French occupation, they say; he's in cahoots with a couple of pachas. I heard that Luaytey kicked him out, but after the government changed to civil occupation, he came back. He's in thick with the sultan, he's got a couple of palaces of his own—and the skunk tried to put over a grafting game with me, to supply a couple of cars to the Sultan's gang. If your lady friend is in with that bird, she's in bad, believe me!"

"Well, go get that 'ere car and Mr. Smith will meet you downstairs," said Solomon. "Me and 'im will 'ave a word or two while you're a-getting it."

"All right," said Keyes. "See you later, Hank!"

He swung out, and I met the gaze of Solomon. He swung around and gave me a look that, from anybody else, would have been called hard. I began to wonder if this little blank-faced man with the mild blue eyes did not have something worth while in him, after all.

"Mr. Smith," he observed wheezily, "did you ever 'ear tell of Emperor Ishmael?"

"No," I said.

"Well, if I was you, sir, I'd find out all about 'im—and werry danged quick about it, too! I don't suppose as 'ow you 'ave a gun, sir?"

"No. Tourists don't need such things—and besides, they aren't allowed."

At this he grunted, and went to a suitcase standing open, and picked up a neat automatic pistol that lay on top in full view. He handed this to me.

"Well, 'ere you be, sir, all ship-shape. Bein' a newspaper chap, I expect you've looked into administration matters a bit out 'ere—justice, government, socialism, graft and so on?"

I had, and said so. Solomon gave me a blank look and puffed at his pipe.

"Well, I expect as Mr. Keyes is a-waiting, so run along. You'll 'ear from me at the Dar Jamai tomorrow, sir, and 'ere's wishing you good luck. I'm werry much afraid as you'll need it."

And with this dubious blessing, I departed—wondering not a little about Solomon.

Chapter Two

THE EMPEROR ISHMAEL

 THE LEGACY of war has bequeathed excellent roads to Morocco — in some places—and as there are no speed laws and travel is scare compared to our traffic in America, Keyes could let out the Hispano and figure on making Rabat for dinner.

"Well?" he asked, when we were out of town and buzzing north past the farms along the sea. "Is the old boy off his nut?"

"Nope," I said. "He told me to look up Emperor Ishmael—look up all about him, and do it quick. Then he asked if I'd looked into socialism here, the administration of justice, and so forth. I told him I knew all about it, and he said to run along. Rather sarcastic."

Keyes chuckled, swept past a bus that was loaded with Arabs alow and aloft, and waved a cheery hand to them.

"No wonder. Your learning is admirable, Mr. Hank Smith! Justice is administered by the Arab courts; the superior courts, or pacha's tribunals, have a French chap along who runs the show himself. Some on the level, but most of the Arabs not. The French civilians and military hate each other. The Arabs are all for the French, except those that are fighting against 'em. I dunno about graft, but I'll bet I could get by with anything if I had a pull. And there you are."

"More or less what I knew already," I retorted. "But who was Ishmael? Not the chap who built Meknez?"

"The same. The Napoleon and Queen Elizabeth of Morocco—he died in 1727, left a thousand children or so, and nobody ever found his treasures, which were something enormous, as he'd saved his money for sixty years. He had Scotch blood, or at least a few Irish wives, which amount to the same thing. He was the first black Sultan, and his descendants, who are considerably whiter, still sit on the throne. That's Ishmael in a nutshell. What sort of an errand is this?"

"It doesn't matter," I said. "It's worth thirty-five thousand francs, so why worry? What about this French chap you know so well?"

Keyes grunted. "Maillot? He's no slouch, if you ask me. We don't like each other, and I'd not be surprised if he was behind my being wrecked. Couldn't ever prove it, though. We're looking up a Miss Pontois at the Dar Jamai in Fez—is that right?"

"Suits me," I said. "I stayed a week at the Dar Jamai. It's the best hotel in the world, bar none. I suppose you know that it is an ancient palace which has been converted—"

"I know all about it," said Keyes sharply. "Why are we looking up the lady?"

"We are looking up the lady, Mr. Bones," I rejoined, "in order to lend her the support of our strong right arm or arms. Perhaps your friend Maillot is about to kidnap her to join the sultan's harem—"

"Don't be a fool, Hank," growled Keyes. "We can get to Fez about two in the morning, with this car. Shall we?"

"Not at the Dar Jamai," I said. "The city gates will be closed at midnight, and so will the hotel; and you have the devil of a time getting in, as I learned."

"Where were you after midnight in Fez?" he demanded.

"I was having dinner," I said proudly, "with Kaid Abdesalem and some other boys of the town. A friend of mine got me in—a bird who runs a bank branch there. Named Angel Souzan."

"My Lord!" and Keyes chuckled. "Where did you meet that chap? How?"

"He cashed a check for me," I said. "And we went out and had a drink. I threw a party at the hotel for him and his wife, and we just naturally got friendly."

"Congratulations, then," said Keyes. "He's a prince, and he's one of the few French or other gents in Morocco who has the confidence of the natives. Yeah, I know him well. He's no angel, in spite of his name—"

"I found that out," I said modestly, and Keyes chuckled all the rest of the way into the Rabat. To tell the truth, Souzen and I and a couple of other friends had experienced a lot of life in Fez, and they were all good scouts, too. No wonder all these Arabs have placid and unworried faces; if the little old severest critic and best friend does any nagging, divorce takes two minutes or less, and there's no alimony graft."

 IT WAS only ninety kilometers to Rabat, which is the official capital of Morocco today, and we got in a little before seven. Having plenty of money, we went on to the Transatlantique Hotel, or the "Transat," as this chain of hostelries is universally known, which was located across from the Kasba and the Arab cemetery. It was the beginning of November, and the tourist season was on full swing, so there were plenty of people in the place.

Tom and I got one of the little tables by the window overlooking the street, and proceeded to celebrate. The Transat hotels put up the best French cooking in Morocco, and provide the best champagne, so we were not surprised to see the big central table all fixed up with candles and decorations; evidently somebody was throwing a banquet. We were just at our second glass of bubble water when in they trooped, ten of them, all in evening gowns and uniforms. A batch of officers and officials, obviously.

Only one man was in plain evening dress, and he wore only a couple of decoration ribbons. He was the most striking of the lot, however—a wide-shouldered, handsome man with jet-black hair and eyes and mustache. His face was bronzed, high-boned, vigorous, and as he had the head of the table he was evidently the host. He held a chair for a lady, then glanced around and saw us. He gave Keyes a bow, and a smiling wave of the hand, and sat down.

"Who's your friend?" I asked. "He looks like a cavalry officer."

"Used to be." Keyes gave me a grin. "How do you size him up?"

"Devil with the women. A regular guy, as the saying goes; a good man to have along in a jam. I'd like to know him."

"Look again," said Keyes curtly.

"Well, he'd be a pretty bad actor if he was an enemy—he's got a cruel mouth," I observed. "I suppose you don't like him because he's a handsome devil."

"You're a hell of a character analyst, Hank. That's Alfred Maillot."

"Oh!" I said.

"Just so. I hear he has a regular castle over in the mountains somewhere, and he's in solid with the sultan—acts as official secretary or something of the sort. Some say he's turned Muhammadan; but that's a lie in my opinion. He's hand in glove with the grafting gang—old Pacha Ishmael down at Marrakesh and the concession crowd of business people in Paris, banks and so forth. He's a big man in Morocco, no mistake about that."

I kept an eye on Maillot, but for the life of me I could see no villainous indications in his manner—though I knew Tom Keyes must be right. We were in no hurry, since we had only a couple of hundred kilometers more to cover, and did not want to reach Fez before the gates of the city were opened in the morning. So we loafed along at dinner and went into the lounge for coffee and cigars.

 WE HAD no more than got well seated when in came Maillot after us. He walked up to us with a smile and shook hands heartily with Keyes.

"Well, this is a surprise!" he said in French. "I am glad to see you—there is something I want to talk over with you. A friend of mine is thinking about two new cars, and I have suggested your model—"

"No use," said Keyes. "I've closed out my agency. Let me introduce a friend of mine—Mr. Henry Smith, an American journalist. Captain Maillot, Hank."

I encountered a firm grip and a warm smile. Maillot hoped I would like Morocco, and displayed that personal interest which always makes a man liked by his fellows. He wanted to know about my trip, my newspaper work, and everything else; then he turned again to Tom.

"But you are not leaving Morocco, Mr. Keyes?"

"I don't know," said Tom. "I'm just looking around for a bit. Hank, here, wants to see some old books, and we're running up to Fez for a day or so—I'll show him a few things in some of the libraries there."

"Then, by all means, take him to El Wazani's palace—here, I'll give you a card." With this, Maillot fished out a card-case and scribbled on a slip of pasteboard, which he handed Tom. "It's impossible for most foreigners to get into the Dar el Menzeh, you know, but this will work it for you. El Wazani has some remarkable books from the seventh and eighth centuries and will be glad to show 'em to you. Well, all luck to you! We'll meet again, I trust."

Maillot bowed and rejoined his party.

"There you are," I said to Tom.

"This bird does his best to be polite and make things pleasant, and you grouse along about how bad he is! Come out of it. Don't be mouldy."

"Never mind your London slang, either," snapped Keyes. "Well, he knows all about you now, that's sure! By the way, had we better give Miss Pontois a ring? The hotels have a quick connection, you know—we can get her on the wire in five minutes."

"Leave her be," I said. "Solomon told her we'd be there. What's your rush? She'll be just another French woman who never learned to use a razor and who never heard of personal hygiene either, and whose friends won't tell her because they don't know any better themselves."

"Huh!" said Tom. "If I had your opinion of women, I'd drown myself."

"If you had my experience of 'em, you would," I retorted. "Why did Solomon tell me to look up all about the Emperor Ishmael?"

"Search me," rejoined Tom. "Hello, there—what's the name?"

The Arab doorman was passing through from the office in the adjoining building, with an envelope, calling some queer name. He came up to us, and I found that Tom had guessed right—the envelope was addressed to him. The man said that it had just been left at the desk by an Arab from the medina, or native city, on whose edge we were. The French occupation very wisely decreed that the French towns should be separate from those of the natives, so that every city in Morocco has its ancient mellah, or Jewish town, its medina or Arab city, and its new French town. The postmen must have a devil of a lot of trouble with their mail.

"That's queer!" Tom passed me the card which had been in the envelope. It bore a line of writing in neat French script.

"Your friend will be at the house of Si Dris el Benouna, Meknez."

Beneath this was the six-pointed star formed of two triangles.

"What d'you make of it?" I asked. "Who's the friend in question?"

Keyes frowned. "Solomon, of course," he returned. "And the old beggar will get into trouble if he uses that emblem as his own—the sultan has a monopoly of it in these parts. Hm! I've heard of this Si Dris chap; he's an Algerian by origin and a *tajer* or banker by profession—quite a fellow by all accounts. Well, shall we be moving?"

"If you like. But how did this card get left here?"

"Solomon telephoned somebody here, or else Si Dris did—don't think for a minute that these Arabs aren't up to date! All right, if you say the word—let's go."

So we left.

The street outside the hotel was full of cars and chauffeurs, most of whom were in military uniform. As we went to our own, Keyes touched my arm and pointed to the car we were passing. On its side was depicted the Seal of Solomon—it was one of the sultan's cars, he said, and probably was that used by Maillot. A little knot of Arabs seemed much interested in us as we got into our car—they were like all the other Arabs in Morocco, enveloped in flowing robes and wearing the usual yellow slippers.

"Know how the yellow slippers started?" said Keyes. "Ishmael chucked the Spaniards out of a few towns they'd been holding, forced the English out of Tangiers, and decreed that all the footgear should be yellow thereafter in token of rejoicing. So it is today. Hi, there! Move!"

The two Arabs in our way moved at the blast of the horn, and we got off.

Even in our short resumption of acquaintance, I had noticed that Tom Keyes did not have the French attitude toward the usual Arabs. Your

Frenchman, whether he is a bus driver or a colonist, is a conquerer in the land and knows it—and makes the Arab know it. The luckless native, in fact, gets practically the same treatment as does the negro in certain sections of the south. Morocco is not a part of France like Algiers, but a separate country; however, the sultan is only a French puppet, and the infidel is here to stay. I had already visited places like the holy city of Mulai Idris, where five or ten years ago not a white man had ever set foot; and with camps all over the country, French towns springing up by magic, and military airplanes buzzing overhead, there is no doubt as to who owns Morocco.

None the less, there are plenty of Arabs who do not love their conquerors, as the present-day fighting in the south still bears witness.

WE FOLLOWED the main highway, Fourteen, and loafed along without hurry, having filled up with gas and oil at Rabat. I liked that town better than any other in Morocco, and said so. Tom sniffed and prated of Marrakesh, which is red and savage despite its palm groves.

"What's up?" exclaimed Tom suddenly. "Is there a car behind us?"

I looked around, startled by his tone. I heard another engine, certainly, but there were no lights on the road; we were winding along the verge of the Marmora forest, with plenty of curves. No lights appeared, but a car with open exhaust roaring was certainly somewhere nearby. It was too dark to see anything. The moon was just coming into full, and was still behind the horizon peaks. Then I caught a glimpse.

"Something back on the road, Tom—"

"Hang on!" he exclaimed. He shut off our lights and engine, and we

pitched out across the road-shoulder to a level spot, and halted. Next moment another car came hurtling and roaring down behind us without lights. I heard a sudden yell, a squeal of brakes, then Tom switched on our lights. We saw an Arab leaning out of the side of the dark car, there were quick red flashes, and I heard the crack and whistling smash of bullets. Then the other car was gone.

"Hurt?" asked Tom.

"No. They came close, though—"

Our car leaped. "Take the gun out of my side pocket next you," said Tom. "Give 'em hell and shoot straight. Ready, now! They won't be looking for us to come on their tail."

Both of us realized that this was no accident; each of us knew the other well enough to waste no time on questions or cursing. Inside of two minutes that car was doing seventy and Tom was taking the curves like the proverbial speed demon. I slipped the pistol from his pocket and threw off the safety-catch. We both knew enough about French law to know that if the other chap opens up on you, you can go the limit.

Then, almost without warning, we swept around a wide curve and came upon the other car drawn up at the roadside. It was empty; our headlights picked up an Arab who was running for shelter of the trees. A spat of flame shot from the trees, and another. As we roared past, I emptied the pistol in my hand, saw the running Arab go down—and then we were gone. Presently Tom slowed down his mad pace.

"Any damage?" he asked.

"No. Couple of bullets plunked into the car somewhere."

"Did you see it?"

I nodded. That large six-pointed star on the side panel of the other car had been beyond any mistake.

"Can't be the same car, though," I said. "Those Arabs—"

"The same gang who were hanging around when we left. They took Maillot's car, sure, and came on to get us; that running without lights is typical. Some of these boys are worse actors than any Chicago gunmen. Maillot had found out something."

"I don't believe it," I retorted. "He didn't send 'em after us, if that's the idea."

Keyes grunted disgustedly. "Sure he did. Most likely, that telephone message from Solomon was reported to him; that bird has agents and spies everywhere. Listen, Hank! If that pudgy little old cockney goes up against Maillot, heaven help him! He'll be washed out in no time at all. However, we'll stick with him—eh?"

"You bet," I said. "Got any extra cartridges for this popgun?"

"Nope. You won't need any more tonight; those birds lost out, and will go back home. Say! I wonder what Maillot's game was in sending us to El Waziri? This chap is one of the old families, rich as sin, and has a dream of a palace; he's on the level, too. Anybody would jump at the chance to see his place and his books—I wonder where the dirt comes in?"

"You're too durned suspicious," I said. "Forget it."

I did not share Tom's wild suspicions at all; it was just too unreal. Of course, the veneer of law and order was thin in spots, and anything was possible, but it was usually a matter of impulse. Some of those Arabs might have been drunk and out for a wild time—this was much more likely than the elaborate hypothesis Tom had built up. The Moroccan Arabs live a life to themselves, they deliberately hold aloof from Europeans, and the less mixing the better, from their viewpoint.

"We'll see when we get to Fez in he morning," said Tom, comprehending my thoughts. "If we run into trouble there, you can bet your boots Maillot has reached out after us. Look here—it's only sixty kilometers from Meknez to Fez. Shall we drop in at a Meknez hotel for some sleep?"

"We wouldn't get very much," I rejoined. "It might be better to look up that all-night dance place on the Boulevard de Fez and get us a little exercise and a drink. Then we can go on about daybreak, get landed at the Dar Jamai, and have a shave and an hour's sleep before breakfast. We can't tackle the dame too early, remember."

"You're on!" said Tom with enthusiasm. "I know the place, and we'll probably run into a hot crowd, too."

Despite what had happened that day and night, neither of us took the matter very seriously. Our friend Solomon was an unreal sort of person, and this business of a French woman telephoning for help was not particularly impressive. So we did not hesitate about having a good time on the way.

When we reached Meknez, we had to go clear around the ancient town in order to reach the new French city on the opposite hill. The moon was up high, and Tom stopped twice in order to drink in the view; and no wonder. Meknez by clear moonlight is one of the most provocative sights in the world to the imagination; every detail is softened, and there out of the middle ages rises the city built by the great Ishmael, almost as he left it, with its enormous walls crowning the hillside for miles, and the minarets of fifteen or twenty mosques rising high above all.

And from this we went on to the new French town, passing the camp and parking near the dance hall. This puritanical establishment was patronized mainly by officers—gaudy ones, in their deep blue of aviation, blue and tan and gold and all the rainbow colors of other services. And naturally, officers are lonely in foreign lands, so Meknez has a floating population of interesting ladies, Russians and French and others. Tom and I ran into a crowd of officers and it was nearly five in the morning when we broke away.

However, we did get to Fez eventually.

Chapter Three

The Jewels of the Sultan

OUR PROGRAM went off without a hitch. When the Ban Suissa, the gate just behind the Dar Jamai, was opened, we left the Hispano parked and safely locked, and walked on down the narrow street to the hotel. We got a room, turned in promptly, and at eight-thirty in the morning showed up for breakfast. An hour's sleep, a shave and a bath had fixed us up in good shape.

We came down to the tiled terrace with its fountain and waving poplars, and crossed to the dining-room—a portion of the old palace to which additions had been made. Up above rose the walled hillside with the twelfth-century tombs of the Merinide dynasty; below stretched the triple city of Fez, across the valley and reaching up the opposite hills, with its morning haze of grayish smoke ascending into the sky.

We found the dining room fairly well occupied; parties by auto and bus were getting off, and the hotel was fairly well filled with tourists. We were given a corner table by the front window, overlooking the ter-

races and the city beyond, and when I caught Tom casting repeated looks at the other corner table opposite, I paid attention.

To tell the truth, I did not blame him. The sole occupant of this table was apparently, an English girl; she looked as fresh as a daisy, and coolly capable to boot, and she knew how to get herself up, too. I liked her neat air and the crisp wave of her brown hair, and when she shot a look our way, there was a quiet steadiness in her eye that was good to see.

"You'd better lay off," I told Tom. "You're here to find a French girl that hollers into the phone for help and uses perfume instead of listerine. That female over there is old enough to take care of herself, too. Done anything yet about finding Miss Pontois?"

"No," said Tom, grinning at me. "But there's the manager coming this way—get him."

I did not need to get him. The polite Frenchman was headed direct for us, and I thought he was going to pass the time of day. He remembered me and gave me a smiling bow as he drew alongside, so I cut in on him.

"Back again, you see! Can you tell us, by the way, if you have a guest named Mlle. Pontois?"

"Oh, but yes, m'sieu!" he rejoined, and waved his discreet hand toward the English girl. "She is here, yonder. But I have a message for one M. Keyes."

"C'est moi," responded Tom. The manager laid down an envelope.

"The bearer is awaiting a reply in the office," he said, and departed.

"Listen, Tom—did you get it straight?" I exclaimed. "That English girl over there—"

"Shut up; she's a woman, not a girl," said Tom, frowning. "What's this blasted message, now? Another of our friend Solomon's tricks?"

He tore open the sealed envelope

and drew out a sheet of paper, at which he blinked. Then he passed it across to me, with a laugh. It was a notice from the local branch of the Comptoir Auto Marrocaine that an overdue bill of twenty-five hundred francs was badly in need of collection and Mr. Keyes was expected to come immediately and take up his note.

"By glory, I'd forgotten about it!" exclaimed Tom. "How'd these Frenchmen know we were here, eh? Can you beat 'em when it comes to collecting the *dinero?* Hm! What did I tell you last night, Hank? I bet a dollar Maillot has had a hand in sicking 'em on me!"

"You're crazy," I returned. "Anyhow, the most important thing is that girl over there being Miss Pontois. Who'd have imagined it? Well, you go pay your bill to the collector—"

"He's probably an Arab," said Tom, frowning. "It's not so simple as all that, feller. This company is located over in the new French town —I'd have to go over there."

"Well, you get acquainted with our lady friend, then," I said. "I'll act as Mr. Tom Keyes and go pay the bill for you. I'd like to make sure our Hispano is all right, and get her filled up with gas, too. Suit you?"

"Fine! Here's the money—"

Tom slipped me the notes from his rapidly shrinking roll, which did not matter particularly, as I had Solomon's money almost untouched. In order to reach the new town, I had to go clear around Fez and out on the other side, and I did not intend to hurry about it; so I told Tom that I would be back in an hour or so.

"Meantime," I added, as I rose, "you can console the lady. She doesn't look as though she needed it, but hop on the job and see what it's all about. And, by the way, you'd better take most of my money—I don't intend to go chasing around Fez with twenty thousand francs on my hip."

I handed over my wad and departed.

OUTSIDE THE office I found an Arab waiting for me, and chatting with the hotel guides. He was high-yellow, rather oily, and wore an old brown jellab; he was a young rascal, and spoke fluent French. He turned to me as I came up and a guide indicated me.

"You are M. Keyes?"

"Just so," I returned, and noted his green vest. "You're a sharif, eh—a descendant of the Prophet? Good! Do you ride in my car?"

"I have a car waiting, m'sieu," he answered. "At the Bab Bou Jlou. If you will walk that far with me—it is only a few minutes—"

"I know where it is," I said, and reflected swiftly. No cars are allowed in Fez Bali, or Old Fez, for the streets are too narrow; to reach the gate which he named, we would have to walk across the upper end of town. However, the morning was fine; and if Tom's creditors were in such a devlish rush for their money, they might as well pay my taxi fare. So I nodded, and we passed down the stairs to the lower terrace and the street level. In another two minutes we were dodging donkeys and camels and veiled women, on our way through town.

Ali, as he named himself, was a gay young blade in his own estimation, anxious to show off all that he knew about vice in general, and he prattled along in a carefree manner about girls and so forth, as we threaded our way among the morning crowds. Around us reeked that peculiar stench of all Moroccan towns —not an unpleasant odor, if you like sour cold cream, but one which grows on you the more you experience it. Ali was much the same; the farther we went, the more I wanted to smash his yellow face. That he was a sharif amounted to nothing—half the hotel guides are holy men of the same stripe, for descendants of Muhammad litter up the whole Moroccan landscape. Ali seemed to think that the only reason Americans came to Morocco was to get a new line on voluptuous enjoyments.

We got into the Rue du Tala, and a moment later Ali touched my arm.

"Perhaps," he suggested with a smirk, "M'sieu would care to see the jewels of the last sultan? They are close by here; my mother's uncle has them in his keeping, and for five francs would be glad to show them to you. None of the French know where they are, of course, and if the present sultan found out about them —whew!" Ali snicked his hand across his throat significantly. "You are an American, so it is quite safe to show them to you—"

Naturally, I scented a whale of a news story in this suggestion.

"Are they real jewels," I asked, "or the sort that are sold in the bazars here?"

Ali held up his hands to Allah. "They are jewels, M'sieu, which descended from the days of the great Ishmael, and with them is a letter which placed them in the charge of my ancestor, a letter bearing the seal of Ishmael himself!"

"Good enough," I said promptly. "If it won't take too long—"

"Three minutes, M'sieu — this way!"

We turned into one of the narrow side alleys, and were instantly in the heart of Fez as it was five or six hundred or more years ago. Most of the houses, indeed, attain nearly this age; the massive iron-studded doors, and the various gates which every midnight divide the different quarters of the city into impassable prisons, speak of the days when sack and plunder were ever-present possibilities. Only a few years ago, in fact, a

Berber army was at the gates of Fez, as the shot-holes in the French forts still testify.

In this rabbit-warren Ali stopped and pounded on a door set in the wall. Presently it was opened by a veiled woman, and an interchange of Arabic ensued, then Ali turned to me.

"Enter, M'sieu."

I stepped in, and with Ali at my elbow followed the overstuffed female along a sharply twisting passage. We came into a small open courtyard with a tiled fountain; two Arabs were sitting on a sofa beneath an arch, and they rose at sight of us. Each of them greeted Ali with the usual shoulder-kiss given a sharif, and there was more talk.

"We must go to the room where the things are kept," said Ali to me. "They speak no French, M'sieu, but are glad to show you the things."

The two Arabs smiled and nodded at me, and all four of us passed through another door and corridor. We halted before a massive door set flush in the wall. One of the two men threw back an iron bar, then got out a huge key and turned it in the lock, and opened the door. He smiled at me and motioned me to enter.

 I STEPPED inside. As I did so, Ali lunged forward, giving me a vicious shove. I staggered under it but just the same, I got my wish—for I caught the rascal a beautiful crack in the face. Then, before I could recover, the door was slammed shut and the bolt shot, and there I was—a prisoner. There was nothing in the room but a stool and a grated window, and a cot.

The calm swiftness of it all, the deliberate smiling deviltry of it, left me dazed.

I stood rubbing my knuckles and looking around. From the window, which was large, I could see only a blank wall eight feet distant; probably a street lay outside. Going close to it, I looked out; there was, indeed, an empty street or alley below, with not a soul in sight, and my prison cell was on the street level.

Since there was nothing else to do, I sat down on the cot and had a smoke as I thought it all over. Clearly, I had fallen into some sort of a trap prepared for Keyes. I was unarmed, but was also unhurt, and since this gang evidently thought they had Tom, the best thing to do was to let them think so and give him a chance to get in his work with Miss Pontois.

Maillot? Possibly. When I thought about that murderous car the previous night, and the clever way this trap had been sprung, there was certainly no accident about it all. In sending us that message at Rabat, our friend Solomon had certainly slipped up.

I suppose that upon finding myself caged in an Arab rat-trap, I should have acted like the prisoners in books, beating at the door and shouting from the window; but in cold reality it takes a pretty desperate or unbalanced character to act in such fashion. I was not particularly worried, and since I actually did not yet know what it was all about, I did not much care. Besides, I was sleepy. So, after looking over the cot and finding it clear of vermin, I stretched out and made up some of the sleep I had lost the previous night.

When I wakened, it was along in the afternoon, as my watch told me. I sat up, yawning, and looked around to see a bottle of wine and a round loaf of native bread inside the door. What was more, I saw how it had got there—near the bottom of the door was a section a foot long and four inches high set on hinges, and it had been left open after my provisions had been set inside.

I examined it, found that it, like the door, was a good three inches thick, and gave up any prospect of leaving by this channel. The house was an ancient one, and this room had been made for its present purpose—there were several huge iron rings in the wall, much rusted away, where prisoners had probably been confined. Satisfied of this, I attacked the bread and wine and made a satisfactory enough meal.

As I was finishing, voices in French came to me from outside the door. I knelt down and peered through the half-open slit, and saw my friend Ali outside. With him was a slovenly-looking Frenchman; they were lounging against the wall and smoking.

"M. Maillot will arrive tonight, then," said the Frenchman lazily. "And he ordered that the mademoiselle be left alone, eh? I wonder what was found in her room last night."

Ali chuckled. "I can tell you, for I was there," he rejoined. "She was writing letters, in the hotel writing-room, and I went through everything in her room, with Ahmed. We got what we went after, my friend—an envelope with an old document in it."

"Oh, you did!" said the other with evident interest. "And you looked at the document?"

"Of course. Am I a fool?" retorted Ali. "It is in my pocket. Here it is —but say nothing of having seen it."

He passed over an envelope. From it the Frenchman took out a bit of folded parchment or vellum, at which he scowled.

"Diantre! But this is in Arabic!"

Ali laughed softly. "Yes. And there is the oval seal of Mulai Ishmael, the sultan who died two hundred years ago. It tells about his treasure."

"What?" Excitement flamed in the bearded face of the greasy Frenchman. "His treasure? The treasure of Ishmael, which was never found?"

"Exactly," returned Ali languidly. "Shall I translate it for you? Oh, never fear—it will do you no good, nor Captain Maillot either! Still, it is what he wanted us to get. This is a verse, my old one, and if you can make anything out of it—"

 HE FINISHED with a promised reward which was quite in keeping with his disposition, but which has no place in the writings of Henry Smith. Then he read off what the document said, and Mr. Smith listened attentively.

My treasure is in my shade—
Nay, my shade is in my treasure!
Search for it; despair not!
Nay, despair—search not.

The Frenchman cursed in disgust. "There is no meaning to it," he exclaimed, in which I agree heartily. "It is a riddle, a plague, a *poisson d'Avril!*"

"So it would appear," assented the languid Ali. "There is nothing more on the document, and to this riddle, this plague, this what you will, the great Ishmael set his seal! Well, we shall let Pacha Maillot pay his promised reward and then see what he can make of it."

I swung the little slot-door shut. It closed perfectly, and kept out all further sound. Also, it kept all sound in.

It had occurred to me that whatever this thing might mean, I knew at least as much about it as Maillot would know; and this information was valuable. Clearly, Miss Pontois had lost the document, of which she might or might not know the translation. I knew it, and settled the words firmly in my mind.

I was being kept here—the supposed Tom Keyes—in order to await Maillot's arrival sometime tonight; what he wanted Keyes for, was at the moment immaterial. The chief thing was now to get out of here, if possible, and carry my information to Solomon. I was pretty certain that Tom would have taken Miss Pontois

over to Meknez by this time for he had no earthly reason to worry about my absence, but I must first make sure.

The sight of those rusted rings in the wall had given me an idea. If solid iron rings would rust in a room, the grating at the window would probably have rusted a good deal more, being exposed to the weather. There were no shutters to the window, and I crossed over to it and examined the grating: It was apparently solid enough, but I saw that at top and bottom, where the iron was set in cement, the rust was thick—and the grill itself was by no means solid.

The stool, however, was a good solid one.

There was no one in the street outside. As I swung repeatedly with the stool, the sound of the blows was only a dead and muffled noise which attracted no attention; and at the third stroke I could feel the rusted iron giving. Inside of ten minutes I pulled the grill into the room, laid it on my cot, and had a free way before me.

It had occurred to me already that there was something odd about this empty little alley outside, and as I swung out of the window and dropped into the street, I saw what it was. At the upper end was a fountain set in a blank wall, and at the lower end was a gate, and the whole street was not ten yards long. It was nothing but a passage, probably between two houses; for the walls on either side were quite blank except for my one window. And the gate, a huge affair ten feet high, was solid—and locked by means of mammoth old padlocks.

And there I was, with nothing ahead except to climb the gate and drop over on the other side—and see what happened.

Which is exactly what I did.

(The next instalment of this engrossing serial will appear in the March issue of FAR EAST *Adventure Stories.)*

RUBY EYES of RHIBI

A Short Story of the Wild Dyaks

By

CAPTAIN L. B. WILLIAMS

A MILE east of Mount Rhibi, that sanguine sandstone promonotory jutting ominous and frowning out over the matchless sapphire of South Sulu Sea, lies Magpie Rock. The Rock, for centuries past has been the bane of navigators bound round the shoulder of North Borneo for the China and Sulu seas, but it is now marked with a gas light flashing red.

But when Dan Marguard found Wepler clinging starved, crazed and all but dead to it, the only watchers keeping vigil there were the myriads of wheeling, screaming sea birds that fed along its base at ebb tide. The lonesome place was known to the Sea Dyaks as the abode of evil water spirits, and that perhaps, is the reason why Herr Gustaf Wepler was privileged to die and keep his head intact. Otherwise the savage Dyaks would have put off in pursuit and there would have been *two* blond heads instead of one, hanging over the smoking fire of old Amabong, sorcerer and high priest of Rhibi.

But the Dutchman had escaped, made the rock, and clung to it for six horrible days and nights—until

Marguard in his *Gadfly* sloop breezed by and picked him up, and he was just in time to thwart the headhunters that waited for him in the jungle fringe scarce a mile away.

Marguard found him at the end of the sixth day, but he had come too late to save the gem collector's life. He realized this while he worked over him in his cabin. The constant battering by lashing tides during foggy nights, plus further wettings during long, soul searing days, had been too much for Wepler. He had contracted a severe case of fever along with the inevitable coral poisoning, and it was but a matter of a few hours after he was hauled numb and bleeding aboard the *Gadfly* that he died. But he didn't die until he had gasped out the most important details of the tragedy which had overtaken him and his partner. And hardened adventurer though he was, Marguard never forgot those wretched last minutes spent with the luckless Wepler.

No, he could never forget. Although Marguard had buried his body in twenty fathoms of water off Lankayan Island, the ghost of the Dutchman seemed to stay and perch in the rigging of the old *Gadfly*. All the way from Rhibi back to Sandaken—and especially during the night watches, Marguard could see him as he laid dying on the narrow bunk, see him and *hear* him. For out of the rigging where the gruesome vision perched came a moaning voice.

"There it is, Dan!" the words rattled through the rigging. "Blood! See? Blood! I'm done and I know it. Vengeance of the Red God of Rhibi—who lost one Ruby Eye and don't know where to find it. BUT I KNOW! And if you'll do as I bid, you'll get that Ruby Eye. Worth fifty thousand it is, and runs to a turtle egg for size. Genuine pigeon's blood mined from a Mogok clay pit

and worth fifty thousand dollars. Fifty thousand—God!"

Marguard gritted his teeth and tried to close his ears to the ghastly tale. But even after he was below in his bunk the Feng Shui would search him out and taunt him.

"Ruby Eyes, Dan. Worth fifty thousand. Then there's poor Carl's head. Wouldn't listen after we got the ruby. But he's paid, poor devil. And although I'm done myself, I hate to die thinking of his head drying forever over a stinking Dyak's fire. Listen, Dan, old friend. You do me one last favor and get that head. Get it and give the heathen a lesson. Remember, that although they got Carl, they never did find that ruby we gouged from the red idol's head. But I've got an idea where that ruby is—maybe you will guess the secret? Anyhow it's worth thinking on and you'll make it your business to get that head for me, I'm sure."

So it was that Marguard had resolved to go back after the head as soon as he had reported to proper authority at Sandaken and satisfied the wailing banshee.

 THE SOUTHWEST monsoon along that section of the Borneo coast lasts from mid-April to mid-October. Marguard had picked up the dying Dutchman in early May. Now, after a long period of careful preparation he had chosen the last days of October in which to make his bid for the withered head of Carl Gartz. The undertaking, carefully kept from his superstitious crew until it was too late to turn back, depended largely on the prevailing winds for success, so it was with extreme care that he chose the hour and manner of making his first landfall.

At midnight, five and a half months after he had reported at Sandaken, he brought up about three miles off Magpie Rock and hove his sloop to in a howling gale. Marguard knew that the storm would last the night out, but would die by morning and be followed by a brisk land breeze. This would make handling of the vessel easy for the two left in charge. And most important of all, it would facilitate a quick getaway from the Dyaks in their swift *praus* after he had made the raid. As to his method of getting clear of Mount Rhibi after he had bearded the old sorcerer in his den, he was not bothered at all; although to the Chinamen's minds, this was the most uncertain feature of the whole wild scheme. But Marguard was supremely confident, so risking his all on the whimsies of the ever treacherous elements, he made ready for the try.

Day breaking bright and clear found Marguard aft with the Chinamen gazing steadily across the mirror-like sea toward the sandstone cliff of Rhibi. Finally Ni-Ling, the tall, Manchu ex-pirate, lowered the glasses he had been using. Slowly he swung about. Then solemnly, and with his harsh saffron face a ghastly mask in the morning light, he began speaking in Mandarin to the man he loved better than life itself—Marguard.

"It cannot be done, Younger Brother. Already they have seen us." He pointed his long sinewy arm toward the crest of Rhibi where a thin column of white smoke purled heavenward. A straight, unbroken line it was until it spread out fanwise across blue dome of morning sky. "The signal fire, Master. A blind dog could see that the land breeze has not yet started. Nor will it this day. Once again I beseech you to abandon this madman's dream that has somehow addled your wits. The chances are a thousand to one against you even if the wind freshens, but without it—"

Marguard cut him short with a gesture of impatience. "Can it, Ling," he answered crisply in English. "The wind'll be up all right. But wind or no wind, I'm bound to attempt it now."

The trader's bold eyes glowed as he spoke and the faint semblance of a smile twitched at his thin lips. "No, my good friends, the thing's not half so risky as you think. With a little luck I'll get over shipshape. All you'll have to do is to stand by and pick me up. Fetch me back here, where, even if we haven't a sailing breeze, we can stand them off. So stop your worrying and get busy. You've plenty to do, and just *how* you do it will have a direct bearing on whether or not *my* head goes to join that of Carl Gartz's over the Dyaks' fire. So hop to it. No more *beseeching!*"

 AN HOUR later the sloop's dinghy grounded on a narrow strip of reddish-brown sand and Marguard stepped boldly ashore. Casually he surveyed the darkly frowning green wall of matted jungle that all but smothered the scanty beach, then set calmly to work.

First he drove an iron stake in the sand and made the boat painter fast to it. This done, he took a small bag of boiled rice from his pocket and scattered it freely about the beach to propitiate whatever evil spirits might be lurking there. For a minute he stood as if listening for signs of approbation. Apparently satisfied he smiled serenely, then turned back to the beach boat again.

He fumbled under the bow thwart a moment and snatched out a squealing snow-white pig and a flustered game-cock. The reddish-brown feathers caught and reflected the sunlight like burnished gold. Both the pig and rooster he staked out in the sand. Then he brought forth from the boat a toy brass cannon and a shining alarm clock. The cannon he loaded with black powder from a crimson bag. Then he wound the alarm clock and sat down to wait.

For ten minutes Marguard squatted there in the sand gazing fixedly at a spot a few feet in front of him. Suddenly the alarm went off with a strident whirr that set the rooster to squawking and the squealing pig to racing in circles around the stake. Marguard paid no attention to the rooster or pig and presently they quieted down again; one to rooting and grunting, the other to clucking peevishly as it pecked at the tether that held it.

The clock ticked on importunely and five more minutes seeped by. Then suddenly the alarm rang again. Marguard leaped to his feet like he had been stung. Like a flash he whipped out a long knife and cut the pig loose from its tether. He grabbed it, drew it quickly to him, and with one deft stroke cut its throat.

Bending over the dead pig and working like a fiend Marguard soon had the animal butchered with its lights and livers laying out on the sand. When this was done he rose with a gusty sigh and picked up the carcass, then striding to the water, he threw it in. After which he washed his hands carefully. That done he came back and sat down calmly by the brass cannon.

For a full five minutes Marguard squatted by the cannon, then he reached over and touched it. Instantly there was a deafening report and a burst of flame. The rooster set up a terrific squalling and fluttered about. Marguard turned and regarded it reproachfully until it finally quieted down again, then he gave his undivided attention to the pig livers lying before him on the sand.

For fully a quarter of an hour Marguard bent over the livers and studied intently the delicate vein markings on the under side. When he glanced up casually, there were no less than fifty wild Dyaks in full war panoply, squatting or standing about. They were undoubtedly headhunters sent to capture him when he landed, but that fact deterred them no whit from studying the pig livers as intently as he did.

Marguard heaved a deep breath, surveyed the war party from one end of the long line to the other. His attention centered on the chief who squatted a yard or so in front of him.

Chief Mulud was tall for a Dyak and magnificently proportioned.

Marguard studied his flat, cruel features briefly. The Dyak's beady black eyes returned look for look unwaveringly. There was, Marguard noted, dark suspicion in those crafty orbs; a suspicion mingled with hatred and contempt. It was very evident that he had been places and seen things, and did not behold the superior white man with the same awe and fear his followers did.

But, if the native was unimpressed by the magic of the white man, so was Marguard unimpressed by the threat offered by a half hundred savages who were thirsting for his blood and coveting his head. He knew it would not be easy to convince them of his powers as a witch doctor, still he was entirely confident he could, so without further ado he got down to real work.

His bronzed face was an inscrutable mask and his eyes twin pools of lambent flame, when Marguard picked up the sliver of bamboo and resumed tracing the spidery veins on the pig livers.

"Can you," he asked without looking up, "also read the omen which is so plainly marked here? If so, tell me what it says."

The Dyak blinked beady eyes, spat a stream of betel juice on the sand and shifted uneasily on his haunches.

"No-o," he faltered in the dialect, "I—I cannot, *Tuan.* Such interpretations are for the learned only. For such as your illustrious self perhaps, or Amabong, High Priest to the Red God Rhibi—who has been angry these many monsoons because of the loss of an eye—"

"*A-ba,*" barked Marguard, glancing up sharply, "*A-ba! A-ba—M'pia!* You *can* read, then, the same as I! Lie not to me of sacred things, O Chief. Lie not to me, nor yet to the Red God, lest he in his mighty anger destroy us all here where we stand. You have read—and correctly—so beware!"

Marguard bored the Dyak through with fanatical eyes as hard and unwinking as points of polished green jade. The native half rose in consternation. But he settled back again and after chewing hard on his betel quid, spat a thin, scarlet stream and replied:

"No, Illustrious, I did not lie. I cannot read omens. The Red One lost his sacred eye and I merely mentioned what is well known to all of us. I—"

"*Mapia-lang,*" conceded the trader brusquely, "It is well. I understand. I did not know what I read here was common knowledge to your tribesmen. That being the case I shall proceed to explain something further which you do *not* know, but should. Attend me now, and offer no profane interruptions. So—" Marguard began again to trace over the veins of the livers with his left hand. "Here," he intoned impressively, "I have found two stories. One which relates of the loss of the Red One's eye, and the other which warns of dire disasters that will overtake any Iban of the tribe of Amabong who stands in the way of a certain white chieftain who is to deliver the Red God of Rhibi another eye. *I* am the white chief—and *here* is the eye!"

 MARGUARD STOOD up impressively and made a swift motion as if he were plucking something from the air. And suddenly there appeared in the palm of his right hand, which was plainly bare before, a glowing green eye about the size of a turtle's egg. The eye *was* an eye, as far as appearances were concerned, for it had a pupil, an iris and a white. The trader held it in his hand tenderly and the chief sucked in his breath sharply. The warriors behind hissed in astonishment and stared fascinatedly. Then, as suddenly as he had produced the green eye, Marguard made another dexterous motion and caused it to vanish.

Marguard then squatted down before the astounded Dyaks and waited for the magic of his performance to sink in. After a time he began to cover the pig livers with loose sand. For a moment after this was accomplished he bowed his head in apparent meditation, then cut the gamecock free from its tether, quietly arose and tended it toward the chief.

The Dyak, who mistrusted all white traders in general and this one in particular, likewise arose. For a moment he had been favorably impressed by the white man's magic, but now the moment had passed. He had been places: Sandaken, Samarinda, Batavia and even to Singapore. He had heard many strange things and observed many more. He knew the cunning, rapacious gem-collectors for what they were. No native shrine with its age-old relics was ever safe when they were about. And hadn't two of this man's daring brothers raided their very own shrine but a few months back? Yes. And now here was this brazen one to lift the sacred Idol's remaining eye. Oh, he knew what it was all about, but just wait!

With burning hatred and mistrust but illy concealed in his hard eyes, the young chief studied the bold features of the bronzed American adventurer before him. That he had learned the rites and ceremonial customs of the Ibans to further his own evil interests he was quite convinced. But then, too, he knew those same customs bound him absolutely to reciprocate all such overtures of friendship without hesitation. To do otherwise was to lose caste instantly, so with what small grace he could summon for the unique occasion, he grasped the head of the unfortunate rooster, and between them they pulled its neck in two.

"*Mayo-Cayo!*" intoned Marguard solemnly when the rite was completed. "*Magunda Saakin.* I am pleased—and signally honored. The Red God of Rhibi has no doubt observed and is also pleased. The omen on the pig's livers was favorable, so I shall go at once to meet the illustrious Amabong in whose worthy hands I shall place the Red God's new eye. Maybe then the holy Amabong will see fit to give me the head of my unfortunate countryman so I can return it to his grieving kin. Yes, I believe it was written. *Salamat!*

Marguard wheeled about abruptly, and strode toward the grounded dinghy. The Chief, much to the horror of his superstitious tribesmen, made an obscene sign; bared his sharp teeth in a horrid grimace and drew his fingers eloquently across his throat. He had obeyed the dicates of Custom and discharged his obligations, but that had not eased the itch in his kris hand nor dulled his ambition to add another fine head to his ever growing collection. But this he would do later—in fact just as soon as this *Boung-lang* (simple one) had delivered the green eye to the witchdoctor on the Mount. It had been written, indeed!

Serenely calm and confident, and displaying the fatuous smile that had deceived and misled many another before Chief Mulud, Marguard returned from the boat carrying a footsquare lacquered box which was elaborately decorated and inlaid with fantastic designs in varied, colored tiles and gleaming mother of pearl.

"Here, oh Chief," he said affably, "is a casket I would have one of your brave warriors carry for me. And gently, too, for it is still another offering for the Red God Rhibi."

He sat the thing carefully in the sand and looked aloft toward the thousand foot precipice which was already casting sombre shadows over the translucent lagoon. For a long minute he stood there gazing upward. Then after adjusting a heavy pack he had brought from the boat more securely on his broad back, he strode swiftly up the narrow beach and vanished into the sinister green silence of the brooding jungle. With avid eyes alight and wolf-like grimace still distorting his scarred, yellow face, Chief Mulud sprang into action. "*Tomi! Sagi! Tulot! Hargi!*" he barked. "*Sunka Roa!* Follow this white devil Bukidnoon and make certain he misses *not* the path to the Sacred Mount. We shall follow after and see the fun, so as you value your lives and wives, let him not escape your vigilance one second. You, Hargi, are fleetest of foot, so carry the box and show the trusting fool the path. *Sunka! Sigi!*"

The four head-hunters he called sprang to do his bidding and Mulud turned to the beached boat. This he looted with the thoroughness born of long practice. After sinking it beyond recovery in the lagoon he was ready to follow. He had no more than completed his treacherous work of gathering up the coveted brass cannon and clock when three of the Dyaks who had followed Marguard burst back into view again. Their faces were the color of dirty ashes as they came pelting up to him.

"*Aue-Aua!*" choked Tulot and glanced behind with terror stricken eyes. "Hargi is dead! He ran ahead with the devil-devil box, disappeared up-trail and a moment later we found him face down with his neck broken. There were no wounds, no marks; neither were there signs of the white-devil trader. Here's evil magic, lord, and we beg that we be not compelled to follow, lest we too be stricken with the silent death. The White One is a sorcerer—an Evil Eye—I for one, saw it in his gaze—which is like nothing so much as that of the giant green-eyed python of the swamps. I—we—"

The chief, who had halted in amazement when the frightened warriors burst into view, searched their sickly faces for a brief space, then leaped into action yelling. Necessarily of sturdier stuff than the rabble and still unawed by the trader's death dealing magic, he was not yet to be frightened away from adding another head to his collection. "*Hay-agh!*" he snarled, "Another trick, that! And you let him escape. Cowards, all three! And you shall answer for it later. Already he is well on his way and if we tarry here cowering like frightened monkeys he will have the god's other eye and be gone. *Sunka! Sunka Roa!* After him. We shall yet trap him and offer him as a sacrifice to the God of Rhibi. After him, cowardly dogs, and the last into the trail shall feel the weight of my kris. *Sunka! Sunka Roa!*"

That was enough for the warriors who seemed to fear the certain vengeance of the chief's crooked knife more than the white man's evil magic and the forest-devils whom they knew must be aiding him. Anyhow they took to their heels as a man, and even the chief was not swift enough to catch the last one as he dove desperately into the matted jungle.

 THE HEAD HOUSE or Shrine, or more properly yet, the den of the sorcerer Amabong and his devil-devil fetish, was, appropriately enough, built of brilliant red sandstone. Carved painstakingly from an upthrust cone in the living rock by some ambitious ancestor of the present fakir, it squatted grim, forbidding and alone on the very lip of the thousand foot cliff that fell away sheer to the purple lagoon washing at its base below. Protected from the sea by a vertical wall of unscalable rock and from land side by a plainly marked Tabu line, the old fakir was safe enough from native disturbance.

But he had learned he was not safe from white-devil gem hunters and for almost six months now he had not been outside the place. Now however, he would soon be relieved of his self imposed exile. Soon a white man would show up, and if his patron devil-spirits had informed him correctly, he would be easily overcome and later be sacrificed as atonement for the Red Eye which was still missing.

So Amabong, sitting on a greasy stone pedestal before the Red One, stirred a pungent brew in a huge kettle of beaten brass and waited. He had observed a ship early that morning and one of his many spies had seen a white man land alone on the beach. It would not be long now—for outside on the wind swept plateau his quick ears caught the swift tread of leather shod feet approaching his door. Amabong chuckled evilly, peered carefully under the pot to see all was in readiness, then settled back to await his visitor.

As quickly as he was in gaining the summit of Mount Rhibi, Marguard was really only a jump ahead of the Dyaks, who, after finding his trail and the dead Hargi, had set off hotly after him. But he was in no wise worried, and really not too much in a hurry. He figured, and rightly, that the Tabu line would hold his pursuers until he had disposed of the sorcerer in his den, so after a brief survey of the bare, sandstone table, he deposited his magic box on the Tabu line, then bracing himself against the boisterous wind, strode boldly toward the low hut.

Seen from the distance of a hundred yards the devil-devil house appeared small. But once inside Marguard found that appearances were deceiving. Dazzled at first by the sudden transition from blinding sunlight outside to the semi-gloom within, he stood for a moment blinking like a startled owl. But if he couldn't see he could smell and suddenly to his nostrils came a myriad of earthly stinks that absolutely defied description. A few he identified, the sickening odors of ancient, decomposed meats and fruits; the awful stench of drying human heads, snake skins, and other filth unmentionable.

Marguard tried for a moment to shut out the almost overpowering stench, but couldn't. However, the spots stopped dancing before his eyes now and he could see the foul nest that housed them. That was what he had come for.

The place was high roofed, rectangular in shape, and literally wainscoated with skulls, dried and drying heads, skeletons of what had been men; mummies, orang-utan bones, skeletons of great jungle snakes and what-not. He surveyed the amazing collection swiftly and glanced toward a tiny flame slickering under the polished brass kettle. As he looked the fire flared up redly and revealed on a pedestal two such figures as had never before come athwart his vision. One of them, the sandstone effigy of the God Rhibi, arrested his gaze first. Standing fully eight feet high, it loomed there like some obscene caricature of the

Buddha, its hideous fat face twisted into a grotesque grimace, its remaining ruby eye glowing like a huge blob of incandescent blood. Marguard drew in his breath sharply and with no little effort dragged his gaze from the glowing eye and looked down on the bent figure of the high priest of Rhibi, who was peering intently into the bubbling pot.

AMABONG PROVED to be an undersized, dried up, evil-visaged Dyak with a twisted, sooty body covered with myriads of scars, tattoo marks and wrinkles. And he looked not unlike an aged orangutan, many of which Marguard had seen on his way through the jungle after he had felled the Dyak with the box. His bleached mop-head was the largest part about him and seemed inadequately supported by a reed-like neck around which was a triple necklace of human finger bones.

Marguard stared down on the twisted, filthy old monkey-man and a shudder of genuine revulsion shook his frame involuntarily. But nevertheless he stepped forward another pace. In a strong voice he made his greeting.

"Hail to Amabong-bong!" he began in the Iban dialect, "Illustrious priest of the Red God of Rhibi, guardian of Mount Rhibi the sacred, and all the Ibans of the tribe of Amabong-bong. I have come, a trusting white man, to replace with a new eye the one another white man stole from the Red God. I hope my coming has caused no inconvenience to your illustrious self, as well as the Red One, and hope you will both look with favor upon one who has gone to no little trouble to bring a new and *real* eye to replace the stolen one. I have spoken and await your pleasure—"

For a long minute after Marguard's flowery oration had ended the medicine man continued to stare into the pot. Then suddenly he bent his gaze upwards and fastened a pair of utterly evil, hypnotic eyes on Marguard. He answered in a voice that was singularly clear and soothing, and entirely out of keeping with the rest of him.

"Well spoken, white man. Well spoken indeed, and in the ancient language of the Ibans. And this *new* eye you have brought with you? Surely you have not braved the perils of the sea-devils, the wind-devils and the forest-devils with no thought of reward. It would not be like a white man to do that, I am sure." Amabong chuckled evilly and bobbed his mop-head knowingly until the necklace of bones around his skinny neck rattled weirdly. "But I know!" he cackled senilely. "I know without asking. I have read all about your mission in the sacred kettle where simmers the very blood of the Red One himself. You have come for the profane head of the white brother devil who stole and lost in the jungle the God's other eye."

He reached behind him quickly and produced a withered blond head which despite the rattan basket-work that held it, Marguard recognized as that of his and Gus Wepler's friend, Carl Gartz. "Am I not right, white man?" he queried, grinning horribly.

"Quite true, Illustrious," agreed Marguard readily. "You are indeed a seer and true prophet. I have come for the head—to take it back for proper burial among his own kind as is our custom. Have I, perchance, by bringing this new eye, properly appeased the Red God so that I may take the head of this misguided unfortunate and go my way in peace?"

"That," said the priest, still grinning, "remains to be seen. The eye, do you have it handy?"

Marguard nodded assent yet puzzled and worried at what seemed an all too ready acquiescence on the part of the fakir, he produced the green eye he had showed the chief on the beach. Not dramatically as he had done on the beach before the gullible warriors, he extended his open palm with the thing glowing in it. But the old wizard would not accept it as he had expected and he was nonplussed for the moment.

"No!" stated the old man shortly, "Drop it into the Sacred Pot. If it withstands the fire of the blood of the Red God it will only then be acceptable. If not—"

Growing more and more puzzled and worried, Marguard stared doubtfully at the old fanatic. But he realized he must eventually comply so he stepped forward to drop his offering in the pot. Then, and only then, did he sense the trick. Like a flash he leaped aside and drew his pistol. And he was not an instant too soon, for over the spot where he would have stood, shot a hissing, roiling stream of molten, pungent substance that looked like lead.

Noting in a flash that he had been frustrated the wily Amabong emitted a yell of baffled rage. Then like a striking cobra lashed out with the keen edged Kamalan he had hoped to behead Marguard with when he bent over to grab frantically at his seared legs. As the trick failed by a hair, likewise he missed his vicious swing with the gigantic knife. Now mouthing horrible maledictions he leaped in with all the fury of a charging leopard, his claw-like talons bent ferociously toward Marguard's neck.

There remained but one thing to do and scant time to do it in, so Marguard fired twice from the hip. Both shots pierced the sorcerer's heart. With a terrible, blood-chilling yell he slid forward on his face and fell twitching in the molten fluid he had intended for his adversary.

 MARGUARD CAUGHT Carl Gartz' head as it rolled from the pedestal, then working swiftly, secured the rattan headbasket to his belt. This done, he leaped over the prostrate form and mounted the pedestal. With the aid of his knife he gouged out the fetish's remaining eye and replaced it with the green one. As soon as he was finished, he dropped down and readjusted the canvas pack to his back and sprang for the doorway.

All this happened in little more than a minute. Consequently when Marguard emerged from the hut, Chief Mulud, who had been impatiently waiting just clear of the Tabu line, had not yet had time to plan his next action. But the instant he saw his enemy leave the devil-devil house he acted, yelled shrilly at his followers, then disregarding the dreaded Tabu line, he sprang like a tiger after Marguard. And from the corner of his eye Marguard saw the long line of head-hunters rise up from their haunches as one man, and like racers suddenly sprung from a barrier, start for him on a dead run. If the chief could defy the age-old tabu tradition so could they. They plunged after him madly.

With sea-green eyes aflame and teeth bared in a sardonic grin, Marguard leveled his pistol and took deliberate aim, then fired at the lacquered casket which still sat on the Tabu line where he had left it. The box exploded on the instant. The plateau rocked and swayed as if suddenly gripped by a rumbling earthquake. The racing Dyaks, stunned by the tremendous concussion, stopped abruptly. Like wilted marionettes they slumped to the ground.

But the effect of the explosion didn't last very long. When Mulud finally staggered to his feet he still had presence of mind enough to know what he was about. There was no known way for the white man to elude them save by deliberately leaping over the cliff and committing suicide. He let out another wild yell and charged madly for the sorcerer's hut. Marguard himself had vanished suddenly after the explosion, but Mulud knew where he had taken refuge and plunged madly after him.

But before Mulud plunged in the door of the fetish house, one of the most curious of his men drew his attention to something white and billowy far below, that drifted on the strong wind current out to where a white-winged sloop lay like a gull on the dimpling bosom of the lagoon.

Young Chief Mulud had been places and seen things. And he had boasted to his men that he could checkmate any trick the white man could devise to escape from the fetish house on the plateau. But he had never seen a parachute nor a man who was brave enough to leap off the cliff with one. For a long while he stared spell bound, fascinated in spite of himself. But when he saw the chute settle like a ball of wind-blown down on the water, he once again leaped into action. He wasn't quite beaten yet, and even as the paralyzed warriors watched, he raced to a huge pile of dry fagots and leaves and set off the signal pyre old Amabong always had ready for emergencies. The wood and leaves caught quickly. Flames leaped and licked upward hungrily. In an amazingly short time a dense column of thick white smoke was reaching heavenward in a signal to the praus standing by in the lagoon below.

With curses and foam spouting from his slit of a mouth chief Mulud left the signal fire and whipped toward his warriors. "Fools!" he yelped, and a light of madness shined in his blood-shot eyes, "You stand there gaping like monkeys, eh? You believe Mulud the Brave defeated, eh? Well, he is not—yet! That's the signal for Tubig and Ulon to put off in the war canoes, so if you want to be at the beach when they bring in the white devil thief to me, you'd better get started. *Hayah!*"

With that he laughed crazily, waved his crooked blade aloft and reeled like a drunken man toward the trail leading from the cliff to the jungle below. The warriors stared after him in amazement, then with nothing better to do, trotted sheepishly after him and soon vanished down the steep trail they had so lately and confidently come up.

 BELOW IN the water Marguard had cut himself free of the encumbering chute with its straps and buckles. Then making sure the head-basket was still safe on his belt, he began to swim toward the sloop which was hovering near. There was no particular hurry. As he stroked leisurely he laughed to himself. It had really been so easy that it now seemed a little tame. The stupid natives had fallen for his every ruse and it had really been a shame to take advantage of them. They had— Then a harsh yell from Ni-Ling. He looked up quickly and saw the Chinaman gesturing frantically, first toward the signal fire on the Mount, then to something that had attracted his attention inshore where a point of land stood ahead and a little to starboard. Instantly the trader sobered and increased his stroke. Also he cursed himself for a fool.

The war *praus*, of course!

Mulud and his men were not so simple after all. If he was to win free he knew he still had some tall work cut out for him. Tame? Easy?

He had been a little premature in his silly gloating, and as he realized this he wondered wildly how many of the craft there would be after him.

Swimming now for all that was in him, Marguard presently made the side and was clawing desperately for the Jacob's ladder hanging ready for him. Koh Hum, the fat Chinaman, was there to help him over the rail, but his face was creased with fright and worry. "Hurry, Master," he pleaded, "the Dyaks have set two *praus* after us."

Marguard made the deck out of breath. He hastily unstrapped the belt with the head basket swinging from it and placed it on the after companion. Then he ran aft where Ni-Ling tended the wheel.

"There!" snarled the old Manchu, jerking his thumb astern and ahead where two giant war craft were converging rapidly upon them, "There they are! Two *praus* loaded to the gunnels with headhunters. I told you we'd never get clear—they're upon us now."

His voice died away in a screaming snarl as Marguard posed on deck with legs spread and eyes flaming. Marguard was quite calm and his tones were level as he expertly sized up the situation.

"So," he said. "Two of them rigged for battle. Well, I see we still have plenty to do before all's settled. Plenty of Samshu and witch-doctors have primed them for a real scrap. Now let's see—"

He wheeled astern, and sure enough, following them at an amazing clip came a gigantic war canoe, not a *prau*, but a great deep-sea cruising *vinta* which as piratical Malays had used in bygone days to take them to the very gates of Manila itself.

He turned grimly to the two Chinamen of his crew. "Well, old warhorses, here's where we've got to show 'em something. Whoever's sailing that *vinta* is a master hand. Light as we are he'll run rings around us in this breeze. Stand by for some real snappy work, for between the two of them we're in for an interesting time." He swiftly surveyed the situation again, then barked suddenly to Ni-Ling. "Hard alee! Come, snappy with that helm!"

 LING SPUN the wheel hard over. The sloop swung into the wind, hung for an instant with blocks clattering and canvas booming, then filled away smartly on the port tack. Marguard and Koh Hum wrestled the boom aft and secured the sheet. Then they left Ling and dashed below. In less than a minute both reappeared, and both were armed. Marguard carried a pistol and a ponderous two-handed cutting kris, while the fat Chino had a carbine and a long knife. Both were ready for sudden battle, and it was well they were, for the prau making to cut them off was now less than two hundred yards distant and the tawny Dyaks were straining mightily to lessen the distance even more.

"Now, Toi," snapped Marguard at his helmsman. "Hold your course till they're within fifty yards of us, then do your best to run them down."

Ni-Ling Toi, veteran of a hundred wild forays during his pirate days, nodded and gripped the spokes with iron fingers. His seared old eyes were aflame with the light of battle and his heart was young again. Gently, very gently, he eased her a spoke to leeward. But the *prau* was traveling with astounding speed. The intervening distance narrowed to fifty yards.

"Now!" Marguard shouted, and strained forward. "At 'em, old turtle! Give 'em the works! *Hay-iee-ah!*"

Ling spun the wheel again and the skipper eased off on the sheet. The sloop wore sharply and plunged toward the *prau* head on. But expertly as the maneuver was executed, it was to no avail. Ever watchful and alert, the Dyak in the stern had anticipated that very move. Shrilly he yelled to his sweating paddlers and threw his weight against the great steering sweep. Then working like machines the warriors backed water and checked headway abruptly. As the sloop bore down on them they skillfully placed their craft so she would fetch up dead alongside.

Marguard swore a tremendous oath, grabbed up the pistol and heavy cutting kris and leaped along the starboard deck with Koh Hum at his heels. Already the first of the Dyaks were over the low rail and charging aft with blood-chilling yells. Marguard fired steadily and repeatedly as he plunged to meet them. Some of the vanguard dropped to the deck, but those behind, about eight in all, surged aft unchecked.

When Koh Hum saw Marguard cast his empty pistol aside he began firing, but perversely the carbine jammed after the first shot. Screeching like a catamount he jerked his long knife out and sprang forward with yellow teeth bared, determined to do as much execution as he could before Death cut him down. But Dan Marguard, famed throughout the Celebes for his agility and expert swordsmanship with native weapons, was to need little help in settling this affair. For a second after dropping his pistol he poised, then for all the world like one of their own kind gone *amok*, he leaped snarling into the fray.

The melee was destined to be a short, if bloody one. The wild Dyaks, charged with firey samshu and tuba wine, had been led into something not exactly calculated upon. Here, they realized too late, was no simple trader to be frightened by awesome yells and brandishing of knives, but instead, a towering, flaming-eyed demon who seemed to know and love all too well this game of hand to hand fighting.

 AS THE howling mob closed in, Marguard met them and brought them to a standstill with two devastating sweeps of the five foot kris. Narrow wooden bucklers fringed with hair of former victims were flung up only to be cut through like cardboard. Coats of tough bark mail capable of turning an arrow or knife point, proved little better than flimsy rice paper. Before they were well aware of it, half their number lay at the demon's feet, while the rest, yelling in terror, turned and broke for the rail. Marguard seemingly as mad as any Dyak gone *juramentado*, pursued them fiendishly, snarling and slashing savagely at their heels.

Three of the Dyaks gained the rail and plunged overboard. The trader, barely an arm's length behind, stormed up just as they hit the water. Swiftly his eyes raked the side, but none hung there. When he looked again the ones who had jumped overboard were swimming frantically toward their half sunken prau far astern. Marguard leaped back from the rail and hurled an oath at the dazed Koh Hum who as yet hadn't got in a single stroke.

"*Hai-ee!* Offspring of a turtle and a slug! Standing there like a mummy—look astern, you fool! Here comes the *vinta*. And by the gods she means to run us down! Below as fast as you can and break out your stink bombs. Jump, you *carabao*, they'll lay us aboard in two shakes! *Hayah!*"

Without looking to see the *vinta* bearing them down astern, Koh Hum scuttled aft like a scared rabbit and dived into the open companionway. Marguard sped aft and shoved Ni-Ling away from the wheel. "Stand by, Toi—wear ship!"

Ni-Ling, who *had* looked astern rereatedly, sprang to obey. Marguard glanced again at the giant war *vinta* and knew he hadn't much time. There was no doubt now as to the Dyak captain's intentions. And Marguard realized with sinking heart that if the plunging craft's knife-like stem came close enough to bite into the hull of the ancient *Gadfly*, they were indeed sunk. But he held the sloop resolutely to her course, and when it seemed they must surely be rammed, he spun the wheel hard down. "Slack away!" he thundered, and old Ling let the sheet go with a run.

Seemingly aware of her peril the sloop answered her helm with a will. Careening like a scared sea bird she swerved sharply to starboard with scant feet separating her from destruction. From astern came howls of baffled rage mingled with the hissing of roiled water as the *vinta* with thrumming cordage and bulging sails, shot past the quarter.

As she tore past Marguard flecked the sweat from his brow and looked to see the Dyak captain's congested, bestial features as he hung dejectedly over the stern of his craft. Defeated by a hair's breadth in his bold attempt to run them down, the Dyak seemed ready to leap overboard in sheer chagrin. And as if to aid him in his decision, Koh Hum charged .ft with two stink bombs in his yellow hands. The *vinta* was still close enough, so with an oath he heaved one of them. It landed squarely in the after part of the *vinta* and exploded with a plop. More wild howls and frenzied screams rent the air, and amidst a dense, choking, acridly burning haze of poisonous smoke, the *vinta*'s crew clawed savagely at one another in their mad struggle to leave the craft which was already burning fiercely.

Koh Hum emitted a yell of unholy glee and threw the other bomb. But the *Gadfly* was footing it away from there top speed and the missile fell short. Koh Hum snarled in disappointment and raced for a high power rifle laying on the after hatch. But before he could begin firing, Marguard, who had sized up things astern again, stopped him.

"No go, Hum, you bloodthirsty heathen! Don't waste good ammunition. You couldn't hit 'em anyway. And if you did it wouldn't be exactly sporting. Let 'em get ashore if they can. And here, if you want something to do, get for'ard and tend that jib. Remember, we've still got to clear that reef ahead, and the tide's beginning to flood strong. For'ard. And you, Ling, handle that boom just like you knew how—So! Let's get going!"

NEXT DAY at noon found the *Gadfly* hove to off Lankayan Island, where Marguard had buried the battered body of Gus Wepler six months before, and where he intended to dispose of the head of Carl Gartz, Wepler's partner.

Koh Hum was aft by the binnacle sewing and getting a canvas bag ready for Gartz's head and Ni-Ling was forward taking soundings to make sure they had the right spot. Marguard was so particular about the matter that it exasperated the crabby old Manchu, who figured they had spent enough time with the two dead men, and the longer they kept the last one's head aboard, the more certain they were to call down some lingering curse on the old sloop which was the only home they knew.

But the skipper had ordered exactly twenty fathoms under the forefoot and the arming in the lead end must show broken shell and hard sand, so Ling knew the sooner he got just that, the sooner the thing would be over and done with. Finally he came aft sourly, coiling his lead line.

"Twenty fathom," he growled. "Twenty fathom, with broked shell and hard sand. If you're satisfied

this is where we buried Wepler, we'll put his partner's head over and finish the job."

Marguard turned from studying the low outline of verdant Lankayan Island and laid his glasses aside. "Why, yes—surely," he agreed, while the corners of his lips upcurled to form that maddening smile Ling so well knew always boded something that would further try his temper. "Yes indeed! You all set, Hum?"

"All set," answered Koh Hum, as he picked Carl Gartz's head off the hatch and put it in the canvas bag. "All ready—here goes—"

Then it came—just as Ling expected. "No!" yelled Marguard suddenly, springing forward in alarm. "Hold on! I almost forgot something. Here, give me that bag—"

He took the bag from the startled Chinaman, fished out the head again, and stood gazing at the gruesome object which had once been part of a human body—alive and vibrant. Then presently he sighed and unsheathed his knife. After setting the thing back on the hatch, he pried the tightly clamped jaws open.

Both Chinamen were puzzled and stared at him as if he had gone mad. For some minutes he probed about in the mouth and throat with his fingers. Then abruptly he brought forth an object which glowed and sparkled in the bright sunlight like a huge globule of incandescent blood. A ruby, it was—a perfectly round pigeon's blood ruby, and a fitting mate for the one he had traded the green eye for up there on Rhibi Mount.

Gus Wepler had been right, as Marguard had always believed he was. His partner *had* placed the thing in his mouth while running from the pursuing Dyaks. When he had stumbled and fallen there in the jungle he had choked to death on the thing. Otherwise he would have escaped with Wepler, swam with him out to Magpie Rock, and there Marguard would have found *two* starved madmen instead of one.

Finally Marguard turned to the gaping and utterly astounded Chinamen. "Here," he said casually to Ni-Ling. "Look 'em both over and see what you think they'd bring in open market at Singapore. Pretty things when they are both together, eh what?"

"By the deathless spirit of Kong Fu Tse!" ejaculated Ni-Ling, once he recovered his breath. "Two of them! Now I know why you were so keen about getting that head!" His eyes glinted with uncontrollable avarice as he rolled the gems in his open palm. "Two of them," he repeated in awed tones. "Why, we're rich! Fifty thousand apiece! A hundred thousand dollars! Why, we can—"

"Only keep *one* of them!" finished Marguard cruelly. "I'm astonished at your thoughtlessness and greed. Only *one* is our rightful share—the one I myself took from the Red Idol. The other goes to the estate of both adventurers. They both had families that need the money. I promised old Gus I'd see that they got it. Anyhow, we're lucky to have one of them and our hides, so we'll be satisfied, I reckon."

"Well," he continued, when neither of the Chinamen moved nor spoke, "Put the head in the bag and cast it overboard. Old Gus is waiting down below somewhere for his pal. And we got to be getting home. Get moving, you two. I see the afternoon Trades are making. Let's get out and grab a bag full of breeze and get started."

BURMESE "KING" LOSES HIS THRONE

There are many types of kings in the world, orthodox and otherwise. One of the strangest was the last outlaw "King" of Great Swinton's Island, one of the Marguie group off the coast of Burma. This little island speck in the Gulf of Bengal is peopled by a wild tribe of savages and their last king, who has just been dethroned and killed by the police, was a Burmese native of mysterious origin who disappeared from the mainland some years ago after a series of bold and brazen robberies.

He showed up later on Great Swinton's Island and was eagerly adopted by the savages there and was soon made their "King."

The police traced him to his remote island and made many attempts to capture him, but each time failed signally. He had organized the native savages and trained them in military discipline. His subjects always put up such stubborn resistance that the meager police forces that were sent to effect his capture were always overpowered, and often times more than lucky to come back with their lives.

But the "King" has fallen now. A policeman lured him to a secret retreat under promise of valuable loot and then shot him dead. The policeman was then offered the "Kingship" in his stead, but turned down the offer and went back to the mainland of Burma.

The HANGING ROPE

'An Ironic Tale
of Stark Retribution

By

L. PATRICK GREENE

 "CURSE YOU—"
The vicious *crack* of a raw-hide whip and the sickening *thut* as the tapered lash cut into the naked body of the prostrate native silenced his voice, but it could not dim the hate which glowed like a burning fire in the tortured man's eyes. That glow represented all the hate which primitive, jungle Africa bears toward the injustice of certain white men, men whose acts are blacker than the African night.

"Curse you—" the native began again.

His voice was drowned by a quick succession of *cracks* and *thuts*. His black flesh parted at the slicing cuts of the whip, like a dead steer's on the block under the operation of a butcher's knife.

There was an angry murmur from the natives who squatted stoically on their haunches about the jungle clearing. One shouted:

"It is enough, white man. He is mad. He is not responsible for what he says. *Wo-we!* It is enough."

Instantly the blows ceased and the squatting natives moved uneasily. They could not meet the cold glare of the white man's eyes. They were cowed by his colossal strength and the evil that dwelt within him.

He stood there, feet wide apart, and looked at them challengingly, threateningly.

He laughed at their confusion; sneered contemptuously at their fear.

There were sixty of them—each one squatting by his load of ivory. He knew that they all hated him, with a hate no less than that which gleamed in the eyes of the man on the ground. He knew that if they rushed him his life would suddenly end. He could not hope to stand against their combined fury.

Still, he laughed at them. He was so confident of his power, so sure that he had beaten from them the very spark of manliness.

He frowned and looked down at the man who sprawled on the ground before him.

That man *had* remembered his manhood. The provocation had been great. The white man, Black Burton he was called, had raided his jungle village; had set fire to the huts; had killed and tortured ruthlessly.

And this man who now sprawled before him had dared to protest; had dared to threaten reprisals.

For a fraction of time Black Burton had been surprised into silence and inaction. But not for long. The lash of his *sjambok*—his raw-hide whip—had answered both threats and protests.

He stood now, outwardly calm, but inwardly a seething volcano of rage. In a sense he felt that he had failed; that he was losing his power. He had expected to hear his victim cry for mercy. That would have pleased him, but it would not have softened him. Actually it would have delayed the native's end a little, that is all. For Burton was an atavism, a throwback to the age when mankind was very young. He found pleasure in the pain of others.

There was something bestial about his appearance. He had a kinship with the gorillas of the jungle. His forehead was low and slanted backward from his thick, bushy eyebrows. His eyes were small and red-rimmed. His nose was short, the nostrils wide.

His face was covered by a tangled black beard. His thick red lips were parted by his laugh and his yellow teeth were like the tearing fangs of a gigantic ape.

The girth of his chest was enormous. The white cotton singlet he wore, stretched tightly across it, was blood-stained; his arms were heavily muscled and abnormally long. His ham-like fists hung almost on a level with his knees.

He flicked the native with his *sjambok*. It was a light, almost caressing, blow but it drew blood. The black flesh quivered.

Black Burton laughed harshly again and drew the lash slowly across the open palm of his left hand. It left a smear of blood.

He licked his lips hungrily.

There was a rustling noise. The circle of natives moved inward. Inch by cautious inch they were closing in on him. Yet he stood there, motionless, as if hypnotized by the material evidence of his brutality.

The jungle seemed strangely silent. Actually it was alive with sound—the drone of bees, the crashing of panic-stricken animals as they raced through the jungle to escape the slinking, flesh-eating cats. A rogue elephant trumpeted shrilly. In the distant swamps, buffalo bellowed. But those sounds seemed unable to pass beyond the green jungle wall which girded the clearing.

The air of the jungle was redolent with exotic scents, the perfume of flowers and the rank odor of game.

But in the clearing was only the scent of tortured Africa, of blood— and the silence of death.

Slowly the circle of natives contracted, but still the white man failed to notice. Their faces were set, their hands clenched tightly. Behind them was the jungle greenness, the jungle shadows. Before them stood Black Burton—blood-stained, body and soul —and at his feet, his almost lifeless victim.

Overhead a brazen sun swam in a sky of pitiless, electric blue.

The silence was oppressive.

AND THEN a native, made careless perhaps by the thought of an easy victory, trod on a sun-dried, rotten twig.

The noise of its snapping beneath his feet sounded like a revolver shot.

Instantly the attitude of Black Burton changed. That ominous report served to dispel the stupor which had possessed him. With a bull-like roar he leaped at the natives directly before him, his right hand rising and falling with awful regularity. He turned that clearing into a bedlam of hellish noises. His brutal, sneering laugh, his lurid curses and bloody threats were fit accompaniments to the *crack* of his whip and the dull *thuts* as the lash bit into unresisting flesh.

Back and forth across the clearing Burton drove the natives. Not one dared to face him; not one thought of seeking the comparative safety of the jungle shelter. Back and forth, round and round the clearing they ran, seeking to escape his blows; yelling for mercy.

At last they huddled together at one end of the clearing. They stood there facing him, eyes protruding, their mouths agape. They were like a flock of sheep facing a barking dog —too frightened to run. There was not one amongst them unmarked by the white man's whip.

Burton laughed at them. He advanced slowly toward them cracking his whip menacingly. He laughed again as they cowered tremblingly.

"You dogs!" he exclaimed in a harsh, grating voice, and he spat his contempt at them. "Haven't you learnt your lesson yet? Do you dare to seek my death? Answer!"

And they bleated timidly:

"Forgive us, strong one."

He licked his lips.

"Forgive?" he laughed. "And what is that? Tell me now—what are you?"

"Your dogs," they replied tonelessly.

"Then see you do not forget it. You are mine. If it pleases me to kill you—then I will kill you. *Wo-we!* I am tempted to kill you all—here and now. It is not weakness that holds my hand. You know that?"

"We know it, master."

"No, not weakness," he repeated. "But I have need of you. There is a trek before us. We are still four hours from my store. If we trek fast we will be at my place before the setting of the sun. That long, at least, I will permit you to live. Now —get to your packs."

They hastened to obey, rushing past him; a panic-stricken mob. One, losing his balance by the pressure of men to the right and behind him, stumbled against Burton and instinctively clutched hold of the white man.

Burton shook him off and, drawing his revolver—it hung in a holster at his belt—shot the luckless native through the head. And somehow, that cold, machine-like killing demonstrated the brute he was, even more than the cruel beatings had.

The carriers stared apathetically before them; unmoved, apparently, by the cold-blooded murder of their companion. It was as if their own feeble efforts at rebellion had sapped all intelligence and strength from them.

At a word from Burton they picked up their loads and balanced them on their heads. They stood there, waiting patiently—like dumb beasts of burden—for the order to trek.

Black Burton stood looking at the waiting line, gently tapping his thigh with his *sjambok*. And each tap left a red smear on his white duck trousers.

He was just about to give the order to march when the man he had t h r a s h e d to the point of death, groaned loudly and, with an effort, sat erect. He supported himself with his left hand on the ground behind him. His right hand was stretched out before him, and he pointed a trembling finger at Burton.

"Curse you, white man!" he screamed. "Listen to the curse of Africa upon you. You have shed much blood. *Wo-we!* The blood of those you have slain paints red the jungle's greenness. But no blood shall flow at your death. And your time is close at hand. Before another sun has risen, white man, you will die. By your pleasure—you shall die. You——"

He could say no more. Strength failed him. He fell back to the ground and stared sightlessly up into the glare of the sun. It is doubtful if he felt even the first of the hail of blows that the anger-maddened Burton rained upon him.

But even Burton's tremendous strength could not indefinitely support such a stress of passion. Presently his savage attack upon the unresisting flesh ceased. He swayed weakly for a moment and drew the back of his hand across his eyes, like a man awakening from a troubled sleep.

Then he shook himself, shouted a series of orders to the carriers and, putting himself at their head, led the way along a jungle trail.

But two carriers remained behind; two beside the dead pair sprawled grotesquely in the clearing.

They had long bladed hunting knives in their hands; they whetted them on the soles of their naked feet.

Then they grinned at each other and approached the dead bodies....

Most hunters remove the skins from the beasts they have killed. They are their trophies of the hunt.

Black Burton was no exception.

IT WAS sunset when Black Burton and his carriers came to the store which, built on a high rise of land, over-looked the wide valley of the river which carries on its yellow flood the wealth of Africa—gold, rubber, white ivory and black.

Burton supervised the stowing away of the ivory he had taken by force from the kraals, then dismissed the carriers to their vermin-invested quarters. He hastened the laggards on their way with vicious cuts from his whip.

Not until then did he turn to face the white man who had stood nearby, watching Burton with expressions of disgust, contempt and fear showing in his mild blue eyes. He was a neatly-dressed, meek little man. Burton had more strength in one arm than he had in his whole body.

"What in hell are you doing here, Fraser?" Burton bellowed. "You keep to your own side of the river. I warned you once before. I won't have you over on this side, spoiling my niggers by payin' 'em high prices."

"I didn't come to trade, Burton," Fraser said softly.

"Then what have you come for?"

"To warn you."

"To warn me? Against what?" Burton laughed contemptuously.

"Death."

Burton stared, puzzled by Fraser's matter-of-fact tone.

"And you'd warn me against that?" he asked incredulously.

"Yes," Fraser replied. "And I'm damned ashamed of myself for warning you. You deserve death. You deserve torture——"

He stopped, intimidated by Burton's silent stare, afraid of his own boldness. He swallowed with an effort and continued:

"You can't go on like this for ever, Burton. Thrashing, looting, killing. I've warned you before that you'd be held to account one of these days and—"

"If you're trying to tell me that the niggers are planning to knife me," Burton interrupted, "you can save your breath. What do you think I am? A white-livered missioner? Hell! I can clear the jungle of a million of 'em, armed only with a *sjambok*. The yellow curs run at the sight of my shadow."

"Well—I've warned you." Fraser said in a tired voice. "I've warned you because I'm fool enough to think white men ought to stick together. Yes, I'm a fool. You're not a white man—"

Shouting curses, Burton rushed at him, brandishing his *sjambok*.

Fraser paled but he stood his ground; his hand rested on the butt of his revolver and its cold touch gave him courage.

Burton sensed this. He knew the little man would not hesitate to shoot.

He dropped his *sjambok*.

He grinned ingratiatingly—and that grin made his face even more bestial.

"Hell!" he exclaimed. "There's no sense in us acting like this. Reckon I'm tired; been trekking too hard—"

"Been flogging too hard, you mean," Fraser interrupted.

"What?" Burton stared at him curiously a moment and then, seeing that Fraser was looking intently at his blood-stained *sjambok*, laughed hoarsely. "Oh, that!" he said. "That's nothing. That's the only way a white man can talk to niggers—with a *sjambok*. They don't understand anything else."

"I hear you killed one—"

"Two," Burton corrected smugly. "One I thrashed. The dog dared to accuse me of murder. He threatened me. He—"

'Yes. I know all that. The drums beat out the message. His name was Bombra. He cursed you before he died, didn't he?"

"Yes." Burton moved uneasily. Then, in a more confident voice, he added: "But what of it? I've been cursed by a thousand niggers—and I'm still alive."

"Bombra was a witchdoctor," Fraser said slowly. "Have you forgotten that? They say he was one of the most powerful in the district. You tortured and killed his people. You put his kraal to flames. You beat him to death. *I* should be afraid of the curse of a man like that."

Burton was silent.

The sun set; the redness of its after-glow faded from the sky. Darkness became absolute.

The drone of mosquitoes filled the air. From kraals hidden in the depths of the jungle sounded the monotonous beating of tom-toms and the weird chanting incantations of a savage people. Down in the river sounded the hoarse bellows of crocodiles.

Lights suddenly appeared in Burton's large living hut. A white clad native appeared in the open doorway and shouted.

"Skoff is served, *Baas*.

Burton started. He laughed self-consciously.

"Come and have skoff with me, Fraser."

He laughed again at the little man's positive refusal.

"I wouldn't have skoff in that hut of yours, Burton," Fraser said, "if I was starving. God, man! What are you made of? Have you no nerves, no imagination? Don't you ever dream?"

"What of, man?"

Fraser's indignation almost choked him.

"You festoon your hut with ropes made from the skins of men you have flogged to death—and you ask me that! The devil's in you, Burton!"

Burton shrugged his wide shoulders.

"You carpet your hut with the skins of leopards you have shot. You cover your bed with a kaross of monkey skins. I don't see that there's much difference between us."

Fraser gasped.

"The skins of animals! The skins of men! No difference? You must be mad. Well, I've warned you, Burton. Don't treat Bombra's curse too lightly."

He turned swiftly on his heel and ran down the hill to the river's ford as if seeking to escape from the devil.

For a little while Burton stood staring into the darkness. Then he walked slowly toward his hut.

IT WAS nearly midnight. Black Burton, lounging in a wicker chair, helped himself to a stiff tot of whiskey from a nearly empty bottle. That bottle had been full when the night was young. He drank the whiskey neat, the expression on his face unchanging.

He slumped even more in his chair; his huge, muscular body was completely relaxed.

He looked around his orderly hut, a smile of smug satisfaction on his face.

All the flying pests of Africa's night fluttered around the stinking oil lamps which lighted the room. He found a modicum of amusement whenever one, its wings seared by the heat, fluttered helplessly to the ground.

From the rafters which supported the high ceiling—his hut was only native in shape, its construction was European—were festooned lengths of plaited raw-hide. Strong ropes—made from the skins of men who had died at his hand.

As he looked at them, there was an expression of pride in his eyes. Those skins were his trophies. In a sense, he regarded them as a big game hunter regards *his* trophies. There was the same feeling of satisfaction, an inward glow of achievement. But his sensations were of an infinitely baser origin.

And, as a big game hunter will dwell on every smallest detail of the chase which led up to the securing of a prized head; so Burton, in his mind, now re-lived each one of the brutalities which had enabled him to add to his collection. He did not forget one blood-letting blow.

His eyes glazed; he looked like a man revelling in pleasant day dreams.

Presently his thoughts turned to the affair of the day; the affair in the clearing at high noon. He thought of the killing of Bombra, the witchdoctor, and of the killing of that other man; the luckless carrier who had stumbled against him.

His thoughts stirred him to action. He rose to his feet and stumbled around the hut, trying to decide in his mind where he would hang his new trophies—after the skins had been sun-dried, stretched and plaited.

At one place where the ceiling was highest, a loop of "rope"—it had slipped off the wooden peg on which it had been draped—hung low. He resolved to put that loop back in its place.

Burton measured the distance with his eye and, lugging the deal table under the loop, climbed onto it.

But the beam was still beyond the reach of his out-stretched hand.

Cursing softly, he reached down and lifted a chair on to the table. He climbed onto the seat and stood there, swaying slightly as the chair creaked under his weight.

Gradually he straightened himself. His hands, stretched above his head, were thrust against the thatch roof.

That thrust steadied him.

He looked along the beam for the peg on which to put the loop of "rope" which dangled down on a level with his neck.

Not finding it, he put his head through the loop and peered up at the other side of the massive beam.

He was sweating profusely. Big beads dripped from his forehead. It was very hot there under the roof.

At the kraal the tom-toms continued the maddening monotony of their beat; a monkey screamed and a leopard leaped.

Burton wiped his forehead with the back of his right hand. His left was still thrust against the thatch, and the unevenness of the thrust made the chair wobble.

With an almost panic-stricken haste he thrust his right hand back against the thatch. He hit it with such force that he was almost blinded for a moment by a cloud of fine dust. Then he felt something cold and clammy twining about his naked arm.

He opened his eyes and saw that a snake, dislodged from the thatch, had wrapped itself about his forearm.

It was only a harmless grass snake. He knew that. But his reaction was instinctive and violent. He exhibited the unreasoning fear of mankind for the sudden death which creeps on its belly.

He tried to dislodge the squirming thing; he tried to brush it off with his other hand.

The chair wobbled under the strain of his weight and his frenzied activities. The table over-turned and Burton dropped.

His downward fall was suddenly checked. That loop of rope caught about his neck . . .

For a fraction of time he hung there—gurgling, clawing, kicking.

Red mists swam before his ears. The drumming of a million tom-toms sounded in his ears. Tortured Africa shouted with one voice—the voice of Bombra, the witchdoctor. He heard again the curse of that pain-racked man—"By your pleasure you shall die."

And then he struggled no more. The red mists gave way to utter darkness; he was engulfed in a great silence.

IT WAS sunrise when the two natives who had remained behind at the clearing came to the hut of the trader. Timidly they knocked at the door.

Receiving no reply, they cautiously opened the door and entered.

They halted then, and stared open-mouthed at the grotesque form which dangled from a high beam.

Then, flinging the bloody bundle they carried at the man who could no longer torture them, they turned and ran headlong from the place; shouting the news of their discovery.

And all that day, the jungle echoed with the songs and happy shouts of a people removed from the shadow of a great evil.

BACKWASH

By
JOHN GUNN

A Tale of Poetic
Justice In the Back
Alleys of Singapore

IT WAS LATE in the spring of the year when the Bum arrived. There was nothing unusual about him, nothing to differentiate him from the countless other beachcombers in the East, save perhaps his very extreme stage of dilapidation. His head was bare, covered by a tangled mop of bristly black hair that straggled down over his lean cheeks in a dark stubble of beard. A tattered cotton shirt, one sleeve missing, clung limply to his flesh; while from beneath a ragged pair of dirty white ducks, two bare feet protruded. God alone knows from what sink-hole of the East he resurrected himself to finally crawl to Philippine Joe's. But he did somehow, irresistibly impelled forward to his fate.

Besides his extreme state of decay there was only one other thing worth mentioning about the Bum—his stature. He barely topped five feet in height and his strong-ribbed, hairy barrel chest gave him the grotesque appearance of some mountain gnome out of mythology.

He was a two-day sensation. Philippine Joe was the first to set him up to a drink. The rest took their cue from the philanthropic dispenser of booze.

The Bum got by easily for a couple of days. He polished the brass rail of the bar and cleaned out the cuspidors that shown like dirty moons in the sawdust, for an occasional hand-out and a place to flop.

Save for his hirsute growth and his build, he was the exact counterpart of countless other sea waifs who had drifted into Philippine Joe's. He was the same, that is, till the advent of Lily, and from that time on our story begins.

Lily, too, was one of the casualties of the East, a harum-scarum bit of humanity washed up by the tide. Her origin was shrouded in mystery, for long years lost and forgotten. If Lily ever had a mother and father no one knew about it and cared less. She was two or three degrees higher up in the social scale than the Bum. Whereas he merely lived off occasional charity, the girl did her best to keep body and soul together by selling ha'penny packets of matches at the waterfront bars.

No one, by any possible stretch of imagination, could have called her good-looking, far less beautiful. There wasn't enough meat on her for that. She had a half-starved child's body, though she had turned twenty-three, and large luminous eyes that shown like deep water sea pools out of her pale, thin face.

But to the Bum her coming was a revelation of all the feminine charms. To him she was not only beautiful but the personification of all the lovely graces. There was some subtle bond between them—outcasts in an alien land. Their eyes met for the first time and something happened. Something new, strange and uplifting happened to the soul of the Bum.

He merely looked at her, at first—followed her slight body around the bar with surreptitious eyes as she attended to her sales. He dared not speak to her. Who was he to violate such a fragile thing by even the contact of speech? When she was gone—with a queer little nod of her head in his direction, the room suddenly became dull, oppressive. For the first time in many moons the Bum was suddenly dissatisfied with his estate in life.

Lily came to Philippine Joe's the next day and the next and the next. And about her the Bum builded himself a rosy, ethereal romance. He never dared hope to realize it in the actuality, never even dared hope to touch her hand. But that was where he was wrong. The inscrutable Fate of the East took a hand in the game to throw them together for life—save for a brief, unavoidable separation. But that comes later.

IT WAS about a week after Lily's first coming to Philippine Joe's that it happened. It was night and the bar was more noisy and rowdy than usual. One giant of a man in particular, Sailor Garrigan, was taking his liquor the wrong way. He became ugly, pugnacious. He trumpeted loudly and boldly through the room that he could lick any six men in the place, and when no six worthies stepped forward to accept his challenge he promptly doubled the quota to a round dozen.

Sailor Garrigan was a mountain of a man, red-headed, pig-eyed and a bully. Philippine Joe should have known better than to sell him more hard liquor, but money is money and Sailor Garrigan had it. As long as his silver lasted the bottle was forthcoming.

Garrigan was proclaiming to the bar in general, with wide expansive gestures and a gnarled fist to emphasize his words, that he was a tough nut. He had pretty well convinced his unwilling listeners of that fact when the door opened and Lily entered with her tray of matches. The Bum hadn't been much interested in Garrigan's bombastic words; he had been watching the door. And now on the entrance of the girl his barrel chest inflated, his eyes lit up with fire and with a grimy hand he smoothed his matted hair. To the Bum, Lily was growing more beautiful day by day. It was a miracle to him how such a lovely creature could thrive in such a vile atmosphere.

She threw him her curious half-nod, smiled tenderly at him as the noise of the room assailed her. It was as if she were thanking him in her shy way for the assurance of his friendship.

The Bum smiled back, a curious twisted thing that showed a warm red line in the black of his beard. Smiles came hard to him—he had almost forgotten how, so long had it been since he had been moved by any emotion but a bitter cynicism. Lily started to make the round of the tables, hesitantly offering her wares to an indifferent public. The Bum watched her with fascinated eyes, watched every movement of her slim body as wraith-like she weaved her way through the crowd.

His eyes narrowed dangerously beneath his heavy brows and his hairy nostrils quivered as Lily approached the bar and the little circle surrounding the drunken Garrigan. Such was the sympathy between them, that some psychic sense warned him that trouble was in the offing.

Sailor Garrigan had just reached the climax of some tale of fabulous adventures as Lily approached the bar. She held up her tray for better inspection, a mute appeal in her eyes. This slight diversion gave the ring of unwilling listeners surrounding Garrigan an opportunity to break away. Garrigan didn't like that. It pricked his alcohol-inflated ego. He glared down on the girl as he leaned easily against the bar, the loose skin about his pig eyes crinkling in anger. His massive underslung jaw jutted forward aggressively.

Lily shrank instinctively before his menacing glare. And that one sign of weakness, that slight show of fear, was all that was needed to cause a violent disturbance to the delicately balanced nerves of Sailor Garrigan. He lurched suddenly forward from the bar and before anyone could interfere—not that they would have—his huge ham of a fist swept the tray from Lily's hand and scattered her precious stock in trade to the far corners of the room. Lily crouched back, prepared for a blow that would be dealt to her person.

Someone in the room started to laugh, but the laugh was never completed.

The Bum had witnessed the scene and every instinct in him rebelled; every nerve and cell in him protested. It was monstrous to him that the girl, who to him was the greatest blessing of life, should be so grossly insulted. He suddenly catapulted himself forward, arms flailing, legs thrashing—a hairy primeval creature—straight at Sailor Garrigan.

The Sailor was taken completely by surprise at the suddenness of the attack. The Bum, head first, landed full in his stomach. The two of them together, midst a clatter of tumbling bar chairs and the tinkle of breaking glass, crashed heavily to the sawdust-littered floor. A throaty clamor of voices rose from the onlookers in the bar, but clarion above it was the bull-like bellow of rage that rumbled from Garrigan's throat.

He clawed himself ponderously to his feet, dragging along with him his diminutive attacker. The Bum, dangling ridiculously at the end of his long arms, struck out furiously with both fists. But his blows were futile. He could not reach Garrigan's face and they fell impotently on the mighty girth of the sailor's chest.

For a moment Garrigan stared curiously at the writhing lump of humanity swinging on his fist. He examined it from all sides as a fisherman might consider a strange and unusual catch. Then, really satisfied that his attacker was indeed a man, he slowly pulled back a ponderous fist and crashed it full into the Bum's face. The Bum crumpled beneath the blow, went limp in Garrigan's outstretched hands, and then, as if dropping a dead cat overboard, the sailor let the slack body crumple to the floor.

There was a general outburst of appreciation from the hangers-on at this graphic demonstration of Garrigan's prowess. The knot of drinkers again gathered around him and he resumed his story.

During the beating up of the Bum, Lily had cowered in a far corner of the room, her eyes fascinated and horrified by the spectacle. Now, cautiously, so as not to attract attention, she made her way across the room to where her defender was slowly coming back to consciousness. She reached one pitifully trembling hand out to him, helped him to drag himself to his feet.

It was then that Garrigan swung around from the bar and caught sight of them. He snarled, his lips baring back from yellow teeth. Lily shrank back but still continued to clutch the Bum's hand. Some atavistic thrill coursed through Sailor Garrigan's veins at the girl's obvious fear of him. He looked at her closely for the first time, found her insignificant indeed. But such was the perversity and meanness of the man, that since she evidently preferred the Bum to himself, he immediately found her desirable.

Slowly he took his eyes off her and turned their baleful glare on the Bum.

"That'll teach you, my bucko, to keep your filthy hands off a sailor man."

The Bum was seized with a furious emotion he could not express. He glared up at Garrigan from beneath his bushy brows, his eyes twin agate balls of hate. It was a challenge, and in return Garrigan's lips again curled back off his teeth.

Lily began to tremble, her hand became moist and wet as she plucked at the Bum's tattered sleeve.

"Come," she whispered. "Please—for me."

And something within the Bum answered her voice. Reluctantly, he turned away from Garrigan and followed the girl out into the night.

 THAT WAS the beginning of a strange friendship between Lily, the match girl, and the Bum; the strangest friendship Singapore was ever to know. That's all it was at first. The two were struck dumb by the bigness and strangeness of the thing that had happened to them. Few words were said between them, but their eyes told the story. They met every day at Philippine Joe's; said a few hurried words together, that was all. But to the Bum it was enough. A little goodness, tenderness, kindness in his life went a long ways. As for Lily—half-starved as she was, sea waif and outcast, she too responded to romance. Never before had man seen fit to fight for her. It was a terrifying, wonderful experience.

But if serenity and harmony ruled the relationship between the Bum and the girl, not so between the Bum and Sailor Garrigan. There was an undying enmity between the two men; a scornful contemptuous disdain on the part of Garrigan and a flame-like bitterness from the Bum. Their diametrically opposed physical natures nurtured and fostered it. It was inevitable.

And all the while Garrigan looked on the girl Lily, with brooding eyes. Far back in his dark mind vague things were stirring, terrible things. Someday, somehow he would strike at the Bum through the girl.

 A MONTH passed and the stimulating effect the girl had on the Bum was manifested in more tangible ways than soft words. He was missed from Philippine Joe's throughout one day, only to come back triumphantly at night to announce that he had gotten himself a job. What? Heresy! The Bum a job? The crowd laughed.

But it was true. Instead of earning his precarious living cleaning cuspidors and polishing bar rails, he was to get a weekly stipend for performing the duties of watchman at one of the Standard Oil tank farms.

He was working, drawing a pay envelope every week. He was again, after a lapse of God knows how many years, a respectable member of society. Sailor Garrigan sniffed at the news.

"You'll be wearing shoes next, Bucko," he yelled across the room.

"Over your grave," flung back the Bum, tossing up his shaggy head defiantly.

It was little exchanges of witticisms like that, that kept the enmity between the two ever burning. But a few minutes later, at the entrance of Lily, the Bum forgot all about Sailor Garrigan and the blood feud between them. Hesitantly, shyly, half-proud, half-ashamed, he told the girl of his good fortune. She positively beamed on him and for a swift second her hand trembled on his.

"I'm glad," she said simply. "For your sake."

"And I am for you," he replied.

And from such simple kindnesses is romance built. It flourished, it prospered, along with the Bum's rise in fortune. He *did* get a pair of shoes and it was Lily who kept his cotton shirts and white ducks clean.

Two months later he married her. It was a simple ceremony performed at the chapel of the Methodist mission. When the ceremony was over, the matron primly gave the regenerate souls her blessing and they departed.

 THE BUM had already prepared for his bride a mansion on Arthur street. True, it was on the top floor of a ramshackle, dilapidated, three-story wooden structure, and it contained but two rooms.

But it was a mansion for them just the same.

Now if ever by chance you have shopped for preserved ginger or jade on Arthur Street, you will know that it is very, very narrow and crooked. The old, three story wooden houses, warped with age, lurch crookedly against one another in intimate fashion and occasionally lean across the narrow alley way that marks the street towards one another, like old neighbors out for a bit of gossip.

Number 21 Arthur Street, at which place the Bum brought Lily to lodge, was the most tipsily leaning building of all that long row of crooked houses that flanked it on either side. It leaned drunkenly, not only against its crowding neighbors, but toppled over on the street at a dizzy angle. From the rakish slant of the windows on the top floor, to the corresponding window of the house across the way, there was but a few feet of intervening space. A short-armed man— even the under-sized Bum—by leaning far over the sill, could have reached from one room to the other.

And it was at this point in his story that Fate again entered the scene.

Sailor Garrigan's hoard of yellow gold and silver was fast disappearing across the counter of Philippine Joe's bar. In fact, he was perilously close to being broke. To conserve his wealth as much as possible, he moved from the shabby hotel Philippine Joe operated in conjunction with his cafe —moved to the top floor of the house directly opposite the one in which the Bum and Lily lived.

The couple were very happy together. Their romance was one of the marvels of Singapore's waterfront. And the bitter realization that the Bum had something that he hadn't, in some inexplicable way infuriated Sailor Garrigan. For long hours on end he would sit on the one rickety chair in his room and gaze sullenly across the street into the Bum's apartment.

The girl grew on him, in direct proportion as his bitter hatred of the Bum unreasonably increased. He suddenly found her desirable, as he followed with hungry eyes her fairy-like movements around the room. But there was nothing he could do about it. The girl ignored him emphatically, gave him no opening for a chance smile, a chance remark. And to make things still worse, the Bum had undying trust in her.

Their fortunes prospered as Sailor Garrigan's declined. Odd bits of furniture were added to the top floor of 21 Arthur Street. While dumbly across the way, Garrigan brooded in sullen silence over his last dollar. But all the brooding in the world could not multiply it and hard liquor still cost money. Garrigan awoke one morning with a sour taste in his mouth and the bitter realization that he was broke—stony broke.

He caught a glimpse of the Bum across the way, sitting down to a breakfast prepared by Lily, and he growled. He watched him malevolently, from eyes red with malice. Then with an oath he heaved himself out of his bed, lurched across the floor kicking the rickety chair savagely out of his way and quitted the room. He barged sullenly into Philippine Joe's, banged his ham of a fist on the bar and demanded a drink.

Philippine Joe obliged him with the first. When Garrigan demanded a second, P h i l i p p i n e wanted to see the color of his money. Garrigan spewed forth a picturesque oath, puffed out his chest, clenched his fists and glared at the proprietor behind the mahogany. But Philippine Joe was not to be so easily bluffed. He returned the stare unflinchingly and finally, with a muttered rumble deep down in his throat, Garrigan turned away.

Now that his money was gone, he was not so welcome in Philippine Joe's. If he couldn't set up the boys to drinks, he couldn't compel them to listen to his stories. All of which didn't sweeten Sailor Garrigan's very sour disposition that morning. He returned in a towering rage to his room, convinced that the world was conspiring to make things miserable for him. And of all the people who galled him, surely the Bum took first place in his animosity.

With a surly oath he righted the rickety chair with his foot, planted it by the window and sat down. Some day—some day he would strike at the Bum. And again in his dark mind stirred the realization that the best way to hurt him would be through the girl.

 IT TOOK two days of acute hunger and thirst to drive Garrigan to it.

Night. An evil street with the dark tides of the harbor lapping mysteriously somewhere before him. The creaking of a ship chafing uneasily at her mooring lines. Garrigan knew that ship, knew that she had just made port that day. Sailors would be coming ashore soon, careless, unseeing, thinking of naught but the nearest bar. Their pockets would be full of silver.

Garrigan crouched back in the shadows as a footfall sounded down the dockway. Something cold and evil glittered in his hand. The step came closer. Garrigan tensed himself for action. Abruptly out of the night the man was before him and he leaped forward. He jammed the point of his stiletto blade into the man's spine—pricked through the heavy pea-jacket to the skin to show that he meant business.

"One peep out of you, mister, and you get the knife," he whispered hoarsely. "Quick! Your roll."

The sailor hesitated a moment.

Garrigan's knife prodded deeper. Slowly his victim brought to light a heavy wallet—held it before him. Garrigan's left hand reached eagerly around for the prize, was about to snatch it when the other suddenly dove for his wrist.

Garrigan never knew exactly how it happened, had never intended it to happen; but a moment later he was panting over the body of the sailor, a hideous stained knife in one hand, the purse in the other. He took one swift look at the crumpled figure lying face down in the dirt of the alley, then stuffed the knife and wallet in his pocket, melted into the shadows and ran.

By devious routes he made his way back to his room on Arthur street. Hurriedly he bolted the door behind him, pulled down the shade that masked the window. Then with trembling fingers he struck a match and applied it to the gas jet that protruded from the wall by the side of the bed.

His hands were red. He looked at them once, winced and turned away, then carefully washed them with coarse yellow soap and water. All evidence of the crime removed from his person, Garrigan felt for the purse to count his prize. A chill shudder ran through him again as his fingers encountered the steel blade. He had not disposed of that yet. Slowly he pulled it out from his pocket, held it gingerly by the hilt and examined it. The bright steel was stained an ugly dark red. Garrigan placed it on the window ledge for a moment while he felt for the wallet. The knife was forgotten while he poured a limpid stream of silver pieces onto the bed and greedily counted them.

Big money. Enough to keep Sailor Garrigan out of work and in drink for a long time. His first impulse was to barge out to Philippine Joe's for the much needed bracer his nerves demanded, but it was then that his cunning cautioned him. Everybody at Philippine Joe's knew that he was broke. It would not be wise to go there rolling in wealth again so soon—so soon after the . . . . .

Hurriedly Garrigan gathered up the silver pieces, secreted them under a loose board beneath his bed. Then his attention was drawn back to the purse. There was that and the knife still to be disposed of. He crossed the room to the window for the blade, lifted it off the sill and buried it in his pocket again.

Then mechanically he turned out the gas jet, pulled up the shade and looked across the alley. The first thing he saw was the dwarfed figure of the Bum moving around in the room across the street, with the slight figure of Lily in the background. A dark scowl crossed Garrigan's face. He watched them heavily for a moment, then something clicked in his mind—the something that had been stirring deep down in his brain for a long time.

For long patient hours he sat there by the window cunningly evolving his plan. The light across the street had long since gone out. But Garrigan did not move. A distant clock struck one, two before he stirred.

It was dark outside. The sky was overcast between the tenement roofs. No stars shone through. The pale blur of the street lamp on the far corner was ineffective in its battle against the night. Without haste Garrigan lifted up the window sash, peered out once up and down the street, and finding it black and deserted, leaned far over the sill with arm outstretched. The tips of his fingers stirred the draperies at the window of the Bum's room and parted them. Then carefully he deposited the blood-stained knife and the empty wallet in the house of the Bum and withdrew his arm.

AN HOUR later a squad of local police, working on an anonymous tip, raided number 21 Arthur street and on the top floor by the window found the incriminating evidence. The Bum and Lily were hauled away to jail and Garrigan, watching from his window as they were dragged away, smiled evilly to himself.

Fortunately for Lily and the Bum, Garrigan's victim did not die. The Bum was remanded to jail until he was able to give evidence. When he did, he was doubtful whether the Bum had been his attacker. The outcome of it all was that the Bum was given a year sentence in jail. Everything considered, that was a pretty good break for the Bum.

But Lily, on the outside, was not making such a good time of it. There was rent to be paid, food to be bought —and no money. She took up her old profession again of peddling matches in the waterfront bars. But the pennies she garnered were not enough to keep the two top rooms at 21 Arthur Street.

There were other ways, easier ways to make money in Singapore, but Lily was faithful—faithful to the Bum. If he was doomed to be away for a year, she would wait. All things must pass in time. Garrigan himself made advances to her, but she was magnificent in the manner in which she spurned him. He never tried again.

The Bum heard an occasional word of Lily in the jail, and a great sorrow filled him. But he was behind iron bars and there was no wishing them away. Slowly, drearily, the days of summer, fall and winter slipped by. Spring again, and the year of his sentence was up. It was a bright May morning when the iron door of the jail clanged shut behind him and he again went out into the world a free man.

Lily was there waiting for him, wan, pale, smiling through her tears at him. The Bum pressed her hand. Few words were said between them. There was no need for words. Hurriedly they made their way along the waterfront to their old house on Arthur street. The top floor was still vacant.

They picked up the thread of their life where it had been broken off a year before. The Bum regained his job as watchman at the tank farm. On the surface everything ran smoothly enough, but there was something fomenting in the back of the Bum's brain.

As luck would have it, Sailor Garrigan was still living on the top floor of the house across the alley. The two men would glare at each other across the narrow street until Lily would come and drag the Bum away from the window.

The Bum knew he had been trapped, framed by Garrigan. But how—he did not know. How had that blood-stained dagger and the purse been planted in his room? That was the question. He applied all his cunning to the problem. Slowly he brought to bear all his plodding logic to solve the riddle.

It was a week after his return to Arthur street that he saw the light. It came to him in an illuminating burst of inspiration. It was so simple, so very simple that . . . . .

Later that night he sent Lily around to the Mission. There was a party there with music and she would have a good time. She protested at first at leaving him home alone, but he insisted. Finally she went.

From the window on the top floor the Bum watched her go, followed her slim body up the street and out of sight. Then, raising his eyes to the house opposite, watched Garrigan cook three pills of opium over the lighted gas jet. He saw him light

the first, the second; saw him vaguely through a pall of smoke as he found his bed and lit the third.

 BY TWELVE o'clock a high wind was tearing at the tin roofs of the wooden houses that lined Arthur street, and a slanting rain flushed the deserted streets. Sailor Garrigan was lost deep in an untroubled opium slumber of bliss and seeing these things the Bum smiled to himself.

Without haste or hurry he rose from his chair and opened the window. A baffled burst of wind tore at his loose shirt and billowed the tattered shade. But the Bum did not mind. He peered once up and down the street and finding it black, wet and deserted, leaned far over the sill with arm outstretched. The tips of his fingers just managed to touch the sash of the window across the alley.

Slowly he raised the frame an inch, a foot, whatever noise he made drowned in the roar of the storm. A bawdy gust of gale zoomed around the corner, rattled boisterously at the pane of glass a moment, then with a high-pitched wail of triumph darted tempestuously under the raised window.

The two inch tongue of flame dancing from the gas jet which projected from the wall—the flame over which Garrigan had cooked his opium pills —flickered frantically for a moment in the rushing current of air, then hissed spasmodically and went out. Slowly the Bum lowered the window and withdrew his arm.

 A SOLITARY floral piece decorated the unmarked grave of Sailor Garrigan. There was much debate at Philippine Joe's regarding the identity of the donor. But the Bum only smiled to himself, and considered the money well spent.

The Epitaph
of Eddie O'Brien

by
JACK D'ARCY

The Story of a
Chicago Gunman
in Burma

 NONE OF us who lived in the remote trading station at Bhamo ever solved the very human problem of Eddie O'Brien. When he died, there was not one among us who did not feel a deep sense of obligation, and that rending tug of the heart that comes to a man when he witnesses a deed of incredible heroism. But for all that, we never understood him, never fathomed his motivation, never knew what made him tick. In appearance he was just another man like ourselves, perhaps a trifle undersized, perhaps his eyes were a bit harder, but nevertheless physically he was an entity—a man.

But it was his mind, his philosophy born of an alien environment which evaded us. Everyone from Parker's houseboy to the R. C. himself would stare at him, a vague baffled frown upon their brows, as if by sheer ratiocination they would read the mind and motives of Eddie O'Brien. But they never did. Even on that day he died, when they were overwhelmed with emotion, when they had definitely accepted him as their finest friend; even then, they were never close to a complete understanding of the man.

Perhaps I knew him better than they. I was less insular than the average civil servant. I had traveled a bit before dragging my traps to this

God-forsaken hole at the source of the Irrawaddy. I knew something of other places which to the R. C. were merely fine print upon the map.

In my time I had lived in the birth place of Eddie O'Brien—Chicago, Illinois. I made no claim to knowing the town well, but I did know something of the political maelstrom that exists in that utterly mad city. And I recognized Eddie O'Brien for what he was. I understood his language even if I failed to understand the man who spoke it. I was the one that acted as general interpreter between Eddie O'Brien and the R. C. For the latter's middle class Etonian slang was as unintelligible to Eddie as was Eddie's underworld jargon to him.

It was Parker, the junior clerk, who first brought word of Eddie's arrival in Bhamo. Up there at the tail of the Irawaddy, less than a hundred miles from the Chinese border, we generally knew of a white man's arrival forty-eight hours before he actually got there. A fact which accounted for the R. C.'s faintly amazed stare when Parker brought the tidings. Mainwaring (the R. C.), and myself were sitting in his bungalow at tiffin, when young Parker entered.

"There's a white man down in the native village, sir," he reported gravely, keeping to his feet as though expecting an order which would deal adequately with this phenomenon.

Mainwaring stared at him for a full minute in silence. Then, evidently satisfied that his subordinate was neither drunk nor suffering with a bit too much sun, he asked: "Who is he?"

Parker shrugged. "I don't know. He talks English, but in a peculiar way. American perhaps. I didn't understand half that he said."

"What did he say?" I interposed.

"Something about coming up the river in a native craft. Said he was starving in Bengal. Couldn't get a white man's job."

"Why didn't he appeal to the conul?" asked Mainwaring.

"I don't know," said Parker.

"Why didn't you bring him along?" I said.

Parker hesitated. "Well—" he said slowly. "I didn't know whether —you see, he isn't—he isn't a gentleman—and he's filthy."

The R. C. grunted. "Go and get him," he snapped. "Gentleman or no, we can't leave a white man living down there with those stinking niggers. Get him up here."

"Yes, sir."

Parker left the hut and walked down the path, his clean white drill suit gleaming in the beating sun. The R. C. looked at me with raised eyebrows. I answered his unspoken question.

"I don't know, unless it's one of these mad jungle fortune hunters that's looking for the elephant burial ground or some other impossibility."

The R. C. lifted his tea cup. "I so hate to have the routine disturbed." he sighed.

I said nothing, but had I realized then what the advent of Eddie O'Brien was going to do to Mainwaring's beloved routine, I would have laughed aloud.

IN A short while Parker returned bringing with him a ragged, unshaven derelict who, notwithstanding his obvious indigent condition, wore a jaunty enough air as he puffed easily on one of Parker's cigarettes. The R. C. received the stranger with his most official frown.

"Who are you?" he queried.

"The name's Eddie O'Brien."

"Where are you from?"

"Chicago."

"Chicago?" said the R. C. "Chicago?"

"Illinois," said Eddie O'Brien. "And I'm just beginning to see what a sucker I was for ever leaving the burg."

Mainwaring didn't bother to listen to this. He embarked upon his next question.

"What are you doing here?" he asked.

Eddie O'Brien sighed the sigh of a man who is weary of it all.

"What the hell," he said easily. "I suppose I might as well come clean. They can't nab me in this neck of the woods. All right, major. I bumped a guy in Chi. Took him for a ride. It turned out it wasn't the mug I wanted at all. It was a big shot. Up there I stared a murder rap in the face. So I took it on the lam, pronto. I had to scram to some joint where they couldn't extradite me. I landed in Bengal, after screwing around in a dozen other countries. And—"

The R. C. silenced him with a wave of his hand and turned a distressed, puzzled countenance to me.

"What on earth's he talking about, Fielding?" he said plaintively.

"He means," I translated. "That he murdered a man in Chicago and had to find a country from which he couldn't be extradited. So he's here."

The R. C. turned again to Eddie O'Brien.

"Well, my man," he said. I don't want to be harsh. You appear to have had a hard enough time. But you can't stay here. If you do I'll have to notify the authorities."

"Okay with me," said Eddie O'Brien. "I'll scram."

"Where to?" I asked.

"Back to the native village. They don't treat me bad down there."

The R. C. shook his head emphatically.

"No," he said with finality. "You can't go there."

"Why not?"

"I can't permit a white man to remain down there living like a savage."

"Why not?" asked Eddie again with ingenuous logic. "If you won't et me stay here, why can't I stay there?"

"If you go down there again," said Mainwaring. "I'll have you brought back here. I won't let a white man ive with the niggers. That's final."

Eddie O'Brien appealed to me.

"Is he nuts?" he inquired queruously. "He won't let me stay down there 'cause the niggers ain't good enough for me. But he's perfectly willing to send me back to the States nd the chair. Is he nuts?"

I evaded the question. After all, t is rather difficult to be asked point blank whether or not one's superior is nuts, when he patently, has none the best of the argument. They remained there, facing each other. Mainwaring, Resident Commissioner of the district, reared on the best English School traditions, totally oblivious to the existence of the rest of the world; and Eddie O'Brien, product of the Chicago gutters rich in, tho unaware of, a merciless tradition of his own. Mainwaring, used as he was to rendering quick decisions, remanded the case.

"Get him shaved and give him a lean outfit," he told Parker. "I'll onsider this."

 THE PAIR of them left the room together. I noticed Eddie's dirty hand reaching out to Parker's cigaret case as they walked out into the molten sun.

"Well," said the R. C. "What do you make of that?"

I grinned over the cold tea.

"A bit out of his place," I ventured. "You've actually seen a gangster in the flesh."

"A gangster," echoed Mainwaring.

"You've read about them," I told him. "The papers from home are full of the doings in America, you now."

He nodded slowly. "That's right," he agreed. "But I thought they were more or less legendary. Good God, the man seems harmless enough."

"So does a cobra basking in the sun," I observed.

"Perhaps. But will you kindly tell me what the devil we are going to do with him?"

"No," I said, and got to my feet. "I won't. After all, you're the R. C. and it's your problem. I'm damned if I'm going to strain my intellect in this heat."

I left him sitting there, his very British bull-dog chin sunk thoughtfully on his shirt front, and his very routine mind grappling with a problem which could not be solved by an expedient recourse to precedent.

At dinner that night, Eddie O'Brien sat next to Mainwaring, opposite me. He was lost in a suit of Parker's whites. His thin face stuck itself out of a cavernous collar, and his little beady eyes darted here and there as he ate. It seemed impossible for him to look at an object for more than a split second. Mainwaring was rather aloof at first, on his official dignity. That pose of his always awed Parker, and I was too interested watching the stranger to contribute much to the desultory conversation.

Over the cordial Mainwaring opened up a bit. He invariably did at the end of a meal when spirits and food sent a cheery thrill pulsing through his well fed figure.

"Old Wang ought to be in tomorrow," he remarked. "We can go to work for a change."

Old Wang, as we called him, was the chief of a border tribe with whom we did most of our trading. His blacks would show up about once every two months, and for a while, our easy routine would be broken by hard work, profound haggling and barter. A runner had informed us a couple of days back that Old Wang's men had taken the trail. At Mainwaring's words, Eddie O'Brien looked up.

"Wang," he repeated. "Sounds like a Chink."

"It isn't," I told him. "We call him that because his real name is nothing for a Caucasian tongue to struggle with."

"Ever have any trouble with the natives up here?" he asked.

I answered thoughtlessly. I intended a mild bit of ragging to lighten the boredom that came upon us in that womanless, miserable hole at the source of the Irrawaddy. When it was over, I would have given my right arm to have recalled the words I uttered then. For it was my next sentence that killed young Parker and sent Eddie O'Brien to his doom.

"Trouble?" I repeated. "You don't know what trouble is until you've seen old Wang's outfit. You said you'd killed a man, didn't you?"

"Half a dozen," said Eddie O'Brien.

"Then," I said portentiously. "You're in the right place, son. When we deal with old Wang, we need killers. He's a bad and tough customer."

Eddie O'Brien's little eyes lit up. He became suddenly interested in the conversation. Mainwaring getting into the spirit of the thing, took up the conversation combersomely.

"Yes," he said. "You want to look out for Old Wang. If his men arrive at night with torches lighted and paint on their faces, don't bother to do anything but shoot. It means war—war to the death, *sans* mercy, and *ans* prisoners."

 HE GESTURED violently with his port as I stifled the smile that came to my lips. For Mainwaring's speech was an improvement on my hasty invention. He had exactly described the arrival of Old Wang's blacks. As a rule it was their habit to achieve a dramatic entrance to the trading station. If they arrived at night and they usually did, it was with torches flaming and

drums beating, an impressive sight which would be rendered more so to Eddie O'Brien if he believed that it meant war instead of a colorful overture to the more prosaic business of trading.

Eddie O'Brien listened avidly to Mainwaring as he added verbal embellishments to my theme. His little eyes darted all over the room. Finally they came to rest on a canvas covered object in the far corner.

"Jeez," he ejaculated. "A typewriter!"

Parker stared at him curiously. Mainwaring followed his gaze, and repeated in a puzzled tone: "A typewriter?"

I understood him.

"Yes," I said. "We use that Lewis gun when we have to. It's the only thing that compensates us for Wang's superior numbers."

"Jeez," said Eddie O'Brien again. "That's my meat. If this Wang guy blows in I'll give him the business with that."

"The business?" said Mainwaring.

"The woiks," said Eddie O'Brien.

"Shoot him," I said.

"Well," said Mainwaring as he rose from the table. "All I have to say is: Be on your guard."

Parker then picked up the joke.

"I suppose we'll stand watches tonight, chief," he asked.

Mainwaring winked broadly at both of us.

"Of course," he said hastily. "Suppose you take the first trick, O'Brien. Stand by till midnight. Don't leave your post until Fielding comes to relieve you. We three are pretty much all in—had a hard day—we'd appreciate it, if you stand the first watch."

"Okay, Major," shot from the side of his mouth. "I'll hold it down till the first relief."

Mainwaring thanked him profusely, and stifling our laughter, we left the mess hut and walked over to Mainwaring's bungalow.

The air, perhaps, restored some of Mainwaring's temporarily forgotten dignity. He frowned as we entered his diggings.

"We shouldn't have done that," he said.

"Why not?" asked Parker. "It's a good one. If Wang shows up with his war paint on and all, the big killer from the States'll probably die of fright."

"I don't like it," said Mainwaring.

"Oh, come on," I said. "We'll just let him stand there. You told him to carry on till he was relieved. We'll let him wait. Wang mightn't arrive anyway."

Reluctantly Mainwaring agreed to see it our way. I went to bed regarding it in the light of an excellent experiment. Here was a self confessed gangster from Chicago—well, we would see what he'd do with a mob of howling natives, who he believed were after his scalp.

I took a glass of port and some quinine and rolled in under the netting. It was a rotten night for sleep. One of those broiling hot affairs with the stink of the river in the air. My nostrils felt as if they were inhaling sodden blankets. However, I slept after a fashion. I remember quite clearly that I dreamed a bit. I was home again. I was standing in front of Buckingham Palace. They were changing the guard. I remember seeing the gaudy uniforms quite clearly. A band was playing loudly. It seemed to grow still louder. Violent. The guardsmen started to howl. An awful din rang in my ears. Then——

I sat up in bed every nerve tinglingly alert. Outside, it sounded as though some howling hell had descended upon us. A flaring circle of light enveloped the sleeping verandah. A myriad of screeching voices rammed into my slowly dawning consciousness. Then I heard an unmistakable staccato hammering. *Tatatatatatatat.* That was a Lewis!

I sprang from the bed buckling on my ammunition belt as I did so. As I ran toward the mess hut, I saw Mainwaring rush across the clearing, a thirty-eight held in his hand.

"What's up?" he called breathlessly.

I didn't bother to answer but continued my mad charge toward the pandemonium beyond. We burst through the rear door of the shack together. Parker appeared from somewhere behind us. Before, back of a barricaded window, stood Eddie O'Brien. His thin shoulder was hunched tightly up against the butt of the machine gun. His left hand firmly held the stock, while his right kept the piston pounding its murderous tattoo into the night.

THE ABANDONED torches of Wang's advance guard lay upon the ground burning eerily in the blackness as the howling natives ran for cover. Half a dozen javelins rent the air and splintered the thin wood of the bungalow. For a moment not a black was in sight so well had they taken advantage of the jungle cover. But we knew they were there—watching, waiting.

Mainwaring jerked Eddie savagely away from his weapon. As he turned around and the light fell upon his face, I saw an expression there that frightened me. If I had ever doubted that Eddie O'Brien was a killer, that doubt was dispelled now. Gone was his insouciance of the afternoon; gone was his careless air. His face was a tense and terrible thing. His eyes were deep burning balls, alive with a lust to kill. A faint cruel smile curved on his thin lips.

"Well," he said in the thick voice. "I gave it to 'em. I let the rats have it the minute I seed 'em. I guess they know that Eddie O'Brien's handling the typewriter now."

Mainwaring was for the moment speechless. Parker leaned over and grasped him by the shoulder. His regular features were almost as pallid as the gangster's.

"You fool," he shouted hoarsely. "You bloody fool. You've done it for fair. You've—"

Mainwaring found his voice suddenly. He held his rage well in hand.

"You've murdered God knows how many natives," he said coldly. "Possibly you've murdered us as well. Time will answer that. What the hell do you mean by it?"

His thirty-eight was held before him in a direct line with Eddie O'Brien's heart. His eyes glinted icily. For a moment the gangster returned his glare stupidly. A vague amazement supplanted the look of triumph that he had worn a moment ago. But if he failed to understand the meaning of Mainwaring's words, he understood the fact of the revolver held at his breast.

"All right," he said. "I don't know what the hell you're talking about. But give it to me if you're going to. Well, why the hell don't you give it to me?"

For a moment Mainwaring stood there undecided. Then for the second time that day Eddie O'Brien appealed to me.

"Is he nuts?" he said again. "He tells me to look out for this Wang bloke. I knock off half a dozen of his men. Then the major blows in and squawks. What's the McCoy on this gag?"

If Mainwaring didn't understand the speech verbatim, he, at least, got the general idea. He lowered the gun, and his face clouded.

"He's right Fielding," he said slowly. "It's our fault. We pushed him into this. We—"

He stopped abruptly. A cluster of whirring spears sang a ziraleet as they hurtled through the air. Wood cracked, and a window lay shattered into a thousand pieces on the floor. Mainwaring rose to the occasion.

"We'll talk later," he said swiftly. "Just now we're fighting for our lives. I'll see if I can white flag them. Hold your fire for a moment."

He tore off his pajama coat, and cautiously opened the door. Slowly he waved the coat up and down. For a moment there was no response to the signal of truce. Then a wild savage yell rent the air, and a single spear, whirled like an arrow through the night. Aimed by a steady expert hand it neatly pinned Mainwaring's pajama coat to the wall of the shack.

He slammed the door grimly.

"All right," he said. "Put another drum on that Lewis, O'Brien. Wang can't be with them yet. These are his young bucks and we're going to have trouble. They're probably parleying now on the best form of attack. Is everybody armed?"

We were. Armed and ready. Eddie clipped a fresh magazine on the gun, and ran a caressing hand over the breech. As Parker and Mainwaring were peering through the window, he spoke to me.

"Was that a lot of baloney about the niggers being tough guys?"

"Just that," I told him. "A lot of baloney."

He grinned through set teeth.

"Jeez, I'm dumb."

"Or we are," I added.

Mainwaring turned from the window.

"Here they come," he said. "With torches. They'll try to force the place. Commence firing!"

"Give it to them!" said Eddie O'Brien.

We did. But they gave us as good as we gave them. Our three revolvers took up a jerky obligato to the smooth legato song of Eddie's Lewis. Javelins and arrows beat a steady ominous tattoo against the walls of our flimsy fortress. From somewhere in the jungle a war drummed boomed menacing music.

ONCE. TWICE, we repelled those dusky figures who advanced with the flaming torches which would drive us out into the open to die at the mercy of their flying spears. Our revolvers were effective, but as nothing to that calculating machine gun in the hands of Eddie O'Brien. He swept a leaden hail across their ebon ranks again and again. His eyes were shining steel fixed upon the sights. His lips were curved and cruel, and the sheer joy of the kill shone upon his pallid sweating face.

Young Parker was standing at my side. I saw him go, and was suddenly sick. He stood in the centre of the window frame blazing away at whatever target offered itself to his gun. Twice I had shouted a warning, but he paid me no attention. A steel point abruptly thrust itself through the window. Its shaft reflected the fires outside as it came, an unbending venomous snake of death. The point flashed by my eyes. The metal was suddenly red. Parker's throat was a gory slit. The haft of the spear fell upon the window sill. Parker made a horrible gurgling noise. He dropped to his knees. His hands grappled with the shaft. They stayed there, limp and helpless. He slumped forward, his head against the wall. He said nothing. Neither did he move. For a minute my stomach came up in my throat. I fought it. Then it went back again. Eddie O'Brien's shout sounded in my ear.

"Give 'em the business."

I fired blindly through the window. I made myself forget young Parker.

Then it was dawn. Suddenly and without reason a crimson tropical day thrust the night deep into the jungle. The spear throwing had ceased a few minutes back, and, as I peered with aching eyes into the glare, I saw nothing animate. The ground was red and black with blood and death. But I saw nothing alive.

Mainwaring was bending over young Parker chafing his wrists futilely, like a frustrated Messiah essaying to revive the dead. Eddie O'Brien ran an oily rag over the hot machine gun, caressing it like a woman with his lean fingers. I leaned against the wall, done up.

With the dawn and just as suddenly came Old Wang. He stood before my gaze alone, a solitary figure in the midst of his dead. His hoary face wore a grim reproach. For a full minute he did not move. Mainwaring stuck his head out the window. Their glances met. The native chief then flung his arms out in a wide gesture.

"Ah," he said. "And why does the white *shaib* not slay Wang as he has slain his men."

"He's askin' us," said Eddie O'Brien. There was a click as he shoved another shell into the breech.

I grabbed his arm. Mainwaring spoke.

"I would talk to you, Wang," he said. "There is much to be explained."

"Aye, much," replied the old black, as he walked slowly toward the shack.

As he entered he looked with compassionate eyes at the body of young Parker. They'd always got along well together. But he said nothing. He turned inquiring eyes to Mainwaring. Mainwaring summoned all the native words in his vocabulary and talked. It was no easy matter. To explain to a black man of another race that his men have been wantonly murdered as the outcome of a joke is no simple assignment. Haltingly Mainwaring attempted to make the matter clear to a mind that could hardly be expected to know what he was talking about.

Though the morning was still cool, sweat stood out on the R. C.'s forehead. He gesticulated violently as if

that would compensate for the meagerness of his sentences. How much of the palaver Old Wang understood I do not know. He waited in uncompromising silence until Mainwaring had finished. Then he asked one question.

"Who fired the gun of the machine?"

He indicated the Lewis. Mainwaring hesitated for a moment. Then Eddie O'Brien spoke up.

"Me," he said with an upward turn of his eyebrows. "None other than little Eddie from the South Side. I woiked the typewriter and how!"

Old Wang nodded. "It was that that slew most of my men," he said quietly more to himself than to us. "Wait," he added. "My men are angry with the *sahibs*—very angry. Bloodshed is no good—more bloodshed is the work of a fool. Wait."

He turned majestically and strode into the jungle beyond, leaving us standing embarrassed, humiliated and rather ashamed. For a long time none of us spoke. Then the side of Eddie O'Brien's mouth opened a little.

"I'll bet I knocked off fifty of them dinges," he began conversationally.

"Shut up," snapped Mainwaring. And there was murder in his voice. Eddie O'Brien scowled at him, but he shut up.

 I FOUND a bottle of whiskey in the kitchen and we all took a swig. After a while Old Wang reappeared. This time his followers were in evidence. As he approached the bungalow, his men set about the task of removing their dead. Mainwaring said nothing, but I noticed his hand gripped the butt of his revolver tightly as Wang re-entered.

"It is difficult," began Wang. "Difficult. But I have appeased them. They accept the peace."

Mainwaring started forward his

hand outstretched, phrases of gratitude on his lips, but the old chief stayed him with a gesture.

"Wait," he said. "There is a condition. They want delivered to them the man who fired the gun of the machine. If he is given up, all will be peace."

There was a long uncomfortable silence. Eddie O'Brien's face contorted into a defiant sneer. His hand rested on the metal gun barrel. Mainwaring tapped his pistol against his thigh. His brow was wrinkled.

"What will they do with him?" I asked.

"They will kill him," replied Wang simply. "I shall wait outside for your answer."

Again he walked from the room and left the three of us standing in a worried silence.

"So," said Eddie O'Brien. "They want you to put me on the spot for them."

"On the spot?" repeated Mainwaring.

"Give him up to be killed," I explained.

"Well," said Mainwaring at last. "I suppose we're all in it together. It's just a question of how long we can last. I take it all the house boys have fled. How much ammunition have we left."

We investigated. We had about thirty more rounds for the thirty-eights, and less than half a mag for the Lewis. Death was striding swiftly toward us through the jungle. Eddie O'Brien would meet it with a scowl. I felt pretty nervous but said nothing. Mainwaring summoned up the British Public School tradition and said: "Splendid. We'll all lunch together in Valhalla."

"What'll they do if I don't go for the ride?" asked Eddie O'Brien.

"We've got little ammunition," I said. "They've got numbers and a fanatical desire for revenge. They'll get it."

"They'll knock us all off then?"

"They'll knock us all off," said Mainwaring evenly. "I'll go out and tell Wang to start."

"Why don't you give me up?" asked Eddie.

Mainwaring stared at him as though he were slightly mad.

"Oh," he said. "A chap couldn't do that, you know."

Eddie O'Brien turned to me. "Is he nuts?" he demanded for the third time in twenty-four hours. "Is he goofy? This morning he was talking about sending me home to burn. Now he won't put me on the spot to beat the rap himself.

"The rap?" said Mainwaring.

"To save your life," I told him.

"The way I figure it," went on Eddie. "Is that if I stay here we all get the woiks. If I take the ride, I'm the only guy that gets it. What the hell. I got nothing to win. I'll take the rap."

He started toward the door. Mainwaring stopped him.

"I won't let you," he said gruffly. "I'm running this show."

"Listen," said Eddie O'Brien. "I'm going to croak anyways. Surely I got a right to say the way I'm going to do it. I started this knocking off, and I'll see it through. I got as much guts as you have. I got plenty of guts. Did you see me knock those dinges over?"

Mainwaring stood hesitant in the doorway. Despite the sporting tradition, life is a sweet thing. Perhaps it was desperate rationalization, justification, but I perceived logic in Eddie's argument. We couldn't save him anyway. But he might save us.

"Let him go, Mainwaring," I said.

For a moment our eyes met. There was a vague reproach in his glance as if he expected me to drop my eyes in shame. I didn't. I looked at him steadily. Then he tore his eyes away and stood aside. Without a word, Eddie O'Brien walked out into the

open. Mainwaring and I followed
him.

Old Wang said nothing as we came
up to him. He waved a signal to a
group of his blacks. Four of them
appeared with a stretcher like affair
made of leopard skin. One of them
held bamboo at each corner. Wang
waved Eddie toward the litter.

"Where are you taking him?" I
asked.

"Inside the jungle."

"May we come?" asked Mainwaring.

Old Wang considered for a moment
then nodded a silent assent. Eddie
O'Brien climbed into the litter.

"They're certainly taking me for a
ride," he said.

We walked, a strange procession,
into the jungle for some two miles.
The four blacks set the gangster
down. They escorted him to a clearing still red with the embers of their
camp fire. They stood him up, his
back against a huge tree trunk. A
dozen splendid black bodies stood before him. Each savage held a spear
unlifted. Wang stood beside them.

Mainwaring grabbed me by the
arm and dragged me through the cor-
don that surrounded Eddie O'Brien.
They didn't stop us. We walked up
to him. Mainwaring held out his
hand. When he spoke his voice held
tears.

"Thank you," he said simply. "We
treated you like a dog. It's our fault.
We shouldn't have ragged you.
You've done a damned sporting
thing."

Eddie O'Brien grinned through
tense muscles.

"What the hell," he said. "It
wasn't your fault. I was dumb to fall
for it, that's all."

He took Mainwaring's hand. I
thrust out mine.

"Mainwaring's right," I told him.
"You've got a lot of guts."

He liked that.

"Sure, I got guts," he said. "What
the hell. I can take a rap standing
up."

He released my hand. I walked
back behind the blacks with Mainwaring. My eyes were rivetted to
Eddie O'Brien's face. It was white,
and the sun trickled through the foliage and made the sweat glitter. His
mouth twitched slightly but that cruel
smile was still there. His high cheek
bones stuck out, and his little eyes
glowed, reflecting those of Death who
stared into them.

Old Wang raised his hand. I could
feel Mainwaring's hand tighten on
my wrist. Wang's arm came down
slowly.

"Give it to me," said Eddie O'Brien.

They gave it to him. Twelve hurtling spears hissed through the air
and burned their way through Eddie O'Brien's flesh. I could hear his
sharp intake of breath. I could hear
the crunch of the bones. I could hear
the tearing of the flesh. I could hear
Mainwaring's sob.

Eddie O'Brien went down, javelins
sticking out of him like pins in a pin-
cushion. No sound came from his
lips as he lay there, a mangled inert
heap. I felt sick. I turned to Mainwaring and unconsciously used Eddie's word.

"Let's lam," I said.

"Lam?" said Mainwaring. I
couldn't hear him. His lips framed
the words.

"Leave," I said.

Mainwaring smiled tremulously.

"Lam," he repeated. "He was a
great guy. He could take a rap with
guts."

He wasn't joking. He was terribly
sincere as he gave Eddie O'Brien the
tribute that he would have liked most.

"Let that be his epitaph." I said
soberly.

We set back through the jungle together. Somehow my eyes were wet,
and my throat hurt like hell.

HELL'S

A

Gripping Novel

of

Grim Adventure

in

New Guinea

By

FREDERICK NEBEL

Chapter One

HIGH SEAS

TOWERS WAS by nature a hard sleeper. But the crack of a rifle, together with the shouts of a dozen or more men, is enough to wake any man.

Towers sat up in his bunk, a bronzed, rangy young man in sand-colored pajamas. While his eyes were still blinking he groped beneath his pillow, got his lean hard hand on a Colt's .38. He could feel the lunge of the schooner through the sea, could see the half-dawn outside the open port, could hear the pounding of feet on the deck overhead.

He swung to the floor, jabbed feet into slippers woven of tropical grass. Fists pounded on the door.

A thick but worried voice was yelling, "A barque runnin' alongside us, Towers, and hailin' us to stand to—"

"Official?"

"Nah, it's some louse lookin' for bounty—"

"Bounty!" snarled Towers as he swung open the door and keened windy gray eyes on Captain Roush.

Roush was a wide and low-built man, dangerous to look at, but only a

BACK DOOR

shell inside. Rum, fever and dirty living had warped his face and body. He had weak milky eyes.

Bang!

Roush shook, said, "That's them—firin' again!"

"Steady!" clipped Towers. He gripped Roush's hairy arm. "Epinard still in his cabin?"

"Yeah—and horro'ful scared."

"Good enough. Now! Can we get away from the barque?"

"Nah. We can just about hold our own—"

"That's fair. We'll hold it then, and pay no attention to the barque."

Roush opened his mouth to say something. Fear and indecision were in his big milky eyes. Towers lanced him with a dark stare.

Towers snapped, "I know! You want to give 'em Epinard, eh? Well"

—he dug his fingers into Roush's arm—"we don't do that! I paid you well for this. I said there might be a fight. Your windbag was rotting in the shadow of Mission Hill, and I gave you a break." He flung down Roush's arm. "Thank your stars it's not a French patrol! And Noumea's sixty miles astern!"

He rocked past Roush and emerged on deck. The breeze whipped at his pajamas, whipped at his mop of dark tangled hair. He looked a gentleman, this Towers, yet there was about him something of the hard. His grandfather had sailed a clipper from New Bedford to China; Uriah Towers was the old gent's name, gentleman Yank. This young Towers had come by the name of Jonathan.

The barque was foaming along to windward, a hundred yards off but trying to run in alongside the three-masted schooner. The barque's rail was lined with a dozen men raked from only God knew what forsaken beaches. The schooner had a kanaka crew—boys picked up at New Georgia and through the Louisiades. She carried a Swede mate named Nils Olafsen, with whom Towers had struck up a warm friendship.

Towers strode aft, briskly determined, his long bronzed jaw set. Olafsen was standing by the wheel, a huge tow-head, calm and dreamy-eyed. A kanaka was tugging at the wheel.

A bull voice roared from the barque, "You heave to, you! All we want is the convict you got on board!"

Towers cupped his hands. "You go to hell, all of you! We've no convict on board!"

"We aim to overhaul you and see!"

"You've no right to overhaul us! Stay clear!"

"We'll take the right!"

"Them be tough fal-lers," Olafsen observed slowly.

Towers came close up to Olafsen. Towers himself was a six-footer, but he looked small beside Olafsen. "Nils, those guys mustn't come aboard."

"Ay t'ank Ay don't like dem fal-lers, Towers." He grinned and rubbed huge palms together.

"Nils," said Towers, "you know I've spent a lot of money getting here. I've got what we came after. Epinard must not be given over. Right?"

"Ay t'ank you be right, Towers."

Bang!

A bullet slammed into the base of the wheel. The kanaka let go the wheel and hopped into the air. The wheel spun violently. The schooner slewed sidewise. Her canvas lost the wind and clapped. Olafsen leaped to the wheel, grabbed it, hurled his weight against it, jaw muscles bulging.

The kanaka, frightened, made to retrieve the wheel. Olafsen, furious, slapped him away.

Roush came lurching aft.

"By God, Towers—"

Towers swung toward him, fists doubled. "Roush, shut up! This is no time to crawl! I warned you this might happen. They've no right to board us! They're just looking for bounty money. And Epinard stays with us!"

The schooner wallowed in the trough. The kanaka seamen, as yet unarmed, cowered behind the deck-houses.

"Break out your arms, Roush," Towers said. "Arm your boys. Give them a fighting chance."

White fury came into Roush's eyes. "I'm master o' this wind-bag, Towers! I'm not going to have it shot up!"

Bang!

A bullet slammed into the 'midships deck-house. Roush turned to run forward. Towers leaped after him, caught him by the shoulder, swung him about. Dark blazing fire was in Towers' eyes. His wide good mouth hardened. His voice throbbed.

"This means a lot to me, Roush! I've come half-across the world to get Epinard from the penal colony! And, so help me, I'll not let him go! Break out the guns!"

"I ain't goin' to have my schooner—"

Towers uncorked a short right that took Roush beneath the chin and sent him skidding up the port runway. Towers went after him, stood over him, revolver pointing down at Roush's chest.

"You heard me, Roush! Give me the keys!"

 THE BARQUE was only fifty yards from the schooner and sliding nearer. Towers hauled Roush to his feet, drove

him down into the after deck-house, forced him to open the gun locker. Towers took out half a dozen Winchesters, as many bandoliers; left Roush cursing and lugged the arms on the deck. The kanaka boys leaped on the guns, and Towers took six more boys below and emptied the gun locker.

Roush stood in the shadows swinging big knotted fists at his sides. "This ain't right, Towers!"

"You fell down on the job," Towers shot back at him. "You turned yellow in a crisis! Stay down here, if you want! Hide under the bunk. I paid you for a round trip out of Port Moresby. Now shut up!"

He pivoted on his heel, followed the kanakas on deck, saw the barque twenty yards off. A gun barked and a bullet whanged by his ear. He dropped flat to the deck, then rose to one knee, lifted his gun and fired over the rail.

One of the barque's men fell away from the rail.

When the barque and the schooner bumped together some men on the barque swung out grappling irons. Others opened fire and raked the schooner's deck. The kanakas, down behind the deck-houses, lifted their Winchesters. Out of twelve guns only two fired, although a dozen triggers had been pressed.

Towers saw this. He saw the horrified looks appear on the kanakas' faces, knew that the guns were loaded with old, faulty ammunition. The barque's men came aboard the schooner. They were rough men, fighting men, and when most of the kanakas' guns missed fire out of three tries, the natives rose in dismay and turned their rifles into clubs.

Towers became a whirlwind of action. He plunged headlong into the barque's men, and a swung rifle landed on his shoulder and knocked him to the deck. A big foot came down on his gun hand, another thud-

ded against his head. He grabbed a man's leg, heaved, and brought the man down on top of him.

Wrestling with the man, he could see a big, burly man snapping orders, waving a revolver. The burly man wore dirty whites, an undershirt, and a white-topped cap. His bronzed face was crisscrossed with scars. Towers saw Nils Olafsen come charging from aft, saw Olafsen slam head-on into three men, carry them six feet along the deck and crash down with them.

Towers got on top of the man with whom he wrestled, drove a blow against his jaw. Towers toiled to his feet, dodged a clubbed rifle, caught the burly man's eye and charged him. The burly man swung up his revolver, but Towers stopped it with a quick left hand, cut loose with a right that exploded on the burly man's jaw. Another man landed on Towers' shoulders, slammed him behind the ear, and Towers hit the deck again. The burly man kicked him in the ribs. The man who had knocked him down began clubbing him on the head.

Towers relaxed. His eyes glazed, and needles of light streaked through them, pierced his brain. He rolled over and lay on his back, seeing the shapes of men as dim ghosts wheeling past. He saw Captain Roush appear on deck holding his hands aloft. He saw the burly man facing Roush, and he saw Roush nodding his head. Then Roush hurried forward.

In a vague futile way Towers cursed, tried to get up. Somebody kicked him down and his head struck the deck. He closed his eyes, groaning. He heard the deep-throated yells of men, the hard stamping of feet. He opened his eyes. He saw a broad smear of flaming scarlet. For a moment it frightened him. Then he knew it was the sun crashing up over the eastern wall of the world.

He began to see the men again, running back and forth. He saw Nils Olafsen lying face down on the deck.

He saw Roush and the burly man, and he saw Epinard tussling between two others. Epinard, that gaunt, bearded man, in tattered whites, rolling his eyes and baring his teeth, straining frantically at the arms of his captors. Epinard—who had spent a year in the penal colony on New Caledonia!

So Roush had turned deep yellow. Even the dazed Towers could see that. He could see how servile Roush was before the big cocksure burly man. Towers labored to a sitting position. He had crossed broad waters to get Epinard out of captivity. He had laid plans, had smuggled notes to Epinard, had arranged with a Canaque to meet Epinard in the jungle after Epinard should escape. And now—this!

The fighting was over. The kanakas, who had been ripe for battle before the discovery of the bad ammunition, now huddled in the waist nursing bruises. The men from the barque lounged about insolently, laughing among themselves.

Epinard saw Towers sitting on the deck and screamed, "*Monsieur*, save me! *Save me!*"

The burly man strolled over and kicked Towers in the jaw. Towers fell back to the deck, groaning, while fresh blood trickled down his chin. He saw no more. Dimly he heard the casual laughs of men, the slow clump of feet. Then even these began to die. Towers felt himself dropping into abysmal darkness, down—down—way down. There was no pain anymore—only a beneficent, strange peace. Towers thought he was laughing—hysterically. But he really didn't know. The darkness seemed bottomless.

Chapter Two

THE OPEN BOAT

 TOWERS CAME to with sea-spray smoking in his face, with thunder exploding in his ears. That was a dream—of course, all that was a dream. Just the same as the way he was rocking from side to side—with frequent violence. And another sound: wind—the high mad wail of wind across the water. All that was a dream . . . .

Yet with the passing minutes Towers began to know it was not a dream, but a chaotic reality. He knew, because he could not move freely, that he was lashed to the thwart of a boat—an open boat. The spray was striking him from behind. Not only spray, but great slabs of sea-water that struck like wielded clubs and made him gasp. Wind winged with sea-spray lashed his head, spumed hissing in the open boat. Thunder cannonaded. Lightning blazed in vast sheets across the black tortured sky.

Towers saw Nils Olafsen at the tiller, heaving with the tiller. The big Swede had lost shirt and undershirt. His white pants were torn and soaked. His feet were bare. Great chest muscles, great biceps, strained. The Swede's big square jaw was set, his blond hair plastered raggedly over his forehead. He rode the boat with a kind of huge, heavy grace. Four feet of a splintered mast jutted up from the boat's bow. A leg-o'-mutton sail had gone by the board.

The bedlam of wind and sea and thunder made Towers' strong voice seem like a whisper. Nils could see him, see the movement of his lips. The Swede opened his mouth, grinned, nodded his head reassuringly. The small-boat skidded up to the crest of a wave, poised for a split-moment, then shot down into the trough. The wild-looking Swede rode it down neatly.

Towers could do nothing but remain where he was, lashed to the thwart. No one else was in the boat. They were alone, and what had happened to put them there, was beyond Towers' conjecture. It was still daylight, but it might just as well have been night, for the sky was blotted out by gnarled smoky clouds through which daggers of lightning leaped at the sea. The sea, the wind, had gone mad—in whose joint grasp the small-boat was a hunk of chaff, liable at any moment to meet doom.

The Swede must have been cradled from infancy by the sea. He thwarted its every sudden move, as if he knew its tricks of old. Towers knew his own life lay in the hollow of the Swede's palm. He was helpless, lashed to the thwart; he would have been helpless had he not been lashed.

For three hours Towers lay in well-nigh breathless tension. For three hours Nils Olafsen stacked his strength and seamanship against the terror of wind and sea. Then the clouds broke up, the wind drove them across the sky, and soon the wind died to a muted murmur, and the sun broke through overhead, blazed on a still restless but moderate sea, glistened on the wet small-boat.

Nils wagged his big head and said, "By golly, dat vas bad blow!"

"Can you get to me, Nils?" Towers asked. "These ropes are laying me open."

"Yah. Ay haf to do dat, Towers, odderwise you vent overside."

"I know, Nils. Thanks, I owe my life to you."

Nils left the tiller and crept forward, drew a clasp-knife, severed the ropes that held Towers. When Towers' arms were free he stretched them high, flexed his muscles. Nils was already going back to the tiller.

Towers said, "What happened? How'd we get in this boat?"

"Dat fal-ler Berks he fired de schooner. Yah, dat he did. Aybe unable to gat up—like you. Cap'n

Roush and tan kanakas take de long boat. So—me and you left, Yon. By 'n' by de fire gat damn hot, so Ay t'ank it about time Ay gat up. So Ay gat up. Ay drag you to do small-boat. Ay manage we get off. Den'—" he waved an arm aloft, looked upward—"de storm."

 TOWERS STARED. The simplicity with which Nils had told a huge story, amazed him. Now Nils leaned on the tiller, smiled comfortingly.

"De storm she be over now, Yon."

"You say Captain Roush left us on the burning schooner?"

Nils nodded, creaked the tiller. There was no bitterness in his big face.

Towers said, "Berks—you said Berks."

"Dat big fal-ler wit' de scars. He taked Epinard on board de barque *Hannah*. Say, Ah be know hof dat fal-ler Berks. He vas chased from de Fijis t'ree year ago, and I hear von time he vas hangin' round Port Moresby. He be long time in de Islands, Yon. Bad, dat fal-ler! Ven Ay gat de small-boat out Ay seen de *Hannah*—she be lay a course vest by nor'-vest."

"Not east—for Noumea?" Towers exclaimed.

Nils shook his head. "No, Yon."

Towers fell back against the thwart as if his lungs had suddenly been deflated. His eyes narrowed, his jaw hardened, his hand rose to the open gunwale and came down a knotted fist.

"I've heard of Berks, in a bar at Apia! They said he was kicked out of Apia for poaching pearl-shell and beche-de-mer on Savaii. And he's left a trail of blood blackbirding in the Solomons. By God, Nils, he wanted Epinard for something else! He didn't take him back to Noumea!"

"De course he took vas vest by

nor'-vest," repeated Nils placidly.

Towers quieted down, like a man accepting philosophically what can not be taken otherwise.

He said in a low heavy voice, "Nils, that was a neat trick Berks pulled! But I've got to get Epinard. Listen, Nils. I understand you took the berth on board the schooner because you were on the beach."

"Yah. Ay did not like dat skipper Roush. He vas yaller. He vas not even a good bad fal-ler. But Ay need yob."

Towers came aft to sit beside Nils. "I've spent several thousand dollars getting Epinard away from Noumea. As he stands, he's worthy fifty thousand or more. There's no telling. But it's not less than fifty thousand."

Nils, looking across the broad swells of the Coral Sea, smiled reflectively. "Dat be lots money, by golly," he said wistfully.

"A damned lot," Towers supplemented. "And I aim to get Epinard so that I can get what he's worth on the hoof. He doesn't know yet—who I am. When I get what I want," Towers' jaw hardened, "he goes back to Noumea!"

Nils looked sidewise at Towers. "Ay t'ank better you geeve up now, Yon."

"Not on your life, Nils! I've planned this for a year. If that old souse Roush hadn't had ammunition from the year One! He thumped his knee. "Now Berks has him. Berks must have known all about it. Word leaked in Port Moresby—and I thought everything was air tight! Nils, I'm a new chum in these waters, and I need a partner. Throw in with me for better or worse and if we clean up, it's five thousand in your pocket."

"Ay don't like bad yobs, Yon."

"Understand, Epinard's wealth doesn't belong to him. And if we win, I get nothing. It's for somebody else—somebody mighty dear to me, Nils! And on top of that, Epinard is practically a murderer!"

Nils said mildly, "Ay like you, Yon. Ay be like your brodder. Ay call you Yon and you call me Nils. But if you lie by me, den I kill you."

"Your hand on that, Nils." Towers reached out his hand, Nils took it.

They looked at each other, whom the sea and the storm had made brothers.

 TOWERS SAID, "Trail's end is somewhere on the New Guinea coast. I must tell you about it, about my sister's husband."

"Yon, you don't have to—"

"Yes—I must, if we're to be brothers in danger. My sister's husband—Malcolm Ward. He came out here—to New Guinea—to search the ruins of an abandoned stronghold in the mountains. He'd run across some papers of William Farr, who was a pioneer in Papua. Farr told of the ruins and of the possibility that jewels were buried in them. Ward, who had hardly any money, worked his way in ships as far as Port Moresby, and then went overland into the mountains.

"He got the jewels and carried them as far as the southern coast. Just where, I don't know. He got the fever there, and lost some of his bearers. This Epinard came into it in a strange way. Malcolm wrote that Epinard was cast on the beach, and Malcolm helped revive him—even though he himself was pretty sick. That was after he'd sent his last native off to get help. All this was told in a letter Malcolm wrote to his wife—my sister. The letter was finished after help arrived in the form of a trader of some kind. Malcolm wasn't clear about that. But he did say something about Epinard being run out of France, or that the French Colonial authorities were looking for him. He seemed to take

Epinard's part—and that would be just like him. He'd showed Epinard his jewels.

"How the letter got away from there, I don't know. He said he'd write again from Port Moresby—a fortnight later. He never did. The next thing we knew, we had a letter, some months later, from a Dutch Resident, saying that his body had been found on the coast, quite emaciated—as if he'd starved to death.

"So I tried to locate Epinard. I did—after long months. He was in the penal colony at Noumea. I posed as one of these men who make a business of extricating convicts—at a price. He was there for life. But I wanted the jewels—for Anne, who is almost destitute."

"Ay be very sorry, Yon."

Towers' eyes were glazed with thought. "I begged a grubstake to come east. I hocked everything. I owe five thousand. But it's not that so much. I can work to pay that back. But Anne and the kid, Nils— they need money—and the jewels belong to them."

Nils was pulling on the oars. "We go den, Yon. Ay go wit' you—anywhere. Ay be good sailor."

Towers said, "Let me take an oar, Nils."

He did—and they pulled westward over the sea toward an island that lay like an emerald jewel five miles beyond.

Chapter Three
THE LURE OF LOOT

PORT MORESBY is no beauty spot, but the raw back door to hell. Bare limestone hills surround it, with on some slopes banana plantations, but above all the unlovely gum-tree. Mission Hill and Argus Hill rise from the harbor.

Some coco palms wave in the breeze. Here come ships from north and south, from the farther coast of Papua and from that necklace of Islands that fling eastward over the turquoise sea. Here come the good, the bad and the indifferent. Here schemes of fortune are hatched and destinies wrecked. Beyond, in the teeming jungle, tom-toms beat, and the moon of other wilder years looks down on the bleached bones of white men who died in the devil-devil houses of the black. Men from the tattered ends of the earth comb the beaches.

Towers was a tall lean man in clean whites walking through a grove of palms far up the beach, beyond the town. Nils was on board the seventon yawl they had picked up in the Louisiades for a song. Towers was almost down to bed-rock in the matter of money, but he had a mission to fulfil. Days in the open boat had burned him nut-brown. Adversity had put grim lines in his young clean-clipped face.

When he reached Yut Lu's place he saw dirty lanterns swinging in the breeze. The beach bar was a rickety low shack set in the palms. It had a broad veranda where a dozen men lounged at tables, drank and talked or fingered grimy cards. The stench of rank trade booze polluted the clean sea wind.

Towers was drifting across the veranda when out of the tail of his eye he saw a ragged white man half rise from a table. Towers turned his head. He stopped short. He saw Epinard staring at him with startled eyes.

Towers made a motion of his head toward the bar inside. The three case-hards with whom Epinard had been sitting, regarded Towers suspiciously. Towers drifted on into the bar, leaned against it, ordered a gin-sling. A minute later Epinard came up beside him.

Towers turned, looked at Epinard steadily for a long minute. Epinard grinned jerkily, pawed at his chest, ran a shaking hand through his hair. Towers said nothing.

Epinard said, "They—they said you had gone down with the schooner. *Oui*—they said that!"

Towers said nothing.

"I—I— Of course, it is the business with you, getting men off Noumea. Business. You must be paid. *Oui*, that is so. There are several men in the same business. It is dangerous. Of course, you must be paid. *Oui*."

"What are you trying to say, Epinard?"

"The smuggled notes—it was done very cleverly. And I promised to pay you ten thousand. I will, *monsieur*. That I will. But I have had setbacks. Berks wanted me. He had heard things. News does get out, doesn't it? *Oui*—ah, *oui!* I escaped here in the harbor from the barque. Now I am laying plans. I have gathered some friends—"

"Wait!" Towers raised a hand. "You mean those birds you were sitting with on the veranda? Nothing doing, Epinard. I didn't get you out of Noumea for pastime. I got you out because I knew you were wise to some treasure." He tapped his chest. "You go with me Epinard."

But, *monsieur!*"

"You go with me! I spent several thousand dollars on you, and I'm not a rich man. Now you and I go and find this treasure. You know where it is. I've got a bottom and a man to sail it. It's business, Epinard. I'm a business man."

Epinard shrank back, looked away from Towers' blunt gray eyes, looked toward the veranda.

Towers gripped his arm. "Listen! Did you tell Berks anything? Did you?"

Epinard winced. "I had to, monsieur. He threatened my life. They held burning candles under my feet —"

Towers flung down Epinard's arm, snapped, "And now you've told some others—that scum you were sitting with! By God, you'll have every man in the South Seas on the hunt!"

"I have a fine plan. These men I have talked with are fighting men, *monsieur*. They have a lugger, and we can all go together—"

"NOT ON your life!" Towers set down the drink he had not touched. "You come with me— back to my yawl. You come, Epinard—or I'll tip off the authorities. Remember, you're an escaped convict, and I'm the only man in this town knows it."

Epinard put a hand on the bar to steady himself. His breath was hoarse in his nostrils. "It amazed me, *monsieur*, how in the first place you ever knew I had knowledge of this treasure."

"I know almost as much about it as you do, Epinard. I know everything about it—except where it is. And I want payment for getting you out of the penal colony. Get going!" Towers nodded toward the door.

Epinard pawed his throat, coughed. Towers gave him a shove and that started Epinard across the bar, out across the veranda. He did not look toward the three men with whom he had been sitting. Nor did Towers.

The two left the veranda and started along the beach, side by side. They had gone about a hundred yards when Towers heard running footsteps behind. He stopped. Epinard stopped.

Towers said, "Remember, you're just going on a visit with me."

The three men came up and one said, "Hey, Froggie, where you goin'?" He was a broad bull-necked man, bareheaded. The other two stood on either side of him, threatening.

Epinard said nothing. He gulped. The wind blew his tousled hair, and palm fronds clicked overhead. Towers looked at him keenly, then looked at the three men.

He said, "He's going with me. We're old friends."

"Oh, yeah?" the broad man sneered.

Epinard said, breathlessly, "Oui, Buck. I shall return later. Wait for me on the veranda."

Buck scowled. "I don't like the way this guy came up to you. Remember, Froggie, we're in on a business deal." He hitched at his belt, grinned and showed broken stained teeth. "Mind if I join you?"

"I—I shall return promptly," Epinard stammered.

"Okey. Then I'll go with you. Jake and Nigger'll join us too. Eh, chums?"

Jake said, "I doan't mind if I do, blarst me!"

The cross-breed was sullen; said, "Sure, Buck."

Epinard withered where he stood, looked helplessly at Towers.

Towers said, "I happened to invite your friend here to a little dinner. I'm sorry we haven't room for more. Some other time, friends."

Jake laughed. "So we're friends, eh? Well, 'at's a bloomin' joke, if you arsk me!"

The dark - faced cross - breed scowled. "I don't like this neither, Buck. This stranger's got somethin' up his sleeve."

Towers eyed them closely. He was a man alone among them, for Epinard did not count. Epinard was a wreck, morally and physically. The three were wary, dangerous—all bore the stamp of hard brutal living. Towers carried a thirty-eight in his pocket, but the three were armed too,

and from the looks of things Epinard seemed not to care whether he went with Towers or not. Epinard had gone into a league with these men, and now they suspected a double-cross. Their eyes showed it as much as their talk.

Buck said, "You—Epinard, come back with us. We don't like this business at all. It looks suspicious."

Towers smiled. "Well, that's not right. If you want to, come along and break a bottle of squareface with us."

"I wouldn't, Buck," the sullen cross-breed put it. "It's a trap o' his."

Buck squinted gimlet eyes. "Maybe you're right, Nigger." He jerked his hard broad jaw. "Come on, Froggie. Come on back and finish what we were talkin' about."

Epinard huddled, throwing frightened eyes from Towers to the three men. He began to edge toward the three men. Towers saw the move out of the corner of his eye. His eyes thinned down, his wide lips flattened across teeth that were clamped tightly together.

He clipped, "You stay here!"

Epinard stopped. There were inarticulate sounds in his throat. The laughter of men came down from the bar a hundred yards up the beach. The three men stood motionless.

Towers said, "This man is my guest, and he's going to be my guest. I don't know who you men are, but I don't like you. And I don't like your guts. You look like three of the lousiest rats I've ever seen on any beach."

"Yeah!" snarled Buck.

Towers took three steps toward him and said, "You heard me!"

BUCK DOUBLED a fist and uncorked it. Towers ducked nimbly beneath the high swing, and while Buck's arm was still in the air, Towers reached out and whipped the revolver from the big man's holster. He leaped back, pressing it along his hip.

Jake and the cross-breed started hands toward hips.

Towers barked, "No you don't! And you," to Buck, "get back there with your playmates. You guys aren't tough. It's just the way you look. You two wiseacres, turn around, pull your guns and drop them. D'you hear! Turn around, damn you!"

He stood spread-legged, neck cords bulging, teeth showing whitely between tight lips that curved backward. Old Uriah Towers must have looked much the same the time he quelled a mutiny of Hawaii. Gentlemen—but hardboiled when they had to be. Cape Cod bred men like that.

Epinard was not in the taut little tableau. He stood on the edge, shaking, pawing at his chest, little sounds aching in his throat. And he was not a particularly frail man. He had height and strong bony arms. But his insides must have gone to rot— the heart of him must have shriveled.

When Jake and Nigger had dropped their guns, Towers told them to march six paces away. He gave the same order to Buck. And when they had done this, he picked up the guns in his left hand.

He said, "Now my guest and I will roll along. You keep walking to the bar. I'll drop your guns on the beach near the end of the town. But stay clear for half an hour."

They had turned and were glaring at him. Buck held his knotted fists pressed to powerful thighs. Nigger wore his dark sullen face, lower lip drooping. Jake's lip was twitching and his spade-shaped face was the color of dry dough.

Towers said to Epinard, "All right. Get going."

"You'll hear from us!" Buck rumbled.

"Strike me pink if yer won't!" Jake cried.

Towers said, "When that time comes, hard guys, I'll have something to say myself."

He turned his back on them, grabbed Epinard's arm and strode briskly along the beach.

THEY REACHED the town. A native in an outrigger took them out to the black-hulled yawl. Lights glowed in three ports of the low trunk cabin. Nils stood in the stern, his pipe making a red eye in the darkness.

He said, "By golly!" when he saw Epinard come on board. Towers paid the boatman, climbed up and grinned at Nils.

"Well, there he is, Nils. I didn't expect this." Towers turned to Epinard. "Get below and we'll talk things over."

The cabin was twenty feet long, with four bunks aft and a small galley forward. Two lanterns hung in gimbals.

Towers was starting a pipe. "You can tell us, Epinard, and of course you go with us. This is Nils Olafsen. You've seen him on board the *White Moon*. I want the truth about it."

Epinard sat on one of the bunks, brushing back his hair. A change of manner came over him. His face brightened, his dark eyes had a deep twinkle.

"I did not want to go with you, Towers, because I had told so much to the other men. Now I am glad I came. I drew maps for Berks because he made me, but I cannot say if they were accurate. I know the place by heart. I can find it. But I am poor at maps. It is almost at the other end of New Guinea."

"Did you tell these three where it was?"

"I told them the details of the

treasure. I told them I could find the place. That is all."

Towers had his pipe going smoothly. He looked down at Epinard with a vague hint of suppressed fury far back in his eyes. Even his voice was constrained. Distrust, too, was in his eyes. He was not entirely fooled by Epinard's servile manner and play at weakness. Therein, he half-supposed, lay Epinard's strength. No doubt it was with these weapons that Epinard had tricked Malcolm.

Seeing Epinard there, Towers knew the sting and lash of inward rage when bottled up. His greatest desire was to leap on the man, choke the breath from his body, beat him to a pulp. But there was Anne at home, and the kids—and a grubstake to be paid back. And he was almost broke now. He had to watch himself, he had to keep the truth about himself from Epinard.

He said, "We're shoving off right away—before morning—before those rats you hooked up with can get a line on us. And remember, no tricks. I must be paid!"

Epinard opened his mouth in surprise. *"Monsieur!* Why, now I think of it, how fortunate I am that we met!"

Dangerous—mused Towers—this sudden change in manner. Epinard was acting now, pretending he was overjoyed. Nails dug into palms of Towers' hands.

He turned from Epinard, said to Nils, "All right, partner. Let's weigh anchor and shove off. You stay down here, Epinard."

"Oui, monsieur."

Towers and Nils went on deck, and Nils said in a low voice, "Dat is a bad von, Yon," and jerked a thumb over his shoulder. "Not bad like Berks, or like odder men, but bad like a snake. Dat von vill neffer fight in de open—not him, Yon!"

Towers laid a hand on the Swede's shoulder. "I know, Nils. So be care-

ful. Never let your gun around. We'll stand watches night and day."

Nils lowered his voice. "By 'n' by Ay t'ank maybe Ay haff to kill dat fal-ler." He spat overside, raised his voice. "Vell, Yon, Ay gat de anchor and ve go places."

Chapter Four

THE OLD MAN OF THE JUNGLE

 FIVE DAYS later found the yawl west of Torres Strait. Dourga Strait w a s behind, too, and Dutch Papua towered in the north—tier on tier of tawny-shouldered mountains. The sea ran in broad channels of indigo and aquamarine. The wind was in the yawl's beam, laying her well over, but driving her at her bows. White water foamed at her bows, gurgled down her low black hull.

Epinard had shaved, put on clean whites which Towers had given him. He was a changed man—outwardly. No one knew what went on behind his smiling face. He was good company, cheerful, optimistic. He cracked jokes. He seemed not to notice that Towers and Nils always carried guns at their hips.

Yet Towers never relaxed his vigilance. He knew that the more amiable Epinard became, the more dangerous he became. No rough diamond, Epinard. A smooth one—polished, inimical in a sly foxy way.

Nils never changed from day to day. He remained the big, slow-speaking, good-humored Swede. At night he sang Scandinavian folk songs. By day he drove the yawl across the wide sun-washed waters with the wind tearing at his straw-blond hair.

It was on the eighth day that Epinard came aft from the bows along the narrow port runway and said, "*Messieurs* the coast looks familiar. That spit of land yonder affords a good harbor I believe, on the western side. The lagoon of the treasure is five miles beyond, around the great arm of land. But we had better put in here. To sail into the lagoon would be foolhardy, because Berks and his men may be there."

Towers shaded his eyes against the westerning sun. "A good harbor there, you say?"

"*Oui.* And quite concealed from the lanes of traffic."

Towers turned. "Let's put in there, Nils."

The yawl beat around the spit of land, took the wind abaft and lunged, breaking white water. Towers and Epinard got at the sails, and the yawl slipped down the western side of the spit of land under spanker and jibsail. At the shoreward end, this projection curved inward, and the yawl warped into a small sheltered cove that could not be seen from the open sea.

A spindle-legged jetty stuck out from a beachless shore. A small outrigger was moored to it. Sago palms hung over the dark shore, and red and emerald parrots wheeled in the spangled sunlight. As the yawl drifted toward the jetty a man appeared at the base of it. He had a long white beard, wore old white pants cut off at the knees and a shirt that had been made by cutting neck- and arm-holes in a gunny-sack. He smoked a long-stemmed pipe and leaned on a gnarled thorn stick. No breeze here—only a hot breathless humidity, the root of fever.

Towers turned to Epinard, growled, "I thought no one lived here?"

Epinard had lost a bit of color. "So I thought, *monsieur.* I do not remember the jetty, nor any habitation."

The yawl bumped against the jetty.

Towers left Epinard and joined Nils in making fast. The old bearded man still remained where he had first appeared.

Towers, climbing to the jetty, leaned his hand on his gun and walked toward the shore. The old man stood straight and immobile, a beak of a nose haughtily in the air. Safety pins, an old watch, a string of dog's teeth, were fastened to his odd shirt.

Towers said genially, "Hello, friend."

The old man stuck his chin higher. "Hello, stranger. I am the king o' the aborigines in Dutch New Guinea. No white man has put in this bight in two hundred years. I know, because I been here that time and longer. I'm glad t' see you. Tell your friends t' come along. I got some palm toddy up my palace. I see you got a nice Colt's there. I had one—'bout a hundred and eighty years ago, but— Well, come along."

"I'll tell my friends," Towers said, staring transfixed at that heroic old figure of a man.

He turned and went back down the jetty, joined Nils and Epinard. Epinard had gone whiter still. His eyes were feverish black coals.

Towers said, "The old gent seems daffy. So humor him. He's talking about being king of the cannibals, and living a couple of hundred years. Don't forget—humor him."

 WHEN THEY walked up and joined the old man, he pierced each of them with fierce blue eyes. A fierce look was always in his eyes, and his voice was like a trumpet. He peered longest and hardest at Epinard.

He rumbled, "Wa'n't you here about a hundred and fifty years ago?"

"Of course—of course," Epinard said. "*Oui, monsieur!*"

The old man looked troubled. He

repeated, "*Oui . . . monsieur*. Seems I heard that kind o' lingo before, too. Well, come along, my friends."

He led the way back through the palms, up a short incline to a low wide hut built of palm fronds and screw pine. He led the way into a large, dim cool room furnished with mats woven of native grass. Neither chair nor table was in the room. He stopped, stood erect, waved an open hand.

"My hospitality is yours, friends. This here is my palace. My aborigine subjects come to see me only at night, and we sit around here and I give orders. Here's some palm toddy."

It was rank stuff with the wallop of old Bacardi, served in home-made gourds. Epinard stood near the door, his eyes glued on the old man. He had not said a word since leaving the jetty. He seemed oddly spell-bound.

Towers, looking at him, asked, "What's the matter, Epinard?"

"Oh—nothing, *monsieur!*"

The old man pawed his beard. "Ay-pan-ard," he murmured, repeating the phonetic pronounciation slowly. He looked up, squinting his eyes; then sighed and shook his head. "Ah—I can't remember. But it must ha' been a hundred and fifty years ago. Well, I'll go on in my garden and get some vegetables. I'd send one o' my subjects, but they're all out. They come only in the dark o' night. 'Scuse me, my friends."

When he had gone out Epinard shivered. "What an uncanny man!"

Nils tapped his head, wagged his head. "De poor old fal-ler has vat you call screw-loose. Dat is too bad. It is too bad ven peoples ain't right by de head."

Towers said nothing. He was thinking rapidly. The old man had peered hard at Epinard when they met him on the jetty. He had repeated Epinard's name, and a cloud had come into his eyes. Then he had

given up.

Epinard started at the cry of a cockatoo wheeling by outside the hut. Sweat was standing out on his forehead. He mopped it away, inhaled deeply.

"I think we had better move up the coast a bit," he said. "This old person may be the hindrance to our plans."

"He's harmless," Towers said. "So long as we humor him, he'll be all right. He's lost his mind, God help him!"

"Still, I think," began Epinard.

Towers shook his head, stabbing Epinard with a dark look. "We'll stay here. We may learn things from him. Besides, the cove is well hidden from the sea—in case Buck and Nigger and the Cockney should come along."

"Ay t'ank ve stay," Nils nodded complacently. "Ay like dat old faller."

Epinard tightened his lips to thwart a grimace. He turned away, went outside. Nils rolled out to lean against a tree and watch him.

When the old man returned with his arms laden he seemed overjoyed at being able to entertain guests. He was fast on his feet, strong, though he appeared to be well in his sixties. He kept talking about his subjects, who came only at night. His mind rambled. He got mixed up on dates and seemed to have no idea of time. He spoke of a trail over the mountains, and native campfires, enemy tom-toms, skulls bleaching over fires. To him, nothing had happened less than a hundred years ago. And the strange fierce glaze never left his eyes. Towers hung eagerly on every word.

 THE OLD man wanted them to sleep in the hut that night, but they declined in a roundabout way and returned to the

yawl, promising to have breakfast with him. Epinard was visibly shaken and had lost much of the easy nonchalance acquired on the voyage from Port Moresby. Towers saw that. Nils saw it.

And when Epinard had turned in his bunk, Towers and Nils smoked pipes in the stern.

"We've stumbled into something," Towers said. "The old man has seen Epinard before, has heard his name. Malcolm and Epinard were on this coast. The old man saw them. Epinard's scared he may reveal something and wants to move on. If the old man could only remember and make me sure Epinard was the cause of Malcolmn's death!" His hand knotted where it lay on his knee. His voice lowered. "Because I know that Epinard will trick us, if the others haven't found the jewels. He's turned color too quickly on the trip. He's been too amiable."

"Ay t'ank so," Nils nodded.

Towers left Nils on board the yawl and went up to the hut. Approaching the door, he slowed down when he heard the old man's voice talking' rapidly inside. He crept up to the door. He looked in and saw the old man sitting on a mat, making gestures, his eyes shining.

"Chief Boe," the old man was saying, "you must not war with the lesser tribes! I won't have it, dang you! We're strong, we are—two thousand strong, and there's no sense pickin' on the little fellers. All you men—you, and you, and you," his finger jabbed around the room, "stop makin' trouble!" He sat back and glared fiercely.

Towers shook his head. The old man was far gone. There was not a soul in the room besides himself. His subjects were ghosts; that was why they came only at night. Life with him was a perennial dream.

Towers had not the heart to break the man's dream. He watched for half an hour, while the old man spoke to many tribesmen, calling them by name, settling imaginary disputes, sending them away one by one.

Finally Towers turned and walked back toward the jetty. When he jumped to the yawl, Nils was not on deck. Towers went down below whistling to himself; stopped whistling when he saw Nils huddled beside one of the bunks. Towers dropped to his knees, lifted Nils' head. Blood was on it.

Epinard had gone.

Chapter Five

THE LOST LAGOON

RAGE TYPHOONED through Towers' blood; was curbed in mid-career by the rebounding realization that Nils lay unconscious in his arm. He straightened the big Swede out, found the welt on the crown of his head, saw an old belaying-pin lying on the bunk. That had done the work.

He got a bucket of water, a rag, soaked the rag and laid it on Nils' forehead. He poured some water between the Swede's lips. He chafed his wrists. Nils was already stirring, muttering.

"Nils! Nils!" Towers shouted. "Wake up, old boy! Wake up!"

"Yon—Yonny . . ."

"I'm here, Nils! I'm all right!"

Nils opened his eyes, opened his mouth. He blinked. He gulped, "Yon—Ay—Yah, dat fal-ler! Ay knowed it!"

"Take it easy, Nils!"

Towers helped Nils to a sitting position. Furrows appeared on the Swede's forehead. He looked woebegone. "Yonny, Ay be dumb faller. But Ay—"

"That's all right, Nils. What happened?"

"Ay come in to gat tobacco. Ay bend down under bunk. Epinard look like he sleep. Ay vas fooled. He gat me day way, Yon—biff!"

"He got your gun, too. Damn him, he's waited days for a chance!"

"Ay be damn dumb fal-ler." Nils struggled to his feet, lurched on deck, gasped in long draughts of air, ballooned his chest. Towers opened a locker with a key, pulled out two Winchesters, loaded them. He went on deck and gave one to Nils. He peered at the dark wall of the jungle. He could hear the fluted whistle and far-off cries of night birds. He could see a yellow moon through the fret-work of trees, like a giant yellow moth.

He growled, "If Epinard's been here before he knows the trails a bit! *We're* strangers, Nils!"

"Ay t'ank for sure now Ay haff to kill dat Epinard."

"The fool!" rasped Towers. "What can he do? I'll get him in the end. He might have known. But greed got the better of him." He gripped his rifle harder. "I'm going! I'll take a chance and look for him!"

A heavy hand gripped Towers' arm. "Yon." Nils shook his head. "Don't go, Yon. It's dark, and dat fal-ler knows his vay, and it vould be easy he should pick you off in de dark."

"I tell you, Nils!"

The big hand tightened. "Yon, Ay say no, and dat is vhat Ay say."

"Let me go, Nils!"

Towers and the Swede wrestled back and forth, and Nils kept saying, "No, Yon. Ay know how you feel. But no. Please, Yonny."

Towers quieted down, stepped back, his chest heaving. He sat down heavily. "Sorry, Nils—sorry. I kind of lost my head for a minute."

Nils' deep complacent voice said, "Ay, know, Yon. But ve gat him— later."

WHEN THEY went to have breakfast with the old man he asked about Epinard.

Towers said, "He went away in the night. He must have got lost."

The old man squinted his fierce eyes till they seemed to shoot living sparks. "I know the trails, I do, friends. We'll have to find him. It's bad for strangers to go a-walkin' in the jungle. But my chiefs were here last night and I told 'em if they bother any white men I'd beat seven times seven bells out o' them. It's hard bein' king o' the aborigines. They're the fightenest men I ever seen."

"You've been here—you say—over two hundred years," Towers said. "Do you remember a man named Malcolm Ward?"

The old man sat back, pawing his beard. "Mal-colm Ward," he mused; then crooked a finger at Towers. "Seems I do, and seems I don't. Just like Epinard."

"What's your name?"

"Me?" The old man laughed. "I got no name. I'm just a king. Kings don't have names."

Towers voice was strained. "Listen. Malcolm Ward. Repeat that name over and over. Say Epinard, then Ward; Epinard . . . Ward. Like that. Try to remember."

The old man repeated the two names a dozen times, then stopped, stared into space with fierce concentration. Then he frowned, ran a hand across his eyes, shook his head.

Towers sighed, went on eating breakfast in silence. But the subject tortured him.

He tried again. "Ward—Malcolm Ward. He was a young man, about my age—thirty or so. He came out of the hinterland with six bearers and a collection of rare native jewels. These jewels had been gotten out of the mountains of New

Guinea. Somewhere along the coast here his bearers were struck down by the fever—all but one. Ward himself got the fever and sent the remaining bearer off to find help. He found help of some sort, because Ward wrote me while he was ill, said he had gotten the jewels, told about the fever, said help had come to him. He also told about a man named Epinard who was cast ashore near their camp from a wreck. He said Epinard was wanted in the French possessions for shooting a man's arm off. But he believed—poor fool— that Epinard was in the right. That was the last letter, from him. Two months later I received a letter from a Dutch resident saying Ward's body had been picked up on the beach —death from starvation. I begun to trace the name of Epinard, and after four months I found that he had been caught by the authorities and was in Noumea. I—got—him out." Towers' voice had gotten thick with emotion. He said, "Can't you remember if you ever saw Ward or Epinard?"

The old man shook his head slowly. "No. It kinda sounds like a dream I had, more 'an hundred years ago."

Towers got up. There was no use. The old man's memory had gone back on him. Towers had noticed an old three-inch scar on his left temple. Maybe that had made his mind a blank.

He said, "Can you show us a trail that leads west along the coast?"

"Yes, my friend, I can. I ain't been on it for a hundred years or more. You see, my subjects cover the trails, and I have to stay here close to the palace, 'cause they come around every night to report."

 HALF AN hour later they took to the trail. The old man led, thumping his thorn stick violently. Nils was behind him. Towers brought up the rear, watchful, for-

ever looking back over the trail behind. The sun steamed in the wet jungle, spearing the foliage with glistening shafts of white fire. Wet rod sopped beneath their tramping feet. Lianas hung like twisted cables across the trail, and the men had to bend, twist their way through. Above, monkeys chattered petulantly, swung from tree to tree, looking down at the men and making pinched ugly faces. The air was stagnant; the smell of rotting earth was mixed with the heady-sweet bouquet of exotic wild flowers. Farther north a series of coyote-like yelps broke through the hot silence.

"Dingoes," the old man said, "runnin' down a kill." Then he stopped, pointed to a broken branch. "Epinard come through here. You can see the branch, it ain't an old break."

They pressed on along the old trail that tunneled the jungle. Faintly they could hear the sea thrashing on a reef. They saw other evidences of Epinard's flight—a piece of cloth hanging from a thorn, a footprint in mud. The old man seemed tireless. He never paused.

At the end of the fourth mile the trail began to rise. They crossed a narrow stream that gurgled down a rocky bed. Soon they could see the intermittent flash of the sea in the sunlight, while the trail became steeper and in some places rocky.

The old man remarked, "It's all just the same as it was a hundred years ago. It won't be long now till we come to the end. There's a lagoon beyond there."

When they had gone another half mile they heard, quite suddenly, the clatter of rifle fire. The old man stopped short, towered and glared into space. Then he broke into a run, and Towers and Nils trotted behind. They came to the end of the trail, on the top of a hill that overlooked a placid blue lagoon. The old man was going right on into the open, but Towers grabbed him.

"Don't show yourself!" he clipped.

"Why not? Ain't I king o' the aboriginies?"

"Sure you are. But don't show yourself—for my sake. I ask it as a favor."

The old man relaxed, nodded. "Puttin' it that way, I'm agreeable."

Nils said, "Look, Yon!" and pointed.

The barque that had attacked the *White Moon* off New Caledonia lay at anchor near the white beach. A lugger had come into the lagoon and was standing fifty yards away from the barque.

Towers said, "Well, Buck and his playmates found it!"

GUN FIRE burst forth again, from the lugger and from the barque. Towers could see men crouched down behind the bulwarks of the barque. Puffs of smoke leaped into the wind. The lugger was a scarred old vagrant of the outer waters. Towers counted ten men on board, kneeling behind bulwarks and deck-houses, pumping rifles, while the lugger drifted nearer the anchored barque. Monkeys, startled by the gunfire, chattered wildly in the trees, and parrots wheeled about frantically.

The old man said, "It's queer my tribesmen didn't tell me strangers were anchored here. My chief held council with me last night." He swayed back and forth, excitement in his voice, his eyes shining fiercely.

The lugger was only twenty yards from the barque. Two men lay motionless on the barque's deck. A man was staggering on the lugger, holding his stomach. The rifle fire was almost continuous.

The lugger bumped broadside against the barque. The barque's men, instead of remaining behind bulwarks and deck-houses, rose *en masse*

and charged the lugger—went aboard it in flying leaps with guns bellowing.

Hand to hand combat—fast and deadly. Guns barked at short range. The screams and shouts of men reached the watchers on the hill. The old man of the jungle moved restlessly back and forth, thumping his thorn stick on the ground, mumbling in his throat. The monkeys leaped about, screamed, waved hands.

The old man shouted, "I'm goin' down! It's un-Godly for white men to kill each other thataway! I'm goin down!"

"No!" Towers yelled.

But the old man had leaped off, into the open, and was charging down the hill in a cloud of dirt and stones. Towers started after him. Nils leaped and dragged Towers to the ground.

"Yon—don't!" he rumbled. "Day von't kill de old man!"

"Nils, they—"

"Dey von't, Yon! Dey vill laugh at him—dat's all."

The old man was so fast on his feet that he had already reached the bottom of the hill and was tearing up the white beach, waving his hands and shouting.

TOWERS AND Nils got up. Towers was like a man on a leash. He was in the throes of indecision—yet he knew that it would be futile and suicide pure and simple to show himself on the beach. Nils was still gripping his arm. It was the second time Nils had stopped him from plunging headlong into wide-open danger. Towers had the impetus of youth, the hot wild blood of youth. Nils was older and a seasoned hand on rough out-trails.

The old man ran up and down the beach. There was no canoe in sight, no means of carrying him to the heart of the conflict. The men on board the lugger were hard at it, but now it seemed that those who had leaped from the barque had the upper hand. Towers could see Berks among his men, and he could see the lugger's crew backing against the rail.

Finally the old man waded into the water, began swimming toward the barque.

The fight came to a sudden climax. The barque's men opened fire at short range, and every one of the lugger's crew who had backed to the rail crumpled to the deck.

"By God!" Towers exclaimed. "That's murder!"

"Berks," said Nils, "has got de name of dat, Yon. He gives no quarter, Ay tal you dat."

Towers muttered vibrantly, "More of the cursed Epinard's work!"

Berks stalked around the deck, prodding the fallen men with his toe. The others lounged about after him.

The old man reached the barque and clambered on board. Then he ran across to the lugger, holding up his hands. Berks turned and regarded him. Towers could see the old man gesticulating wildly. The barque's crew gathered around him and began laughing. Berks laughed, bull-throated. He brushed the old man aside and strode back to the barque. His men trailed after him. The old man of the jungle, persistent, caught up with Berks, grabbed his arm, waved a hand furiously. Berks turned and said something to his men, and four of them grabbed hold of the old man and threw him overboard.

Berks went below, came out again and returned to the lugger. Two men went with him, and they bent down over a form on the lugger's deck. It looked as if Berks was administering to the man. After a few minutes they picked the man up and carried him back to the barque.

Towers said, "It looks like Buck. He's alive and you can bet he's in for a rough deal. They haven't found the treasure—that's certain—and they've an idea Buck might know about it."

The old man had reached the beach and was stamping indignantly toward the base of the hill.

Towers watched him until he disappeared in the growth below, and said, "He'll be here in a couple of minutes. Berks did wrong to treat him that way."

They waited, staring meanwhile at the barque, where men sat around drinking from bottles they had brought from the lugger.

Nils craned his neck. "Ay don't hear de old man, Yon."

Towers puckered his forehead. He said nothing. They waited five minutes—ten minutes—twenty.

Nils said, "Ay t'ank he vent home anodder vay, Yon."

Towers' lips were tightening. "I don't think so, Nils." His fists knotted. "I think that Epinard must have been half-way down the hill. He waylaid the old man!"

Nils' eyes widened. "By golly, Yon!"

Chapter Six

DEVIL DRUMS

TOWERS, WITHOUT a word, crawled through the brush and went cautiously down the hill. Nils followed. They went slowly, rifles ready, ears alert, eyes stabbing the thickets. It took them twenty minutes to reach the spot where they had seen the old man enter the growth at the base of the hill. To go farther would be to reveal themselves to the men on board the barque. And there was no need to go farther.

Towers said, "That's it, Nils!" He swore softly. "Epinard was laying for him! He drove him away. He would have killed him here if it wouldn't have made too much noise. He'll take him off—pretty far—and finish him!"

"Yon, dat ain't goin' be!" Nils gritted.

"Epinard's afraid of him. The old man knows something—something vital." He started upward. "Come on, Nils."

There was only one direction Epinard could have taken—north. South lay the sea. West lay the open beach. Nils and Towers had commanded the east brow of the hill.

The two white men, climbing the hill, searched the brush, and finally found the imprint of a boot-heel in the earth. Here, possibly, Epinard had crouched and watched the battle on the lagoon. Here, possibly—it was half-way up the hill—he had accosted the old man of the jungle.

From this point Towers led the way north across the side of the hill. Nils was at his heels, sometimes at his side. They prowled through the stagnant suffocating heat, their faces shining with perspiration. Droves of insects hovered about them, followed them. The everlasting monkeys chattered overhead. The jungle steamed beneath the walloping blast of the tropical sun, and a pool of black water, motionless as they approached it, suddenly was lashed by a black slimy thing that snaked off into the brush.

Through Towers' mind flashed thoughts of Malcolm Ward, who had traversed two hundred miles of this primordial hinterland. How he must have suffered—and persevered! And how he would have laughed it off. Laughing young Malcolm Ward! Carrying a fortune from the Papuan wilds, only to die on the white beach. And leaving a young wife and a child at home to mourn his passing. Tow-

ers' sister! He remembered the letters Ward had written Anne, painting a rich future in the mountains of Northern California. He'd known a valley there, and a spot where a man could see the sun come up in a blaze of glory . . .

And Epinard! Had Epinard caused his death? Ward was always a fool for the under-dog, a believing, naive soul.

Nils said, "Look, Yon! Dey been here!"

He plucked a small piece of cloth from a thorn bush, held it up. Towers prowled around the bush and found a newly broken twig. He bent down, pawed the ground.

"Epinard's boot-heel again—and the old man's slipper imprint—pointing north. . . . Come on, Nils."

They plunged farther inland, bored into the deeper matted jungle. Presently they heard a voice beyond —the loud angry voice of the old man of the jungle. His words were indistinguishable. Another voice—not so loud; and the sounds of the men's progress through stubborn brush.

Then, quite suddenly, there was another voice—or rather, a long-drawn yell. Nils stopped short. His neck muscles bulged and he gripped Towers' arm.

"Dat be native!" he muttered.

Then many voices—strange, wild and strident.

 TOWERS WHISPERED, "Quiet now, Nils!" and started through the bush cautiously. Nils slipped after him, and at the end of five minutes they could see a clearing through the trees. They could see, too, a dozen-odd blacks, with spears and shields, standing around Epinard and the old man. The old man was gesticulating and talking in stentorian tones with great authority. He lapsed from English into a queer dialect, then back to English again.

He shook his thorn stick above his head. The blacks looked puzzled. One laughed. He apparently was the leader, with his head-dress of paradise feathers and a necklace of human finger bones. His face was tattooed with pale zebra-like stripes, and a brass ring hung from his nose, and tufts of human hair sprouted from his shield.

Epinard cowered behind the old man, his face fear-ridden. No fear showed on the old man's face. He glared and stood erect, shaking his white old head, making his words ring with the utmost finality, while monkeys mocked him in the tree tops.

The native headman then spoke in his own tongue, stepped forward and laid a hand on Epinard's shoulder. His wild black eyes flashed. His tone was dramatic. The old man shook his head, laid his hand on the headman's arm, removed it decisively from Epinard's shoulder. Epinard was cringing, biggering. He looked much the same as he had looked on board the schooner when Berks was dragging him off, near Noumea.

Towers whispered, "They want Epinard, and the old man is trying to talk them out of it."

"Yah, Yon. Ay gat part de lingo. De yief say de old man be friend; he many times treat sick brodders. But he say dat Epinard no friend."

Towers' hands tightened on his Winchester. "If the old man loses, we've got to save Epinard. The beggars 'll roast him and hang his skull over their devil-devil fires."

"Ay, say dat vould serve him right, Yon."

"But—remember—he belongs to me, not to the blacks. I didn't come this far to lose him."

They watched, breathless. The old man was red in the face from talking. The headman listened but did not seem in a receptive mood. He put his hand on Epinard's shoulder again. If he brought a white victim to the devil-devil house, that would give him the right to add another paradise feather to his crown. He spoke briefly, and three natives closed in around Epinard while the others shoved the old man away. It was obvious that, though the old man was daffy about his being king of the aborigines, he still was known by them and in a small measure tolerated. No doubt the blacks had been drawn from the hills at sight of the barque anchored in the lagoon.

Epinard was screaming. Two of the blacks were dragging him off, while the headman spoke sternly to the old man of the jungle. He pointed to the south, his gesture indicating that the old man should go.

Towers said, "Nils, it's time we stepped in."

Nils raised his gun, set his jaw and nodded. Side by side they advanced silently, careful of each step. When they came to the edge of the clearing Towers held his rifle to his shoulder, nodded to Nils, and jumped into the open shouting a sharp command. Nils was beside him, deadly cool, rifle raised.

The headman whirled. The natives whirled, raised their spears.

Towers said to the old man, "Tell them to let go Epinard!"

Startled, the old man was speechless for a long moment. Then he repeated the command in dialect. Growls smouldered among the natives. Towers repeated the command, and the old man translated in dialect.

THE HEADMAN towered with rage, bared filed teeth in a low snarl. He made a quick turn and thrust his spear at Epinard. Nils' gun boomed, jerked at his shoulder. The headman staggered, dropped his spear. The spears of the other men swung around toward Towers and Nils.

Towers fired. A spear shot low between his spread legs, the end of the shaft smacking his calf. Another native near Epinard raised a tomahawk, and Nils blazed away, shattered the tomahawk. Nils ducked as a spear whizzed past his cheek, sank in a tree back of him, quivered there.

Epinard ducked and dived into the jungle. The old man of the jungle whirled and sped after him yelling for him to stop. The remaining natives backed into the jungle, turned and sloped off, howling wildly. The headman and another lay on the ground—dead. The headman had been too eager to roast white flesh in a devil-devil house.

Towers and Nils turned and struck the back-trail. They could hear Epinard and the old man crashing southward. Towers yelled. Then the sounds suddenly ceased, and ten minutes later Towers and Nils came upon Epinard and the old man in a close fierce struggle.

Towers clipped, "Lay off, Epinard!"

Nils went right on walking, caught Epinard by the back of the neck and yanked him away, held him up with one hand and slammed him on the jaw with the other.

He said, "By golly, dat make me feel good!"

Epinard covered his face with his hands and moaned.

The old man, dripping perspiration, stood with his hands still clenched, his eyes glaring at Epinard. "What a fool you be!" he shouted.

Towers said, "It's all right. He's done for now."

The old man spun on Towers. "And for him you lit into them aborigines!"

"They were warned," Towers said. "Epinard belongs to me—not to the blacks. And, enemy or not, I'll not see a white man baked alive!"

He walked over, took Epinard from Nils and held him at arm's length.

Epinard's lips shook. His eyes stared frantically.

He choked, "I will tell, *monsieur!* I will show you the treasure. By *le bon Dieu,* I will!"

"You bet your life you will, you double-crossing pup!"

The old man said, "It was him waylaid me on the hill and put his gun against my back. The blacks took his gun. They wanted him for long pig, they did." He stared toward the north. "This will start a heap o' trouble, this will. A headman was killed. I must be getting old. My subjects don't listen to me no more . . . and only last night we all held council." His voice dropped, his face dropped, he hung his head. "We'd best get back to the coast. There's trouble breedin' in the hills."

Towers said, "Back to the yawl."

 THE OLD man nodded, started off. Nils walked behind him. Epinard walked behind Nils and Towers brought up the rear.

It took them four hours to reach the hidden cove, and as they were standing on the jetty the old man lifted his head and listened. He pointed a gnarled finger northward.

His voice was hushed when it said, "Hear them!"

Drums—far off in the hinterland. Drums beating—drums of the jungle.

"It means war!" the old man exclaimed. "My subjects have turned against me! There must be a new king in the jungle! I'm gettin' old."

Towers said, "We'll clear out of the cove till it blows over."

"You go!" the old man said. "I'm goin' to stay in my palace and tell 'em what I think o' them. Only last night I said there'd be no fightin'. And the way them aborigines talked to me today! 'Twas disgraceful! Me, I'll tell 'em a word or two!"

"You come with us," Towers said,

"The blacks 'll carve you."

"I'm stayin' right here," the old man insisted. "You go. I got things to tell 'em." He turned on his heel and started toward his hut.

Towers took a step after him and grabbed his arm. The old man heaved around and glared.

"You let me go now!" he bellowed.

Towers put both hands on him. The old man began to struggle, but Towers hauled him along the jetty, got him down into the yawl, while Nils came down with Epinard. The old man was furious, bewildered that he should be manhandled. He was speechless with amazement. His wide fierce eyes settled on Epinard.

Epinard shrank back. The old man came toward him, holding out a hand, eyes and mouth wide open. His hand touched Epinard's face, and Epinard cried out and flung himself to the deck as though something had stung him.

The old man groaned, raised a hand to his face, covered his eyes, shook his head and muttered, "I don't know. It's like a dream . . . but the drums . . . and Epinard's face . . . . It must ha' been a hundred and fifty years ago."

Towers said, "What, my friend— what was a hundred and fifty years ago?" His eager eyes were fixed on the old man.

"Somethin'—" He shook his head, lowered his hand, stared fiercely at Towers. His mouth snapped open with—"Mal—Malcolm Ward!"

Epinard bit his lip, clawed at his throat.

Towers gripped the old man's arm. "Yes! Ward—Ward! Malcolm Ward!"

For a split-second the glaze seemed to vanish from the old man's eyes. His breath whistled in his throat. A wild light leaped into his eyes. Then the glaze sprang back, and the old man slumped, groaning.

He muttered, "The drums . . . the drums! My subjects have turned against me!"

Towers mopped his face. He looked at Nils and said, "Almost, Nils. Almost."

"Yah, Yonny," Nils said, though he was staring point-blank at Epinard.

Epinard was gasping for breath. Sweat poured from his face.

Far off, the drums of doom were beating, while the monkeys chattered and the bright-hued parrots wheeled in the spangled sunlight.

Chapter Seven

THE TREASURE HOLE

THE JUNGLE, the hills that rolled back from the beach and became mountains, were swallowed up by the darkness. The sea foamed like white liquid fire on a snag-toothed reef. The moon had not come out nor were there any stars in the hidden sky. Sea and jungle were brothers in the darkness.

The jungle drums had ceased their booming at sundown, making the silence now more inimical, more freighted with danger.

The barque had heeded the warning and put to sea. She lay about two miles off the coast. Towers had seen her put out and drop anchor in the twilight hour. Now she was beyond sight, on the other side of the darkness. The yawl had not put out until after dark, and now she lay a mile off the coast, and quite near the lagoon of the treasure.

The old man of the jungle had said, "The drums stopped at sundown, which means the warriors left and started down. They should reach the coast about midnight. They come from beyond the second mountain."

As the yawl lay to within a mile of the lagoon, Towers turned this statement over and over in his head. The old man very likely knew what he was talking about in that respect, even though he kept on bemoaning the fact that his "subjects" had turned against him. Towers ran his meditative eyes along the dark wall of the jungle, puffed musingly on his pipe.

Finally he rose and looked around at the dim shapes of the men. He said, "It's eight o'clock now. We have—say—three and a half hours before the blacks reach the coast. We can take the outrigger and slip into the lagoon. Berks and his men can't see us." He was looking at the dim face of Epinard. "You said you knew just where it was, Epinard."

Sparks showered as Epinard's hand jerked the cigarette from his lips.

He whispered hoarsely, "But at a time like this, *monsieur!*"

"At a time like this," said Towers dully. "The lagoon is clear. By a stroke of luck things have worked out for our benefit. Berks, an old hand in the Islands, sensed trouble in the booming of the drums. So he pulled out and is lying to off the coast. We can get there, and since you know the exact spot, we can locate the chest of jewels in an hour and be back here by eleven-thirty."

Epinard stood up, shaking. "But if the old man's reckoning is wrong!"

"My reckonin' ain't wrong," put in the old man. "I been back to their village. 'Twas a hundred and thirty years ago. It's over beyond the second mountain. If they travel fast they'll get to the lagoon by midnight."

Towers turned to Nils. "How about you, Nils?"

"Ay be ready," drawled Nils through his pipe.

Epinard shrank back.

Towers said, "Then we'll go." He turned to the old man. "You stay on board the yawl. We'll need somebody here."

Epinard started to argue, but Towers cut him short. Then Epinard wanted a gun, in case the blacks surprised them. Towers laughed shortly. Nils chuckled.

Towers said, "We should give you a gun!" Then he added, "If it comes to that, I'll give you mine. Cut out crabbing and get down to the outrigger."

 NILS WENT first, carrying pick-ax, crow-bar and spade. Towers had to shove Epinard into the outrigger; then followed himself, carrying Nils' and his own rifles. The old man remained on board the yawl hefting a revolver which Towers had lent him.

Nils paddled—quietly, showing no white water. Epinard sat in the bow, his whole body quaking. Towers knelt in the waist. They slipped through the dark smooth water toward the jungle coast. The off shore breeze brought a smell of dank sweet earth and wildflowers; it was the breath of the East that is strongest in the dark hours.

"*Mon Dieu,* it is dark!" chattered Epinard.

"Quiet on the tongue!" Towers snapped in a tense whisper. He was a lean grim man kneeling in the waist, bare-headed, purposeful in a quiet tense way.

Nils, who was his brother in danger, moved the paddle up and down with ghost-like silence.

They won to within a hundred yards of the coast, then turned and followed it westward toward the dark headland that bulked at the entrance of the lagoon. No moon. No stars. A perfect night for a *coup d'etat.*

Rounding the h e a d l a n d, they hugged the shore and slipped into the lagoon. Then Nils headed straight across—still careful of every stroke. Epinard writhed in the bow, his hands gripping the gunwales, his terrified eyes staring toward the forbidding jungle. No doubt the scene back-country, when the natives had almost gotten him, was still vivid in his mind.

Near the shore, Nils rested on his paddle, and all listened. The lugger lay dark and silent fifty yards to their left. After a moment Nils dipped the paddle again, took a long stroke, and let the canoe glide toward the sandy beach. Its bow slushed into sand.

"Get out, Epinard!" Towers clipped.

Epinard stumbled to the beach and stood cowering in the darkness. Towers followed, tense, alert. He was not unconscious of the danger, but any qualms he held were bottled up inside. He had crossed half the world to reach this very spot, and his blood tingled, and a wild recklessness throbbed through his veins.

Nils came last and drew the canoe half out of water. Towers told Epinard to carry the digging implements, while he and Nils carried their rifles.

Towers said quietly, "Now this is the beach, Epinard. We're here. You know the spot by heart. Find it."

The implements clanked in Epinard's hands. He crouched and threw frightened glances about in the darkness. Then he started west on the beach. Towers and Nils tramped doggedly behind him, feet crunching in the sand. They paused when they came to a hole that had been dug six feet into the sand. Here Berks and his men had broken ground looking for the treasure. But Epinard, after a slight pause, continued. They passed two more similar holes, and then came to a grove of palms.

Epinard stopped, shuddering. It was dark in the grove, and the grove was alive with strange whistlings and cries of night birds. Towers prod-

ded him in the back. Epinard whimpered and stumbled forward. He was now counting off the trees, and when he had counted six he turned left and began counting again. He stopped at another newly dug hole, gasped—then choked off the gasp.

"No." he said. "But they were close." He pushed onward for ten feet, and then stopped in front of a large bush. He said, "It lies beneath this bush."

Towers said, "The truth, Epinard, or so help me—"

"By *le bon Dieu*, this is the spot!"

"Ay vill dig," said Nils.

He stood his rifle against a tree. Towers leaned against the same tree and held his own rifle on Epinard. "And you stay where you are," he said; then added, "How deep?"

"No more than three feet."

 NILS STARTED off with the pick, swinging it mightily in the darkness. Epinard did not move. His eyes peered hard at every lump of earth that Nils turned up. His breath was a hoarse sibilant whisper in his throat.

Presently he said, "I am glad, *monsieur*, it is you winning this. I have been foolish, but my nerves have not been too good—after the time in Noumea. I know now you are honest. Once I doubted it. But soon you will get your payment—and I will give it gladly."

"Less talk," Towers muttered.

He was glowering in the darkness. He had kept the truth of his identity a long while from Epinard. Soon he would bare his secret, and all the suppressed emotions of months would rush out. Espinard still thought he was one of those men who made a business of helping convicts escape from Noumea—at a stiff price.

Tense minutes there in the darkness, when each man knew that blood-hungry blacks were sweeping down from the hills. Nils was soaked with perspiration, and after a while Towers took a hand, while Nils held the rifle. And it was Towers who struck something that rang against the point of the pick. He dropped the pick, picked up the crowbar and began prying into the earth. He got around the edges of something hard and solid, and after ten minutes he bent head first into the hole, caught hold of a handle and lugged up a heavy metal box two feet square.

Epinard cried, "*Voila!* That is it!"

Towers said, "Swing it on your shoulder, and quick about it."

Epinard did not have to be urged. He got the metal box on his right shoulder. They left the digging implements, and with Towers and Nils carrying the rifles, they started back toward the beach. Epinard seemed to forget the danger. He hurried, gasping for breath, dripping perspiration, and emitting short excited laughs. Towers and Nils were big quiet men, hawk-eyed and still wary in the jungle through which they moved.

They reached the outrigger safely. Epinard fell down with the box as he lurched in, and whimpered where he lay. Towers and Nils waded into the water shoving the boat clear; leaped in nimbly. Nils took up the paddle and did not let haste spoil his smooth stroke.

The outrigger was moving swiftly across the dark lagoon, past the dark shape of the lugger, when a low choked cry broke the silence.

Nils held his paddle poised. Towers stiffened and looked toward the lugger.

There was no mistaking the "Help! Help!" even though it was weak and muffled.

Towers muttered, "Nils, there's somebody on the lugger! Berks and his scum pulled out for the night and left somebody here for the blacks to chew on!"

Without a word Nils swung the outrigger toward the lugger. He did this instinctively, because there is an unwritten law in the fag-end tropics that no white man shall throw another to the black.

Epinard cried, "*Sacrebleu!* If we do not go straight back to the yawl the natives—"

Tower's threw out in a low snarly voice, "Pipe down, Epinard!"

When the canoe grazed the lugger's hull Towers told Nils to stay in the stern and himself swung up over the lugger's rail. It was dark, but he could find his way toward the groans a man was making. He stumbled over something. It was a man. He bent down. It was a dead man. He stumbled over five other dead men before he came to the one that was alive. It was Buck.

"So it's you," Towers muttered.

"G-God, Towers, cut me loose! Them devils left me tied for the blacks, and all me dead pals here. I been seein' ghosts!"

Towers was already cutting Buck loose, and he was saying, "One crooked move when you get up and you'll join your pals!"

"I'm through!" Buck cried thickly. "God, what a devil that guy Berks is! Imagine him leavin' me here!"

"Ah-r, you're all the same—a lot of cut-throats. Still—quick about it! We'll run this wagon out through the entrance, so the blacks won't get the dead. On your toes, Buck! The anchor!"

Towers ran to the rail and said, "Nils, there's one live bird here. We're going to run the lugger out. Go ahead and hang outside the lagoon."

"Yon, Ay t'ank—.."

"Get going, Nils!" There's no time to argue!" Towers left the rail and joined Buck at the windlass. The ebb tide would help them. But when they had the anchor aweigh, Towers said, "Now run up a rag of canvas."

Buck hung on every word Towers said. He seemed not so dangerous as he had appeared on the beach at Port Moresby. He was a very frightened man who had looked into the jaws of death; and he had not the guile of Epinard. He was intent only on saving his skin, and he jumped to with the eagerness of a boy, while Towers stood aft by the wheel.

The rag of canvas caught the offshort breeze and the lugger moved slowly toward the lagoon's entrance. It had not reached the neck in the bottle when a thunder of wild voices broke out from the shore.

Buck cried, "It's them!"

"We've got to get clear!" Towers yelled.

Chapter Eight

THE RED NIGHT

 THE NATIVES were tearing around the lagoon's shore toward the neck in the bottle. A spear came out of the dark and whanged into the deck a foot from Towers' right heel. But he clung to the wheel. They had reached the entrance, were laboring through, when the moon appeared through tattered scud, grew brighter, and lighted the waters.

Towers groaned. In the moonlight he could see the barque standing to at sea. And he knew that those on board could see the lugger!

Nils was waiting five hundred yards beyond in the outrigger.

The lugger got through the neck in the bottle. The natives, given courage by the fact that their challenge was not returned, jumped into the water and began swimming.

Towers lashed the wheel and clipped, "We're in deep water now!

Throw the bodies overboard!" He leaped to the task as he shouted, and one by one the dead bodies of white men went over side.

Being hillmen, the natives had not boats; but they could swim. Half a hundred were in the water, chasing the lugger.

Nils was paddling to meet the lugger, and Towers and Buck were hanging overside ready to drop when Nils came alongside. The outrigger came up in a foam of water, and Towers went into it sprawling. Buck followed with a bang, and the outrigger shipped water. Towers and Buck picked up spare paddles and dug into the water.

Epinard sat in the waist, limp from fright, unable to lend a hand. The other men strained shoulder and back-muscles and drove the canoe mightily toward the yawl. They could see sails ballooning on the barque, while the lugger kept plowing out to sea under the stiff quarter wind.

Had the moon not appeared, things might well have been different. And yet Towers, gouging dark water with his paddle, began to think that the moon's appearance, after all, was a kind of benediction. The outrigger, pretty much in the shadow of the headland, could not possibly have drawn the attention of Berks and his men on board the barque. What had drawn their attention, no doubt, was the sight of the lugger putting to sea—a lugger which they had left in the lagoon manned by dead men and one live but bound man.

Fleet as the wind was the outrigger driven by able arms. The wayl lay rolling gently to the long ground swell, her two masts dark against the brightening sky. Looking back, Towers saw that the natives were boarding the lugger, swarming over it. Their cries shattered the night. The wind had gotten into her sails and was driving her at a lively gait —so much so, in fact, that many of the natives turned back and swam toward the shore. But at least thirty must have gotten aboard the lugger.

Towers sensed that something dreadful was in the wind for somebody. With all these blacks on the beach, and with a large number on board the lugger, things were primed to happen with blasting effects.

Because, as the outrigger bobbed up alongside the yawl, Towers could see the barque bearing down on the lugger. And when he got on board the yawl and found a pair of marine glasses, he saw that all the natives aboard the lugger had dropped down behind the rails. He reasoned that while the lugger was visible to the barque, yet those on board the barque could not possibly have seen the natives board her. And the natives were waiting for the barque to reach them! A trap for Berks and his men!

The old man of the jungle was pacing up and down furiously, declaring, "They come as I said they'd come!"

Epinard, sapped by the ordeal thus far gone through, sat slumped in the stern of the yawl, the treasure chest at his feet. Buck hung back in indecision. He wore nothing but a torn pair of pants, and his stubble was caked with dried blood. His eyes jumped about wildly.

Towers' blunt voice s n a p p e d through the dark——"Epinard, get below out of sight. Take the chest with you and stay below. You have a bad habit of getting under a man's feet."

Epinard showed no signs of having been stung by the insult. He willingly lugged the chest below, disappeared.

TOWERS LOOKED at Buck standing in the stern. He said, "We have two rifles and a revolver among us. We'll not give you a gun. You can go below with Epinard or you can take the wheel."

Buck moved on his feet. He said, with a bit of rough challenge in his voice, "I'll take the wheel, mister."

Towers thought, "Well, at least he has guts."

Then he said aloud to all hands, "Much as Berks deserves the trap, we must try to warn him—if we can get to him before he reaches the lugger."

Nils said, "Dat is de law off de Islands," grimly.

Towers and Nils hauled up the anchor, then ran up the sheets, and the yawl heeled to the wind and began breaking white water with her bow. Buck stood spread-legged at the wheel. Some of the toughness had come back to him. Hard-case though he was, he had some makings in him.

Foaming beneath the moon and the stars, the yawl made for the barque. But with the passing of minutes Towers saw that barque and lugger would meet before they could reach them. Yet the yawl kept on, the wind strumming in her halyards, bending her canvas. The old man stood rooted to the deck, his long beard blowing, a fierce light in his eyes. The revolver was gripped in his hand.

"I am white," he said. "I figured I could run the aborigines and keep peace 'tween them and the whites. But when it comes to this, I'm white —and the aborigines must pay!"

Nils said, "Dey be close now, Yon!"

Towers went up to the bow and yelled, "Hallo the barque! Stay clear of the lugger! There's danger on board."

No reply came back. The sea slushed and gurgled along the yawl, rolled away gleaming whitely. The yawl was thirty yards from the core of things when the barque ran broadside against the lugger.

Towers said, "My God!" softly.

He saw the men of the barque rise

up. He saw the blacks on the lugger rise up like a dark wave of doom. Shouts of dismay—wild jungle cries —rushed across the water. Guns barked. Flame clashed through the darkness, and half a dozen blacks went down.

The barque's men did not even get to the lugger's rail. But the blacks cascaded down upon them, shouting wildly. The yawl kept plowing toward the barque, and Towers fired a high shot to draw the blacks' attention. Buck was braced grimly at the wheel. Below, Epinard was whimpering.

 THE YAWL hove to ten yards from the lee rail of the barque. Towers saw white men and black in close combat. The old man of the jungle raised his revolver and fired, and a black near the rail toppled.

The old man said, "They mutinied against me!" bitterly.

Berks and his men were mowed down by thrice their number. Many of the blacks now swarmed to the barque's lee rail, looked down into the yawl. Two hurled spears. One spear stuck into the wheel, made Buck duck down. The other spear passed between Towers and Nils, and the two men dropped down behind the low trunk cabin. When Buck dodged the stern of the yawl swung towards the barque, thumped it, and half a dozen blacks came hurtling down. Buck fell flat to avoid a spear, and the old man of the jungle swung his gun aft and blazed away at a black who was standing over Buck with upraised spear.

Towers had his rifle to his shoulder. Its muzzle belched flame and lead as three more blacks came down to the yawl. Nils' gun barked and stopped a black who was lunging toward the old man. Three more blacks charged, and one fell beneath the old

man's fire. Another got in a blow with a club that sent the old man hurtling to the deck. Below, Epinard was screaming.

Buck was up and in hand to hand struggle with a big fellow who wore six paradise feathers in his headgear and a necklace of dingoes' teeth. Five blacks charged in a body toward Nils and Towers, and the two men, shoulder to shoulder, cut down three of them with fast shots. The other two came right on, blind with rage and lust, and knocked aside the gun barrels.

Towers cut loose with a right hand blow that sent the nearest black spinning to the deck. Nils wrenched back, clubbed his rifle and dropped the other in a bloody huddle. Towers got his gun straightened out in time to blow up a black who was sweeping toward Nils with a tomahawk, and Nils shot low to break the neck of a black who was bending over the old man with a poised spear.

They had not time to reload before four more blacks came down from the barque. Buck got a spear through his back and fell screaming to the deck. Towers and Nils, themselves streaked with blood, clubbed their rifles and made a flying charge. Their blows were winged with fury. They were two white men alone against savages, and their swinging guns mowed down the blacks with deadly effect.

By this time the yawl was drifting away from the barque. Towers had closed with a big fellow, and they were toiling back and forth on the roof of the cabin. Nils was close-locked with another aft. The man whom Towers fought was taller than himself, black as coal, his face striped white, rings on ears and nose, bared teeth filed to sharp points.

In a wild turn, they fell from the cabin, struck the narrow runway, and pitched into the sea. They sank beneath the surface, came up treading water and fighting with their hands. There was another splash—Nils and his man toppling off astern.

Towers' opponent was trying to gouge out his eyes, while Towers kept shifting his head and pressing into the black's throat with thumbs of both hands. Time and time again they went beneath the surface, fought beneath it, until bursting lungs drove them to the top again. But Towers retained his fierce grip, pressed harder, until the black rolled his eyes, stuck out his tongue and relaxed. He sank from sight.

Then Towers heard a thrashing close behind. In the moonlight he could see a black atop Nils shoulders trying to keep the Swede's head under water. Towers plunged toward them, shot himself half out of water and laid a hard wet fist against the black's ear. The native toppled and slipped beneath the water, and Nils, gasping for breath, said:

"T'anks, Yonny. By golly, dat vas close!"

THE YAWL, they saw, was forty yards or so away, and both started swimming after it. The outrigger was bobbing along astern, and they had caught up with it when they saw Epinard appear in the stern. Nils and Towers got aboard the outrigger, and they were beginning to haul it toward the yawl's stern when Epinard raised a rifle and leveled it at them.

Towers saw a hand rise and grip Epinard's leg. The gun barked, but the shot went wild. Then Epinard whirled. A jerk of the hand brought him down to the deck. In that moment Nils and Towers were able to draw the outrigger closer, until Nils rose and caught hold of the lugger's stern.

Towers was climbing over the stern. He saw that Buck, with the spear still in his back, had both hands clamped around Epinard's ankle. Towers was getting to his knees when he saw Epinard break free, stagger up, turn to reach for the gun which he had dropped. But Towers was too close. Epinard saw that. He screamed, turned, raced forward. Towers yelled for him to stop. But Epinard plunged right on into the sea.

Nils, when he got on board, jumped to straighten out the canvas. Towers ran forward and saw Epinard twelve yards off the beam, swimming away. He shouted for him to come back. But Epinard kept on swimming.

Then Towers saw a black shape rise. It was the native with whom he himself had struggled in the water. Epinard saw the black, too, and cried out as they met. Dark hands encircled Epinard's neck. The yawl, under a stiff wind, was beginning to make white water.

Towers raised his rifle, tried to aim. But Epinard was in the way. Then both black and white sank beneath the water, and as Towers watched he thought he saw bubbles rising on the moonlit water. That was—then—the end of Epinard.

Towers turned and found Nils beside him.

Nils said, "Vell, Ay neffer killed dat fal-ler after all."

"The fool!" Towers muttered. "The awful fool!"

He went aft and stooped over the old man, who lay on the deck, quite motionless. He knelt down and put a hand inside the gunnysack shirt. He felt the heart. Then he listened. He said:

"He's alive, Nils."

There was a groan farther aft. Towers rose and went back to where Buck lay.

He said, "Thanks, Buck."

"It's hurtin'," Buck said faintly. "I did my best, Towers. Don't hold too much against me. Epinard met up with me in Port Moresby and talked o' loot—and I fell in with him. I been huntin' treasure for years, Towers. I been a tough guy, but I hope I kinda squared myself with you."

"We'll bring you around, Buck."

"Nah . . . not me, Towers . . . ."

A laugh that started in his throat ended in a broken rattle. He stiffened, convulsed—then relaxed, and a glaze came into his eyes.

Towers gripped him, held him for a long minute, then let him go slowly. There was no use. Buck had gone on.

Towers rose, grimaced, stepped over a dead black man, and saw Nils coming out of the cabin. Nils had a white look in his face.

He said, "Vat you t'ank, Yon? Epinard opened the chest. De chest is filled wit' rocks!"

"What!"

"Rocks, Yonny."

Towers winced and swung clenched fists at his sides.

The old man of the jungle stirred on the deck—moaned.

Towers strode past Nils with blank eyes, went down into the cabin. He saw the chest open. He saw stones lying on the floor. He saw stones in the chest—and a key in the lock. His hand shook as he ran it through the stones, and his eyes clouded.

He staggered back on deck, saw the lugger and the barque standing far apart in the moonlight.

Nils said, "Neffer mind, Yonny," in a quiet soothing voice.

Chapter Nine

THE EMPTY CHEST

TOWERS HAD a dull sensation as of the world crashing down about him. It was a hazy sensation. And he did not care. He stood staring into the darkness, while Nils stood beside him, one hand on Towers' shoulder, the other on the wheel. Towers' face brooded, and bitterness probed him to the core. Anne—the kid—and his own grub-stake to be paid back. Now—why, now he would have to work his way homeward. He reflected that ever since he had touched Port Moresby, hell raw and unadorned always lay beyond. These set-backs were what slammed good men on the beach.

He started suddenly, blinked his eyes. "The old man!" He felt a wave of shame at having forgotten the old man. He ran into the little cabin, got a bucket of water and some brandy. Bending down, he saw that the native's club had gotten the old man about two inches from his original scar on the left temple. He bathed the old man's head, while Nils tacked the yawl back and forth five miles off the coast. It was in Nils' mind that they would salvage the lugger and the barque.

Towers carried the old man down into the cabin, laid him on a bunk, opened the ports to let in the clean night wind. He found the heart beats becoming normal again. He kept laying cold wet rags on the old head.

The chest of stones and dirt angered him, and he carried them out on deck and heaved them overside. Then he went back to watch over the old man. He himself was ragged, streaked with blood, but he paid no attention to his own cuts. He did not care about himself anymore. Maybe he would let his beard grow and comb the beaches too. Some day, there might be another treasure hunt. He shuddered, reflecting upon the number of rum-soaked derelicts he had seen on the sun-baked beaches waiting for the rainbow's end.

The dark hours dragged by while Nils drove the yawl up and down within a four mile radius. And through the dark hours Towers stayed beside the old man, bathing his head, uncertain sometimes whether the old man were dead or alive. But always he found the elusive heart-beat.

Once he went on deck, pitched the dead natives overside. He weighted Buck's head and feet, murmured a prayer, and gave Buck to the dark waters. Then he returned to the old man, and was sitting there when dawn cracked; and he was still there when the red sun gonged into the world.

Far off lay the dark coast, behind which rose the tawny-shouldered mountains. The wind, having changed through the night, had pushed barque and lugger ashore. Towers left the old man and went on deck with marine glasses. The coast, the slabs of white beach here and there, looked deserted. Nils was driving the yawl nearer the land.

Towers started at sound of a cry below. He turned and looked toward the cabin. He was starting toward it when the old man appeared— warily, his eyes wide, a shocked white look in his face. He reached the deck and stared hard at Towers. He turned and stared at Nils. He looked around the yawl. He looked toward the coast.

His voice rushed out, "Where's that dirty muck Epinard?"

"He drowned," Towers said, mystified.

"Where's young Ward? I told him to beware. By Godfrey, this is queer! I—"

Towers rushed toward him. "What's the matter? What happened?"

"It was Epinard struck me. I knew he would. And I warned young Ward, the believing fool. But how did I get here?"

Towers' eyes were shining brightly. "I'm Towers, Ward's brother-in-law—"

"Yes, he was speakin' of you."

"Man, you've just come to! You've been out for almost a year. You lost your mind for a year. We came here —Nils Olafsen and I—and found you in a hut. You called yourself the king of the blacks. Epinard was with us." He related briefly the complications, the treasure hunt, the fight with the natives.

 THE OLD man stared transfixed. The glaze had gone from his eyes. In his eyes now was a tortured look, as if he were trying mightily to remember things.

He said, "I can remember things only from just before I was whacked on the head. The rest—about the natives and Epinard comin' again— is like a hazy kind o' nightmare, and it ain't noways clear. Me king o' the blacks? Gosh, not me! I'm the gent they call 'Cannibal Bill' in the Solomons. Cannibal Bill Moore."

He laughed—jerkily, and swayed a bit on his feet. He saw the lugger and the barque ashore, and then he lifted an ear.

"I hear drums," he said. "It's the victory beat. It means the blacks have got some white men."

"They must have gotten some of the crew of the barque," Towers said.

Cannibal Bill said, "The drums are far off. It means the beach is clear. Let's put into the lagoon there." There was a twinkle growing in his eyes. He was no longer the crack-brained old man of the jungle.

As the yawl was making for the lagoon he said, "Epinard got his, eh? And you got him off Noumea so's he could lead you to the treasure? Well, well, young man, that was a kind o' bright idea! I knew Epinard was crooked all along. One of Ward's bearer's run across me up the coast where I was pokin' around for ambergris.

"I'd sailed me a small cutter all the

way from Port Moresby—alone. So the bearer says a white man is hard hit. Epinard landed here between the time the bearer left and him and me returned. Ward was pretty bad and couldn't be moved, so I sent the bearer off in the outrigger for a bay fifty miles up the coast where there was a doctor. I mind Ward give him a letter to mail. It figgers out then that the bearer got lost."

"I received the letter," Towers said.

"Then he must have reached the bay, mailed the letter, and started back with the doctor. I mind there was a storm about then. They must have got lost in the storm.

"I had no gun, and Ward had a gun but no ammunition. Epinard had no gun. I didn't like his eyes and the way he was so nice. I knew he was plannin' somethin'. Ward figured he was goin' to die and got me and Epinard to bury the chest o' jewels, in case some pirates landed or the blacks got warlike. I mind how Epinard watched me when we buried the jewels.

"One day Epinard went out on the reef fishin', and I dug up the jewels, put 'em in a gunny-sack, loaded the chest with stones and put it back in the hole. Epinard said he couldn't get any fish off the reef. He got me to take the cutter out, 'cause we needed food. And while we were out there he clouted me on the head and I fell overboard. He had no gun, so he couldn't shoot. I swum kind o' blind, and the sea was runnin' heavy, and it carried me down the coast. I mind when I was almost fagged I met up with a hunk o' driftwood and hung to it. Then I mind the surf drivin' me toward the rocks, and then I mind a terrific bang on the head from the rocks, and after that —well, there wasn't anything. I must have wandered far away in the jungle, 'cause I never seen Ward again."

"Epinard must have followed you down the coast," Towers said. "He must have looked for you, to finish you. He never found you. I remember he could not handle a boat. The cutter must have gotten away from him, and a ship must have picked him up. Before he could get back to dig up the chest, the French must have clamped hands on him and pitched him in the penal colony. But he stole the key to the chest from Malcolm."

 WHEN THEY went ashore from the yawl, Towers led the way to the spot where they had dug up the chest. He pointed to the hole.

"Epinard led us here under threat of his life," Towers said. "We found the chest, lugged it on board. Epinard opened it while we were fighting. You know what was in it."

Cannibal Bill chuckled and picked up the digging implements they had abandoned.

"Just foller me," he said.

They followed him back onto the beach and halfway up the hill. He found a blazed tree, paced off from it and sank the pick in the ground.

"I'm kind o' weak, boys. You dig," he said.

Towers grabbed up the pick and began breaking ground. Nils wanted to help. Towers shook his head. He dropped the pick and took up the spade. He dug down three feet. The point of the spade caught on a piece of rag. Towers dug a wider hole.

The gunny-sack had rotted, but the jewels were there, mixed with the earth. The three men dug with their fingers, sieving the dirt and making a heap beside the hole of emeralds, rubies and diamonds set into ornaments of hammered gold. Towers' face and torso gleamed with sweat. Grim satisfaction—and not wild delight—was in his eyes.

"I've gone through hell for these," he said. "Ward's wife is dead broke and needs them. They're for her, except my passage home and a bonus to Nils here, who helped me. And a certain amount should go to you, Bill."

"Me?" said Cannibal Bill. "Not me. They belong to Ward. I swore on the book a long while ago that I'd never treasurer-hunt. I seen a barque and a lugger on the beach. There ought to be some money in them, if you don't mind. But the jewels—nary a one does Cannibal Bill take."

They made a bag of his gunny-sack shirt and carried the jewels aboard the yawl. They inspected each one closely, while the heat pulsed about them and the sea boomed far-off on a snag-toothed reef.

"If I know gems at all," Towers said, "there should be a little more than fifty thousand dollars here."

"Ward's wife 'll need it," Cannibal Bill said.

"Ay t'ank yes," Nils nodded dreamily. "Yon, Ay no take the five t'ousand."

"Nonsense," said Towers. "You will. It's coming to you."

Nils shook his tow-head complacently. "No, Yonny. Ay tal you vhat. Ay neffer been by America. Ay like to go. And Ay neffer travel in ship but Ay vork. Ay t'ank vonce Ay like to be passenger. Ay t'ank Ay get good yob in America. Ay like to go vit' you as passenger, Yon—and dat is all Ay vant."

"Nils, I tell you—"

"Yon, Ay tal you vhat Ay tal you, and dat is vhat Ay tal you. Ay go by America and gat good yob." He stood up with an air of calm finality

and went out on deck.

Cannibal Bill said, "The Swede says what he means, Towers. Take him on. Give him five thousand now and what would he do? Why, blow it in on the beaches, be good guy to a lot of bums. But take him to America, get him a job, look after him a while, and it 'll do him a lot better. Don't tell me, Towers. I been too long in the tropics to know. He'll find himself a nice Swedish gal, marry her and go farmin'. Mark my words. So do that, Towers, and you'll be doin' a heap o' good."

When Towers went on deck he put his arm around Nils' shoulder.

"All right, Nils," he said. "We'll go to America together. We'll be brothers there, just as we became brothers in the open boat. I know a couple of nice Swedish girls that would make good wives—"

"Yah," Nils nodded, beaming. "Ay t'ank Ay like to see nice Svedish gal, Yon. Ay be see none since Ay ships me out of Stockholm tan years ago." He put his huge arm around Towers shoulder. "Yah, Yonny. By yimminy, Ay haf good time by America!"

 THEY STOOD side by side, silent now, looking out across the mirrored sea. Somewhere deep down lay Epinard, who had never known honesty and simple faith—and who, having tricked others, could not have helped tricking himself in the end.

The monkeys chattered, swinging from limb to limb, and the red and emerald parrots wheeled across the white beach.

This is the third story of what we hope will be a long series of yarns by new authors who have never before appeared in print. We would appreciate our readers' opinions and comments regarding this new department.—THE EDITOR.

The MAN FROM SUVA

By

TOM CAMDEN

Yellow Treachery West of New Guinea

LEN RANSOM slouched in the 'rickshaw staring thoughtfully ahead at the bobbing shoulders of the coolie who was taking him into the hills. Behind him lay Singapore—steaming melting pot of many races. Ransom might have enjoyed the ride out into the country, if he had not been so consumed by curiosity.

Ling Soy, most powerful of Chinese traders, had sent for him. They had always been on bad terms. Their respective trading interests were in constant conflict.

His 'rickshaw boy left the road and turned in between the pagoda gates of a walled estate; an estate bought with the spoils of pirating—Ling Soy's palatial home overlooking the Lion City. A hundred yards up a graveled driveway, the 'rickshaw stopped.

Ransom vaulted lightly to the ground, ordered his boy to wait, and turned toward the gilded entrance of Ling Soy's rambling house.

A servant met him at the door and ushered him into the dimly lit reception room. He waited while the weazened little Chinaman disappeared to announce his presence. The house held the silence of death, broken only by the sleepy chirp of a bird in a cage that hung near the window. Ransom had the uneasy feeling that unseen eyes were upon him. With studied indifference he leisurely moved closer to the wall, his back to it. The servant reappeared, bobbing and smiling like a mechanical doll.

"Follow, please," he tittered in his best English.

He led the way down a hallway and into a well-lighted library. Bookshelves reached from floor to ceiling.

Behind an elaborately carved ebony desk, sat Ling Soy, well-fed, placid in appearance, and a little past middle age. Ransom had seen him before—at a distance.

The heavy lids of Ling Soy's sloe eyes drooped ever so slightly. Something smoldered for a brief instant deep in the black orbs. Then the Chinaman's gaze shifted. He looked out through the window toward the lights of Singapore for a moment before he turned back to his guest.

"Maybe you will kill Dutch Joe some time, eh, my friend?"

Ransom's lean jaw set. "Maybe I will—but *you* lay off, Ling, he's my meat—savvy—my meat!"

The Chinaman beamed benignantly upon the white man. Contemplatively, he took in the strong, rugged face with its broken nose slightly askew but still not unattractive; the scarred, gnarled fists toughened by salt water; the muscular arms with their crisp crop of coarse red hair. Ling Soy had long ceased to wonder why the Americans and the British dominated even the far reaches of the world. He had learned that those two countries bred men—barbarians, according to the celestial light and philosophical learning of his own tranquil and honored ancestors—brute-men with shrewd brains who refused to die gracefully. Some of them refused to die at all. He hated them, but in spite of his mandarin superiority, he admired some of them; even respected a few.

"Come, Ling, why did you send for me?" Ransom asked impatiently. "We aren't such damned good friends. There was a time when you'd have had my throat cut and grinned like Buddha while it was being done."

The Oriental smiled faintly. "Maybe I would still like to do that thing, my friend."

"We understand each other, anyway," grunted Ransom. He took a damp bandana from his pocket and swabbed the sweat off his face and bare neck. "Let's get down to business."

"If you will sit down—it is more comfortable to talk so," Ling Soy observed.

Ransom drew a carved stool from a corner and sat down, his back against the wall. He lit a long black cheroot, and waited, staring hard at his host's inscrutable face.

"Dutch Joe now takes most of your trade in Sarawak and Dutch Borneo." Ling Soy paused significantly.

"Well, if he has, that's my business," Ransom said coldly. "He's cutting in on you too, plenty, isn't he?"

"He killed John Taylor, your best man," the Chinaman went on imperturbably.

"One of his men killed Taylor," Ransom corrected. "Say—what in hell are you driving at?"

Ling Soy ignored the question. "Dutch Joe is pearling near Aroo Island, west of New Guinea. It is a very rich bed. His divers have brought up much shell—many good pearls."

"Well?"

The Chinaman pointed his long nailed forefinger at the American. "You and I will have those pearls—*you* will kill Dutch Joe."

Ransom sprang from his seat and leaned across the desk, scowling angrily.

"See here—I'm no damned cutthroat pirate! And who are you to give me orders!"

Ling Soy regarded him placidly.

"I have heard that when you find the man who murdered your brother —you will kill him."

RANSOM'S TENSE body relaxed s l o w l y. The s c o w l disappeared. A strange expression filtered into his weather-

beaten countenance. A hard light burned behind the slate-gray eyes as he stared intently at the Oriental.

"You mean——?"

"Dutch Joe is that man."

Ransom drew in his breath sharply. "How do you know so much, Ling Soy?"

"This is the Orient, my good friend —there are many ways of knowing many things."

The other searched the cream colored face shrewdly.

"How do I know you're not lying?"

"Ling Soy does not lie, Len Ransom!"

The white man almost added aloud: "Not much." But he kept the observation to himself. He watched the Chinaman open a drawer of his desk and take out a small package wrapped in a piece of cheap silk. Silently Ling Soy handed it to his guest.

Ransom unwrapped the silk and saw a faded photograph. His hand trembled as he held the picture closer to the light. He could not be mistaken—the last time he had seen that picture had been in the cabin of his father's trading schooner many years before. It was the photograph of himself and his younger brother Tom. The brother he had not seen since childhood. Separated, by the sudden death of their parents, he had lost all trace of him, until a month before when a Dutch shell buyer, Van Tromp, had told him of a Tom Ransom who had been knifed in Suva.

"It vas a tam fonny t'ing," Van Tromp had said, "but de poor poy vas talking about somepody vat vas named Len chust before he died. I thought maype you know him, yah?"

Ransom had sworn an oath, then, to cut the heart out of the man from Suva who had murdered his brother.

He looked up, his face a little pale. "Where did you get this?"

"It was brought to me from Suva by one who saw your brother die— and *Dutch Joe killed him.*"

For several moments Ransom stared silently at Ling Soy. Then a muttered oath tumbled from his lips. Once again his face was hard as a granite mask. He carefully wrapped up the photograph and put it in his pocket.

"You say Dutch Joe's pearling off Aroo Island?"

Ling Soy nodded. He saw what was in Len Ransom's face, and his soul was complacent.

"I think you will kill Dutch Joe pretty quick, eh, my friend?" he repeated softly.

An hour later Ling Soy escorted Ransom to the door. A strange alliance had been formed. Together they would be strong enough to dare much. The Chinaman wanted pearls —the white man blood.

 THREE DAYS later two auxiliary schooners hauled in their mud hooks and left Singapore, bound for an island off the west coast of New Guinea. Square-jawed, red-haired Len Ransom stood on the poop deck of the *Lucy R.* Ling Soy lounged in the owner's cabin of the *Sea Dragon,* sipping tea with an unusually bland expression upon his placid mask of a face which might well have mirrored the utter tranquillity of a beneficent soul.

Only once did the two ships lose sight of each other. That was when they struck the tail end of a typhoon that whipped across the Java Sea. For a day and a night they were separated. When they came within hailing distance again, good winds carried them swiftly toward their destination. Ransom cracked on under a full head of canvas, making the *Sea Dragon* strain every timber in an effort to keep pace with the *Lucy R.*

It was late one afternoon when Aroo Island was sighted. The two schooners hove to while Ransom got into the dinghy and went alongside the *Sea Dragon*. Ling Soy met him at the rail. They went below to make their final plans. It was their first opportunity to talk together since they had sailed from the Straits Settlements. The Chinaman had marked on the chart the approximate location of the shell beds where they expected to find Dutch Joe and his crew engaged in pearling. It was scarcely half a mile offshore in approximately ten fathoms of water that covered a chain of coral reefs.

Ling Soy's ideas of attack were elaborately cautious. He favored putting in at the far end of the island and making a journey on foot to a point where, through binoculars, they could spy upon the pearlers without arousing their suspicions. That way they might ascertain the other's strength after which an attack could be planned more intelligently. But Ransom was for descending upon Dutch Joe that very night under cover of darkness. His impatience finally prevailed over Oriental cunning and caution.

At sundown, the two ships weighed anchor. With sails furled, they proceeded toward the island under the power of their auxiliary engines. The *Sea Dragon* led the way, for Ling Soy's mate was familiar with these waters. When darkness fell no lights were lit. They were running dark. It was past midnight before a light was discovered riding high upon the mast of a shadowy hull that lay off the *Lucy R's* starboard bow. Motors were shut off. Heavily muffled anchor chains were let out with painstaking care.

Several boats put out from the two schooners. There was Ling Soy and his score of Chinese coolies, and Ransom's Malay crew in three boats. Ole Jensen, the *Lucy R's* mate was the only other white man. With muffled oarlocks they moved silently upon the swiftly running tide toward their unsuspecting prey. Coming alongside they swarmed over the rail like monkeys.

Ransom was among the first aboard. At the rail he turned to Ling Soy.

"Remember — Dutch Joe's my meat!" he whispered fiercely.

A sleepy lookout aboard the pearler managed to shriek a startled warning before steely hands gripped his throat and prevented further outcry. But the damage had been done. A rudely aroused crew rolled out of the forecastle to fall upon the borders with knives and belaying pins. There were yells, curses, imprecations, in half a dozen dialects and languages.

A voice roared orders from the poop. Ransom leaped toward the after deck. A naked form sprang toward him. A long knife flashed. Ransom's pistol barked. The man shrieked and pitched forward, but not before the flat side of his knife struck Ransom's hand to send his gun clattering to the deck.

Ransom did not pause to retrieve it. Unarmed, he plunged on toward the poop. In the darkness, he was met at the head of the companionway by a white man dressed only in a pair of trousers. Even his feet were bare. There was the glint of steel in his hand.

"Are you Dutch Joe?" shouted Ransom above the din of battle.

"Yes—what the hell do you want?"

"You—you —— ——!"

He sprang up the companionway toward the pearler. Dutch Joe's gun spurted fire. Hot lead seared Ransom's cheek. With a snarled oath he leaped upon his enemy.

They came smashing together like two charging bulls. Ransom drove a hard right to the jaw that sent the other staggering back against the rail like a drunken man. But Dutch

Joe came back as if catapulted from a giant sling-shot. He sent blow after blow in rapid succession to Ransom's head and body, driving him back along the poop deck toward the stern.

The two men had the after deck to themselves. Forward on the main deck men of many races fought. Malay, Chinese, South Sea Islander, Japanese. Divers and crew. Their mixed battle cries and growls of pain rose above the clash of knives, the thwack of belaying pin on skull, the crack of pistols, the impact of fist on bare flesh.

Suddenly Ransom ducked low and closed with his man, encircling his big torso with his arms. Carried backward by the momentum of Ransom's rush, they crashed violently to the deck. It was a rough and tumble battle with no odds given or expected. Dutch Joe drove his knee into Ransom's groin with a force that sickened the latter. For a moment he yielded to the spasm of pain and nausea. In that instant a big fist smashed into his jaw and Ransom's senses reeled from the shock. Calloused fingers clutched at his throat.

With a sobbing intake of breath he thrust the palm of his left hand against Dutch Joe's chin, forcing his head back. His fingers pressed against the other's eyeballs. Slowly, with desperate stubbornness, Dutch Joe's throat hold yielded. Ransom's strength was returning. He drove his gnarled right fist into his enemy's taut, exposed throat.

The two men broke away and sprang to their feet. For a moment they appraised each other in the gloom, like two wary beasts waiting for the first move of attack.

From somewhere forward, Ransom heard Ling Soy's voice giving orders in gutteral Chinese. The sounds of conflict amidships had died down.

As he leaned breathless and bat-tered against the hatchway leading down into the skipper's quarters, Ransom's hand touched the cold round end of a belaying pin. He barely had time to grip it securely, before Dutch Joe charged him. Quick as lightning Ransom raised the belaying pin above him and brought it down hard upon the pearler's head. Dutch Joe fell at his feet with a low moan. His body quivered convulsively for a moment, sprawled face down upon the deck.

 SPENT AND exhausted, Ransom swayed unsteadily on his feet. The wild yells and curses which had punctuated the free-for-all were completely stilled. The conquest of the pearling schooner had been swift and complete. A voice spoke at Ransom's elbow. He turned his battered face toward Ling Soy. The Chinaman's clothes were unruffled, the placid face expressionless, save for the sloe eyes that stared down at the prone body of Dutch Joe.

"So—you did kill him?"

Before Ransom could reply, a woman's white face appeared at the after companionway. She tried to penetrate the darkness and identify the two men standing nearby. Then her eyes fell upon the sprawling form lying so still upon the deck. Her hand flew to her mouth, stifling the cry of horror that rose to her lips. Oblivious to everything else, she ran to the body upon the deck and knelt beside it. She took the shaggy head in her arms and pressed it to her breast.

"Oh—Joe!" she moaned.

Ransom flinched visibly. He heard Ling Soy giving orders to his coolies in rapid Chinese. Two of them sprang upon the girl and dragged her away from the still body. Suddenly Ransom leaped forward. His bruised and swollen right fist shot out to the jaw of one of the coolies. The other he seized by the neck and hurled him crashing down the companionway leading onto the main deck. Then he whirled upon the astonished Ling Soy.

"You and your yellow rats keep your filthy hands off her—savvy?"

He thrust his chin belligerently into the mandarin's face. He was not aware that Ling Soy made the slightest move until the muzzle of a short-barreled automatic was thrust against the lean, hard muscles of his belly.

"Don't move, my friend," came the Chinaman's expressionless voice. "You are my prisoner."

"You — yellow - livered, double-crosser!"

The muzzle of the gun was pressed a little harder against him.

"Don't be a fool, Ling Soy! My men'll make shark meat out of you and your crew for this!"

"Your men are not capable of being much assistance to you," replied the Chinaman. "They are my prisoners. More than half the crew on this boat were my men."

Ransom was beginning to think he understood a little more about Ling Soy than he did before. Still for some unknown purpose the Chinaman might be bluffing. Ignoring the gun which menaced his vitals, he called out to his men.

"Jensen! Lay aft here!"

A string of oaths from somewhere amidships came in reply. "I'm sorry, sir. But this gang of yellow cutthroats have got me tied fore-an'-aft!"

Ling Soy chuckled mirthlessly. He issued swift orders and half a dozen brawny coolies fell upon Ransom. Despite his struggles, he was soon bound hand and foot and propped up against the low deck house. Dutch Joe's woman came up to him and raised a tearful face.

"Who are you? How do you come to be with these Chinese pirates?"

Ransom was inarticulate. He could scarcely bring himself to meet the woman's eyes. He had never before seen a girl just exactly like this one.

Ling Soy came up to them. He spoke to the grief-stricken, frightened girl.

"You are Dutch Joe's wife?"

She nodded silently, too overcome by emotion to speak.

There was a flicker of triumph on Ling Soy's face when he spoke again to his erstwhile ally.

"You do not seem happy to meet the wife of your brother for the first time, my esteemed friend?"

Ransom glanced quickly at the girl and then at the prone body upon the deck before him. He turned upon Ling Soy in deadly quiet.

"Quit sparring, damn you! What is your game, anyway. He was not my brother. Van Tromp, the shell buyer, saw my brother knifed in Suva."

Ling Soy chuckled sardonically. "Van Tromp spoke the words I put into his mouth. Dutch Joe *was* your brother—that is why I planned to have you kill him." Ling Soy's face was no longer placid. An ugly scowl of black hatred had filtered into the yellow countenance. "Many years ago in Penang, your father did a very great wrong to Sung Lee. For this thing he died— Sung Lee, whom you know as Ling Soy, saw to that. You have played your part well—for that you will be rewarded. You will be the last of the Ransoms to die..."

The Chinaman spoke to his coolies. They picked up Dutch Joe's limp body and heaved it overboard.

"For the sharks," commended Ling Soy, as the body splashed into the water. "Now, Len Ransom, I shall give you a little time to meditate upon many things before you go to your Christian Hell."

 RANSOM WAS carried below and thrown upon a bunk in one of the cabins beneath the poop. Torn by an avalanche of emotion, dazed and horrified by the terrible thing he had been tricked into doing, he lay quiet as a dead man. For the first time in his life, Ransom felt utterly, miserably helpless. From an adjoining cabin the sobs of a broken-hearted girl came to torture him. He would be glad when it was all over. But if he were going to die —he would like to go *his* way—fighting for her.

He was barely conscious of the door opening and closing noiselessly. After a moment he realized that someone was in the cabin with him. He could hear a man's heavy breathing. A big hand gripped his arm. A hoarse whisper warned him to silence.

When Ransom turned his head, he started violently. There, close to him in the ghostly moonlight that came through the open port, he saw the big head and shoulders of Dutch Joe. But the man was dead! He had killed him. The body had been thrown into the sea.

Still Ransom knew that what he saw was no apparition. Ghosts did not breathe heavily like living men. This one's hair and clothes were wet with sea water. The bronzed face glistened faintly with moisture. The man was alive—very much alive.

It was the first opportunity he had had to study the pearler's features. It *was* Tom! The family resemblance was strong. A younger, handsomer counterpart of himself. Square-jawed. Red-haired.

For a long silent moment the two brothers stared at each other. Slowly the younger grinned.

"What—how the devil——?" burst out Ransom, unable to restrain himself longer.

"Sh-sh!" cautioned the o t h e r.

"Those yellow devils will hear."

"I thought you were done for!"

The younger man chuckled. "I've got a hard head. That crack you gave me just made me sleepy for a minute or so. I came to on deck while the Chinaman was talking to you. I overheard most of what he said—enough anyway. I played 'possum. Crawled back up the anchor chain."

"Good boy!" murmured Ransom. "Quick—untie me."

Soon his hands and feet were free. He stood up. The brothers were the same height; two powerfully built men, though the younger was narrower of hip, slightly lighter of carriage. A strange pride beat in Ransom's heart as he surveyed the figure before him in the gloomy little cabin. They clasped hands silently. Nearly twenty years had past since they had done that.

"Tom!"

"That sounds funny—I haven't heard it since I was a kid. I'd almost forgotten it."

There was the sound of someone moving about in the main cabin. Tom raised his hand in warning and motioned his brother to lie down in the bunk. Then he took a pistol from his belt and moved cat-like to one side of the door. It opened and Ling Soy stepped into the room. He went to Ransom's side and gloated down upon him. But his expression changed as the muzzle of a pistol was jabbed into his back.

"Keep quiet, or I'll put a bullet in your spine!" Tom's voice hissed behind him.

Ling Soy's face became a mask. His body remained motionless.

Ransom sprang to his feet; frisked an automatic from the Chinaman and helped bind and gag him. Then the prisoner was thrown face down upon the bunk.

Tom led the way into the main cabin. It was deserted. He moved swiftly on. First he went to a door on his right and knocked softly. A muffled, tear-filled voice sounded inside the cabin. Tom smiled gently.

"It's me, Sybil. Everything's all right."

A little cry of joy came from the other side of the door.

"Keep quiet, honey," cautioned Tom. "Just stay inside until I come for you."

With Ransom trailing him, he moved quickly across the cabin and opened a secret panel. He took out two repeating rifles and a couple of boxes of shells.

"They are already loaded," he whispered, passing one of the guns to his brother. "Come on—let's fill the yellow devil's bellies with a lead breakfast!"

The first streaks of the tropical dawn were lighting the sky over Aroo Island when two grim, red-haired, square-jawed men crept up onto the poop deck of the schooner.

One moment the early morning air was still, save for the slap of water against the ship's side. Then death fell with terrifying swiftness upon a group of coolies eating rice on the deck amidships. Hot lead poured from the two rifles on the poop. There were cries of agony, confused yells, and the shouts of Ransom's crew held prisoner in the hold below. For two minutes the rifles blazed—then silence.

Later that morning, the bodies of several coolies and one mandarin, that dangled at ropes' ends from the masthead, were cut down and cast into the sea. Long phantom shapes cut through the water, stained crimson the morning tide.

Tom Ransom turned to grin at his brother. "After this, I'll be eating no more shark fins!"

The ROYAL CUCKOO

A Novelette of Flying Wings
North of New Guinea

by

Ace Williams

Chapter One

RIFF-RAFF

THERE ARE men who are continually roving, tramping to the ends of the world and back again, moving always—and for no apparent purpose at all. Civilization and its attendant accessories pall them, and they seek out the remote corners of the earth; where they hope, possibly, to find the fabled El Dorado of their half formed dreams. Some are called soldiers of fortune, others adventurers and explorers. But if they happen to stoop low in their travels, smoking of hashish and opium, and spilling their seed on the lands they have trod, the better sounding title falls away from them. Then they are known as tropical bums, tramps, riff-raff—even scum.

To one of these classes Snark Smith belonged. Snark wasn't his given name, for it had been once S. N. Arkwright Smith. But his fellow flyers of the squadron in which he served in France dubbed him Snark. And Snark it was now, if anybody at all chose to call him by a given name—which thing very few people did. Long, lean, hungry looking, with a far-away unfathomable cast reflected in his deep set eyes, he stalked the remote corners of the earth with no apparent purpose in mind. But he differed from the others in whatever class you choose to put him because he did his stalking a-wing; in a ramshackle contraption of wood, linen, and scraps, that he had put together himself from cast off parts and had nerve enough to call an airplane. And an airplane it was to him, for it flew, and he flew it.

What matter that the linen wings were patched with muslin bits that still held the faded imprint of Pillsbury's Gold Medal Flour? What difference if the gas tanks were more than one-half made up of soldered squares clipped from empty five gallon cans scattered over the fringe of the world by John D.? Nor did it matter that the fifty gallons of gas that swished about in his fuel tanks had come from a barrel that an island trader had very carelessly left unguarded. The fact that he hadn't paid the trader for it didn't bother him in the least. Things like that never worried him.

But inactivity and lack of movement did. To stay more than two weeks in any one place was positively annoying. And not to have the wherewithal, be it money, transport or endurance, to make the next land that beckoned from below the ever alluring horizon line, flooded him with the most wretched feeling of despair imaginable. But at the moment this story begins, Snark Smith was not in despair. On the contrary a sort of subdued light flamed in his eyes; and the corners of his thin lipped mouth were slightly upturned, just vaguely revealing the feeling of satisfaction that must have glowed within him.

SMITH'S EYES took in a rare sight. For there on the four walls surrounding him was the most astounding and spectacular display of color he had ever seen. It was just as though all the rainbows of the sea and sky had been gathered together and compressed to make one single scintillating diadem of beauty —thousands of bird of paradise skins hung one upon the other to almost fill the small room of the trading post store.

"Ah, tell me," he spoke to the Dutch half-caste who presided over the assortment, and the tone of his voice betokened the awesome grandeur of the display. "There are many varieties, I see. Which ones are the most valuable?"

"Z' Rouge Magnifique," answered Jan Van Zandt, "undt also z' Superbe undt z' Epimaque are very scarce. Undt on zees bird here I vill make you a bargain."

The half-caste trader reached up on the wall and took down a string of feathery pelts, threw them on the counter before Smith. The corners of Smith's upturned lips spread farther toward his ears, and he laughed, laughed openly in the surprised half-caste's face.

"But I don't come to buy," he replied. "What will you pay for some just like them?"

Van Zandt blinked his eyes, then stared at Smith, his fat jowls drooping. "Vat? You haff pelts for me to buy?"

"No, but I come to ask prices and find out the best varieties. It is only the best and scarcest varieties that I will bring you."

Van Zandt gazed past Smith out at the bobbing seaplane, in the harbor, the one in which he had come, then he shook his head negatively from side to side and grunted.

"No, not efen wiz zat airplane will you be able to get zem. Oh, five, seex maybe? Yess. Zen z'natives zey get your head."

Then he centered his gaze on the tall form of Smith and let his eyes rove over him, only to shake his head again in the same manner. The smile faded from Smith's tanned features. The far-away look dimmed in his eyes and in its place ignited two little pools of flame. His brows narrowed and his thin lips pressed together.

"Thanks!" he spit out coldly. "But I didn't come to you for advice, only prices. Now what's your offer for skins like those?"

Van Zandt jerked upright now, observed the newcomer again. And

very probably because of those two little pools of fire he saw in Smith's eyes, he changed his manner. Or possibly it was that he had nothing better to do, for white visitors came very seldom to remote Ternate in any kind of transport. This man had come in an airplane—the only one that the Dutch half-caste had ever seen, if you except the Dutch Island Patrol plane that he had glimpsed overhead several times in its very infrequent flights over the Spice Islands.

"Vell," he began and beckoned to Smith to sit down beside him on a narrow bench that extended along one wall. "You musdt know zät ze price vat ve pay, eet ees much differendt zen ze price vat ve zell——"

Smith dismissed the halting explanation with an abrupt wave of his lean, gnarled hand. "That I don't care. Tell me where these birds come from and we'll haggle about prices later. I will get you more than enough to fill this room here." And he made a gesture with his lean hands that encompassed the whole interior of the trading post store.

The Dutch half-cast peered at him from beneath shaggy brows that drooped lazily. His beady inquisitive eyes probed questioningly through the scanty lashes.

"Go on," Smith chided. "Open up, tell me where the most wonderful skins come from."

Then proceeded a lengthy explanation of how the bird of paradise skins eventually reached the marts of trade. From far in the innermost jungle fastnesses of New Guinea came some of them—most of them. But the scarcer, more valuable skins came from the little known islands to the north; islands that were seldom touched by white man. The skins were traded from tribe to tribe, brought down through the jungles to the river mouths. Other tribesmen picked them up there, and eventually they found haven in some white trader's hands. At this point the half-caste grasped hold of Smith's arm, squeezed it tightly while he bent his flabby neck and looked up into the tall pilot's eyes.

"Ah, I vill tell you a secret——" His pudgy fingers gripped tenaciously the rippling muscles beneath Smith's tunic sleeve, and the beady eyes narrowed to flaming pin points. "Z'ere ees vun bird zat ees more valuable zen all ze rest. Vunce ever' two year zere comes to me seex of ze skins. And ze seex are worth more zan all ze skins you see hanging here."

Smith gasped.

 AH YES, that was a business. Better by far than copra, tin, benzoin or pearls. Bird of paradise skins—he had figured it out before and had come to the Spice Islands for that precise reason. But he had never imagined that there was a species of bird so valuable that six skins would equal a fortune. He shook loose Van Zandt's grip on his arm, and in turn grasped the half-caste's flabby biceps, pinched them until the fat trader squirmed.

"Tell me," he fairly shouted. "Tell me where they are to be found, and I will bring you six times six." The little pools of fire in his deep set eyes leaped to swirling flames now. His tan face flushed crimson beneath the bronze coating.

Van Zandt blinked, stuttered out a reply.

"Ah, but zat ees ze secret. No vun hass efer seen ze bird alive. Only ze skins zey come here, but zey are *magnifique* wiz ze colors of royalty— purple undt gold. Brilliant as ze sunrise, yet soft as moonlight. Undt only seex do I get undt zen only ever' two year."

"Tell me," repeated Smith and poked his rigid forefinger in the half-caste's ample paunch, "tell me where they come from."

Van Zandt only shook his head from side to side negatively.

"Efen I don'dt know. Usually I know ze country where ze best birds come from, Tenique, ze Red Horse Mountains. But ze most valuable, ze Royal Cuckoo, no. No vhite man hass efer seen it alive. It ees traded from tribe to tribe oudt in ze Forgotten Islands. Undt ze sea gypsies zey bring it to me. But only seex skins ever' two year. No more, no less."

Snark Smith shook his pointed finger impatiently. "You have them here now," he asked. "And you don't know where they come from?"

Van Zandt lowered his eyes and continued to shake his head negatively. "But ze Royal Cuckoo, zat elegant bird, I haff ze pelts here if you would like to see zem. But to catch zem alife, zat ees anozzer matter. It ees better zat you stay here undt safe your head."

"My head is my own to risk as I please," Smith snapped, and the little pools of fire in his eyes leaped in flame. "And I don't thank you for the advice. I'm free, white, and over twenty-one, and not used to taking advice from those whose blood runs thick with the dirty slime of the tropics——"

The fat half-caste jerked his flabby neck back and blinked his pig eyes as he stared at Smith inanely.

"Show me," Smith ordered, and his voice now had the tone of command. "Show me the pelts of this marvelous bird—this Royal Cuckoo, as you call it."

Van Zandt got up from the bench hesitantly, as though unwilling to do the simple bidding. But the light that flamed in the tall pilot's eyes, and the grim intent indicated by the manner in which they followed his every movement, caused him to withhold the inner feeling of resentment that surged through his half-caste veins. He opened a door that led off the main room of the trading post store, kicked it back with his sandaled foot, then stooped in and dragged a small chest out into the center of the main room.

"Ah, yess," he replied as he fumbled for the key in his pocket. "Certainly I vill show zem to you. But firsdt I musdt ask you ze favor. You vill tell nó one zat you haff seen zem here?"

A smile flushed over Smith's bronze features when he answered, "No, no one." His eyes fastened on the lifting lid of the chest as Van Zandt straightened up. But he wondered at the simple intelligence of the half-caste.

Van Zandt had cautioned him about telling the tale to anyone, yet, here he was showing the pelts to him. And he had never laid eyes on him or the plane before. Smith was just about to mumble some jesting reply when the lid of the chest was thrown open. The lilting repartee was choked off half way up his throat. There before his eyes was a bursting bomb of color, radiant as pyrotechnic and brilliant as the sunlight—the mounted pelt of a Royal Cuckoo. Small as a robin it was—no larger, cloaked with a scintillating armor of dazzling splendor. The breast was feathered with golden plates, fragile and leaf-like; and row upon row, flaring out in great tufts, ribbon-like and sheer, on either side; royal purple at the base and terminating in veritable cataracts of flaming passion at the tips.

Snark Smith blinked and turned his gaze away.

"I will find the place they come from, and bring you enough to fill this room."

Van Zandt lowered the lid, locked the chest and slid it into the adjoining room. "Many haff told me zat before," he said. "And some of zem, a long time afterwards, I haff seen zere smoked heads. Ozzers—" Van Zandt shrugged his bulbous shoulders. "Vell, ze ozzers, I haff not efen seen zere heads."

Smith laughed again, laughed openly in the fat trader's face as he had done before. He thrust a stray wisp of blond hair back with a quick swipe of his lean hand, then stalked toward the door that opened on the harbor vista, where waddling *prahus* and lateened junks were milling about with their strange cargoes and yet stranger crews. Riff-raff, gathered there under the blue dome of the tropic sky, far from the distant corners of the earth from whence they had come for some reason or no reason at all, and engaged now in business nefarious or legitimate, whichever they chose.

"Your story is good," Smith said, "and true, so far as you know. But in this day of fast transport, airplanes and wireless, there is no such thing as an inaccessible spot where a man can't go alone and return the same way, with his head still fast on his shoulders and thinking."

Van Zandt stood with his pudgy hands on ample hips and watched Smith go, then when Smith turned his head and shouted back over his shoulder: "I'll find them" the half-caste swirled the tip of his dirty finger around the rim of his right ear.

"I haff seen zem like zat before," he mumbled to himself. "But never haff I seen zem come back."

A faint smile of satisfaction rippled in his beady eyes when he sat down on the narrow bench and waited for Smith to get in his plane and take off.

Chapter Two

FLYING BLIND

 THE TALL pilot set his spark and throttle levers, then walked back on the hull and tickled the engine carburetors until he flooded them. When the gasoline was overflowing—the gasoline he had taken from an island trader and forgotten to pay for—he stepped further back on the hull and put his lean muscular hands to the propeller tip. A couple of powerful twists sufficed to fill the motor cylinders with a priming charge. Then he set the switch on contact, and gave the propeller a powerful twist. The engine sputtered, coughed, turned over unevenly in sharp staccato movements. But Smith rushed to the pilot's seat and jimmied the throttle and spark levers back and forth rapidly. The motor began to turn up more evenly, and finally settled down to an even throated purr.

He looked about him on all sides to see that his takeoff path was clear, then waved his hand at the fat half-caste still sitting on the verandah of the trading post store. And he smiled as he jerked open on the throttle with the other hand. The little seaplane leaped eagerly across the dimpled surface of the harbor, and shot into the air easily when Smith rocked the stick back and forth. It might have been made of second hand parts and scraps, and its looks were nothing to comment upon, but it flew and handled like a dream.

As he gained altitude the smile faded from Smith's countenance, and in its place came an expression of somber intensity. His eyes scanned the dials and indicators on the instrument board intently, they rested longest on the vibrating float of the compass. He straightened his course automatically and waited for the vibrating float to still. When it did, the lubber line centered between the letters N-NW. North—north-west, he was flying, at least by compass indications, and that was just as good a direction as any, so he pulled back gently on the control stick and let the seaplane climb for altitude.

"Out in the Forgotten Islands," Van Zandt had said.

And up to the north, north-west of Ternate laid the ten thousand black specks on the heaving green of the great Pacific which had been designated by the mariners—"The Forgotten Islands." Small volcanic cones most of them were, just the tips of which still protruded now since the thousands of years when a once expansive land had shrunk beneath the surface to form a new ocean floor. Remote, inaccessible, and most of them unpeopled, they came by the name naturally. "The Forgotten Islands." And upon but a few of the mariner's charts were they even indicated. The ones Smith had showed but a few scattering dots north of the East Indian Archipelago, and the words, *Forgotten Islands*, had been written in by pencil on what would have otherwise been blank space. Yet, there were ten thousand of them. And upon one of them was the habitat of the Royal Cuckoo. And six pelts of the Royal Cuckoo would equal a fortune.

The thoughts of that salient fact caused Smith to fidget in his seat and pour on all juice to his roaring motor. The plane answered and leaped forward with greater speed.

Perhaps it was because he was too interested in locating the black speck ahead that meant the end of his trail, or possibly it was that he feared nothing, man made or Heaven born, that he didn't look back over his shoulder as he flew along. For while he was searching for a black speck ahead and scanning the surface of the sea intently in his passing, a black speck bloomed in the blue void behind him. The further he flew in a direction, north, north-west, as indicated by his magnetic compass, the larger grew the black speck behind him. In fact it expanded and bellied out until it dissolved the blue of the sky and dimmed the rearward horizon line.

Smith would have seen if it he had glanced behind, but his gaze was fastened ahead, where the sky was still cerulean and the horizon an opalescent rim upon the deeper sapphire of the sea. And somewhere in that vista, flared and faded a blazing magenta of color—the vision that danced before him as he visualized the forgotten island where stalked the Royal Cuckoo, in all its imperial glory and great worth.

The storm—they break like lightning in this region—caught Smith and his surging seaplane when he was not more than three hours out of Ternate. A blanket of ebony folded in from behind and enveloped him. At the same moment, and before he had a chance to react to the sudden transition from light to dark, something that seemed like a giant hand appeared to grasp his tiny plane and shake it frantically. It was lifted a thousand feet in an instant and was hurled downward almost immediately, crackling and groaning in every brace and strut to the accompanying roar of a series of rumbling thunder peals that seemed to blast in all at once.

How long he fought there in that heaving welter of blackness above the foaming sea, no one, not even Smith knew. He passed out at the controls when something like a terrific bludgeon descended on his head.

Then all was still and quiet as death.

SOME THIRTY hours later, after many fitful moments of wakefulness that were followed immediately by blank spells of unconsciousness, Snark Smith came to fully. Where he was he had not the slightest idea. All that remained of his seaplane was a bit of watertight hull and a mass of ribbon-like shreds of linen that had once covered the wings of his plane, but was now tangled about the hull in wretched disorder. The engine itself had broken from its fastenings and plunged into the sea, apparently. And it was good that it had, for undoubtedly the remaining bit of hull would have been dragged to the bottom with it, had it not been wrenched free.

As it was, free of the weight of the heavy motor, the remaining bit of watertight hull had kept him afloat through his unconsciousness, and the current of heavy running seas had spun him about through a nest of narrow, basaltic islets, where jagged black teeth of rugged lava stuck out upthrust like spiny fins on a giant serpent. The howling gale was still whistling and moaning weirdly and driving him along at a merry pace—when finally he struck.

The debris was washed ashore by the morning tides onto a narrow shingle of rough beach, strewn with coarse pebbles and jagged coral, and it required all of Smith's waking efforts to haul himself out of the surf before he was ground to bits on the tearing edges. There on the shoreline just barely free of the water he collapsed, sank over on the hard rock shelf from sheer fatigue and exhaustion.

When he next awakened, the sun was beating down on his salt sprayed head, and a thunderous voice boomed in his ears. Snark Smith opened his eyes and blinked them, rolled his head hazily from side to side in a vain effort to shake the cobwebs from his tortured brain. Finally a semblance of consciousness returned and he saw standing above him a giant of a man. Belted in a simple cincture he was, and a great mass of shaggy red beard covered his face and chin.

"Get up!" he thundered at Smith, and kicked him in the ribs with a shoeless hoof, big as a rhino's and hard as steel. "What business have you here?"

Smith made an effort to rise to his haunches and he attempted to frame a reply, said something about being a trader or something like that. That he had been caught in a storm and was wrecked but finally managed to make the shore in safety.

But the words as he mumbled them were apparently unintelligible to the giant of a man who questioned him, and he kicked Smith in the ribs again —another belt from his hard hoof that shook the fatigued pilot from head to foot and came very near jarring all the consciousness from him.

"Where's your shipmates?" the giant boomed. "I don't see any wreckage along the reefs here. You're just one of those sneaking pirates that's been tryin' to poach on my own private terrain for the last three years."

"I came alone," Smith answered weakly. "There ain't anybody with me. And I didn't come aboard a cutter or junk. I came in an airplane—"

"Airplane?" the giant stammered in reply, while a strange light flashed in his blue-as-the-sea eyes.

Then he became suddenly silent and scowled down at Smith sternly, sizing him up from head to foot. Smith weaved upwards now, unsteadily. His head swung in circles and the blood pulsed through his temples terrifically, with the pounding roar of a chugging locomotive on a steep grade.

"Get down there!" the giant boomed and spun him around with a blow from his balled fist, big as a smoked ham and just the same color. "You're one of those thievin' fortune hunters come to spoil my island. But you should have brought along a gang and a couple of machine guns, maybe a cannon, too."

"But I tell you," Smith replied, "I didn't even know where I was coming. I don't even know where I am now. You have taken advantage of me before you heard my story."

The giant smiled at him grimly, and it was a most unpleasant grin. "I had a notion to break your head first off, then tell the Governor about it later. But the King's Counsellor put in a plea and the High Court decided to let you live just for the fun of it. There'll be lots of time for you to die later."

"Where are all these people?" Smith asked hopefully.

The giant threw back his head and laughed long and loudly.

"Right here," he bellowed. "I'm the whole works—Governor, Counsellor and Judge. Schmidt."

And the way he sounded his name was like a sharp detonation. It might just as easily have been Scat or Pfft, or any other derisive rejoinder. The effect on Snark Smith would have been just the same.

"Yes, Schmidt!" the giant repeated when he noted the questioning look that came to Smith's eyes. "Came here ten years ago, on my own with no help from anybody, and haven't asked for any since. I don't owe anybody anything and nobody owes me. I am not wanted East or West, and I'm not hiding out from anybody. This is my island by right of possession and you're a poaching trespasser who had best watch his step."

So saying the giant gathered Snark Smith up under his arm as an ordinary mortal would lift a bundle of groceries and carried him up the hill off the barren rock shelf. And the thing was done easier than it might have been if Snark Smith had had but a faint semblance of his original strength still with him. His heart was willing but the raw, bleeding flesh was weak, so he submitted meekly and bided his opportunity for revenge to come later.

UP ALONG a meager path through the lush, tropical growth they meandered until they came to a clearing, in the center of which stood a house neatly built of bamboo and roofed with thatch. And along the front of it was a wide verandah. There sat a girl, with two long black braids of glistening hair hanging down her back. A brown girl she was, with face round as the moon and lissome figure clothed in a purple cloak of dazzling splendor.

She stared at Snark Smith with growing amazement, and he stared back from his perch beneath the giant Schmidt's arm with a growing amazement of his own. For the resplendent purple cloak that was slung so carelessly yet gracefully across the lissome figure of the girl was made all of bird skins—skins of the Royal Cuckoo which he had set out to find.

Over five hundred of them went to make up the glorious garment. Five hundred golden rainbows joined together and neatly sewed to make the most resplendent garment he had ever imagined. No cloaks of ermine or sable, or royal satins, could begin to compare with it. The courts of the richest kings had seen nothing like it. Yet here it was, slung carelessly across the shoulders of a little brown thing on a Forgotten Island north of Guinea—a fortune in feathers.

Its great beauty and stupendous worth was the first thought of Snark Smith. He scarcely noticed the woman at all, and that was not unusual with him for he had never noticed any woman—for long. This was a native woman, and native women were just that and nothing more. But as he stared in wonderment at the marvelous robe, he saw that the supreme beauty of the feathered cloak was no more than fitting for the beauty of the flesh that it adorned, and so of lesser worth after all.

Her lips moved and she spoke. Although he caught not a whit of sense from what she said, a thrill coursed down Snark Smith's spine and he felt the warm blood tingling in his finger tips.

"Ah, it isn't dead," she cried when she noticed Smith's eyes rolling in their sockets. And her voice was like the breeze that sifts through palm fronds on blue summer days.

Schmidt released his hold on Smith and let him drop to the brown earth with a thud, then he laughed again, laughed raucously.

"No, Eventide," he chuckled back, "not all of them that are washed up on the beach are dead. This bit is still alive, so I brought him up to you for a plaything."

The brown girl leaped off the verandah, ran to where the huddled form of Snark Smith was stretched out prone on the earth. Then she stooped down and touched him.

"It's alive! It's a man!" she gasped.

Smith stirred. She drew back as though she had been stung. And the giant Schmidt bared his yellow teeth in hideous laughter.

"Aye, Eventide, if you can call what's left of him that. But a poor excuse for one even so. Why look at his spindly shanks and skinny arms?"

To demonstrate his point, Schmidt reached down and twisted Smith's arm, twisted it until a horrid grimace of pain flashed on the smaller man's features.

"Don't!" the native girl shrieked, sank her teeth in the giant's arm and bit him.

He stared at her in amazement for a second, then flung his massive hand around and caught her flush on the face, sent her spinning and reeling backwards toward the verandah.

Now Snark Smith had never been much betaken by women—even white women. And this little wild thing that the giant Schmidt had called Eventide was a brown-skinned native. But some unplumbed well deep within him was stirred into activity when the girl rushed to his defense, and the pulsing blood surged through his veins in turbulent torrents when he saw the giant send her reeling backwards with a hefty slap from his open palm. He gathered all the strength within him and leaped erect. His right fist lashed out like a whisking rapier and landed flush on the giant's chin.

Schmidt calmly shook his head and flicked his finger across his face as if he were brushing off a fly. "Is that the best you can do?" he rasped derisively. "And all these long years I've been aching for one to match blows with me, stand up to me and trade right and lefts, give and take. Exercise, you know. But—Bah!" And Schmidt punctuated the last expletive with a ponderous swing of his ham-like fist that thudded against Smith's right ear with the crashing din of a train wreck. He went out like a smashed lamp.

The native girl came forward again and stooped over him, smoothed his feverish brow with her delicately pointed finger tips, brown as mahogany but soft as eiderdown. The giant Schmidt just stood and looked at her, with his great ham-like hands perched on his massive hips. But Eventide had no eyes or words for him. She bent over the prone Smith and cooed in his ear, sweet musical little notes that meant nothing to him, for he was out and didn't hear them, and wouldn't have understood them if he had been conscious.

"So you like him," the big man spoke finally and screwed up his thick lips in an angry snarl. "I was going to kill him right off and I should have. But I thought you'd appreciate me bringing him to you—"

"I want him," she broke in, and stroked his ashen cheeks more vigorously. "I want him because he's a man."

The big man was silent for a moment. Although his lips were moving rapidly no words issued forth. But apparently that was the way he did his thinking, for suddenly he acted.

"Well, you shall have your puppy dog," he answered, then forthwith stooped down and gathered Smith under his crooked right arm. "But I'll put him away for you where he'll keep."

Chapter Three

THE PIT

HE STALKED out of the clearing with the limp and unconscious form of Smith dangling grotesquely from the arch of his armpit. Into the lush tropical growth he plunged, taking no heed of the rough and thorny briars that scraped and scarred his victim's exposed hands and face. And it might be mentioned here that Smith took no heed of them either, for he was still under the anaesthesia induced by that powerful blow he had taken on the ear. For perhaps several hundred yards Schmidt stalked through that thick tropical growth until he came to a sort of cliff that fell away, sheer and abrupt, to depth of thirty feet or so. A natural ravine it was, walled on four sides and lined with vines and thorny creepers, with the poisonous red berries of the trailing arum in scarlet abundance. Into this natural pit the giant dropped Snark Smith, just as he would dispose of a bundle of garbage. After he had dropped him, he walked around the rim of the pit and pulled up all the trailing creepers that overhung it. Then he left and went back to the clearing.

There was a wide smile on his broad face when he stepped up on the verandah and addressed the little brown girl. But though he spoke she paid no heed, only hung her head and pouted like a little child who had been muchly spoiled by overly fond and adoring parents.

"I am keeping him for you," Schmidt repeated. "But I'm keeping you safe from his touch. Sweet you are, Eventide, and wise in the ways of the jungle and this tiny island; but you know nothing of the outside world, nor the scurvy touch of the rotten whites that so seldom have tainted these shores."

He attempted to stroke the long braids of her hair, but she drew back from him and hissed in his face, showing two even rows of teeth, white as alabaster and lustrous as pearls.

"Spitfire," he chuckled at her while his broad frame shook with rollicking laughter. "You are just like all women—"

"But you told me I wasn't," she broke in, and thrust the resplendent cloak of bird of paradise skins challengingly over her bare shoulder. "He's a man and I want him!"

She stomped her tiny bare feet in emphasis of her demands.

"And I have acceded to your demands," he replied. "I have put him where he is safe, in that pit in the jungle where runs the little spring. And while he is there he can work for us. The well needs digging. I'll put him to work when he comes to, and in that way he can earn his board and keep. You can go and look at him every day."

"Oh," she gasped in evident relief, "I thought you had killed him."

And when the giant reached out to stroke her hair this time she didn't draw back.

 SNARK SMITH came to, fully, a couple of hours after he was dropped in the pit. He rose up on his haunches, leaned his back against the hard lava outcroppings of the natural prison cell, and looked around. The blood pounded through his temples tempestuously, and every bone and muscle in his lean body ached, while his hands and face were bleeding and raw. Ceiled by the open blue sky of heaven above he was, but the sheer walls of the natural ravine made the cell just as effective as any steel-barred one. Then as he looked at the high rim of the cell, just as though it had come to taunt him, appeared a tiny bird—a Royal Cuckoo in all its living splendor and dazzling brilliancy.

Smith smiled painfully and immediately there surged in his mind a picture of the fat half-caste, Jan Van Zandt, and a few of the last words he had uttered rang in his ears.

"Zen z'natives zey get your head."

The Royal Cuckoo twittered for a second or two, then took wing and flew away. But a soft padding sound reached Smith's ears now. And presently the moon round face of Eventide appeared above the rim of the pit.

Smith struggled erect now, doffed his hand to her in salute.

"Did he let you come?" he asked incredulously, although the solidified salt spray irritated and burned his cracked and scratched lips.

"What? Let me?" she replied surprisedly. "What is that?"

Snark Smith repeated his query and watched Eventide's eyes cloud over while her smooth bronze brow knitted in a charming interrogative frown.

"Let me," she said. "Who, let me? I came because I wanted to see you and talk with you. I came because you are a man. You are, aren't you?"

Smith smiled again, even though

the effort was painful in the extreme. Astounded by the absolute simplicity of the native girl, and wholly absorbed by her perfect beauty and naive charm, he put her another question.

"How long have you lived here? And from where did you come?"

She listened with an air of intentness, while the reflection of the sunlight on the resplendent robe she wore arched a vivid rainbow across the blue dome of his cell.

"How long?" she repeated. "What is that?" And her English was so perfect that Smith couldn't believe the question was so ambiguous to her.

"How many years have you been on this island with Schmidt?"

"Years?" she asked hesitantly, then a sudden light flashed in her black-as-ebony eyes. "Oh! Herr Schmidt's ears!" she replied quickly. "He has two big ones. And they are so funny."

The lilting laughter that sifted through her even teeth filled the open pit with soft musical notes of a strange wild melody all their own. Snark Smith shook his head hopelessly and gazed up at her benignly.

"Child," he asked, "don't you know anything?"

"Yes," she came back quickly and flaunted the gorgeous garment of purple, golden feathers in his face. "I know everything. Herr Schmidt has told me all there is to know. I know about boats and ships and trains. I even know about airplanes—"

"What—what?" Smith broke in and jerked his head back so that he might better survey the seeming fairy who lilted above him. "You say you know all about airplanes? But you have never seen one?"

She tittered some more and flung the classic robe carelessly across her well rounded shoulder. "Oh, yes I have. I have sat in one."

"Not here," Smith said unbeliev-ingly.

"Yes, right here," she replied. "But I only did so when Herr Schmidt was sleeping. He won't let me go near it when he is awake. Says it is his plaything and for me to leave it alone. But now he has brought me you for my plaything." She crossed one bare leg over the other and sat down on the rim of the pit. "So I don't care whether I ever sit in it again. It's cold and hard anyway. And I like things soft and warm. Things that talk to me like you do, the birds and monkeys."

THE FACT that he had been compared so easily with the twittering birds and chattering monkeys m i g h t have afforded Smith much amusement if he hadn't become so tensely serious when Eventide mentioned the airplane. He wondered whether it wasn't some strange fantasy of her child-like dreams that prompted her to speak as she did, so he put her another question to test the truth of her assertion.

"Tell me, Eventide," and his own voice was soft and pleading now, "tell me what that airplane you sat in was like. Was it like a bird?"

She shook her head swiftly and the long black braids swung out horizontally. And the cloak she gathered more closely about her.

"No, no," she replied, seemingly disappointed. "The birds have feathers and are warm to the touch. But that airplane—it is cold and hard, made of tin and wood and cloth. Not pretty at all. And when you sit in it, there is a stick that comes up between your legs and wiggles around when you push your feet." She grasped an imaginary control stick with her hand and indicated to Smith how it acted by cat-like movements of her nimble and flexible wrists.

The statement was enough. The

proof was self-evident. There was an airplane on the island, or how else would this naive and simple little brown girl know so much about one. He stood silently in the bottom of the pit, utterly amazed and spellbound, too concerned with events that had transpired to utter a word in reply.

Eventide leaned down over the rim of the pit, stared at Snark Smith quizzically. The feathered robe fell away from her shoulders and bared her full bosom. Smith, with a pained look on his face and a queer twinkle in his eye, stared back at her.

"Why don't you talk with me?" she pleaded.

A hundred thoughts were surging through Snark Smith's agile brain now, and some of them were conflicting. A dozen feelings welled up inside him and cried for expression. He had come out from Ternate in search of the habitat of the Royal Cuckoo. And, strangely, he had found it without great effort. But his thoughts now were not of the Royal Cuckoo or the great fortune to be gained by the sale of the pelts. Instead they were of the little brown girl who leaned over the rim of his pit and stared at him so innocently. Finally he spoke.

"Eventide, do you love him? Do you love this man you call Herr Schmidt?"

Her eyes widened and she leaned farther down in the pit.

"Love him? Love Herr Schmidt? What is that—love?"

Snark Smith put his hands on his hips and shook his head hopelessly.

"Oh nothing, Eventide," he replied, but deep within him—for the first time in his life—there surged a feeling that was very much akin to love. Love for the little brown girl who leaned over the rim of the pit and peered at him so innocently.

But the soft, melodious words that were on the very tip of his tongue were purged out before they were spoken, when a hand big as a ham reached over the rim of the pit and snatched the girl out of sight.

"Get!" he heard a great booming voice thunder. "Get back to the house and prepare the evening meal. I bring you a puppy dog for a plaything and you neglect all your duties. Better that I had snapped his head off first thing. A dead man wouldn't be so interesting."

Then there was a crackling in the bush, followed immediately by the soft pad of swiftly running feet, and something that sounded very much like a series of sobs.

A mad surge of anger coursed through the lean frame of Snark Smith. That unplumbed depth within him had been touched again and he boiled with rage, pounded one doubled fist into the palm of the other until his knuckles reddened. Then a massive head appeared above the rim of the pit, and a deep basso voice blasted in on his ears.

"Like her, don't you?" the giant Schmidt bellowed and bared his yellow teeth in an ugly sneer. Then he cackled fiendishly. "I knew you would. It's just part of your torture before dying time. It's what you get for buttin' into business that is not your own. A man picks out a solitary island for himself with a woman of his choice to keep him company, and all the white trash in the world come sniffing around."

Smith didn't answer, but held the air of listening. And the more he listened, the hotter and more turbulent his pulsing blood stream boiled within him. Not that he was in love with the little brown girl on the remote Forgotten Island north of Guinea—for Smith would not admit this fact even to himself. He had never been in love with any woman and considered himself too old for such things now. But there was a spark of chivalry within him and an intense feeling of sympathy for the underdog, be it black, brown, or white—or even half-caste.

"And I should have known better than send those Royal Cuckoo skins out into the world," the bearded giant went on. "I might have known that thievin' white traders would follow the trail like a dog follows the spoor of wailing bitches. But I had to have things for the house, things that only money could buy. Six skins every two years got them them for me. And I thought I was clever. I took the pelts to another island and traded them there. I figured I would throw the poachers off my track. And I did—until you showed up. I was of a mind to kill you first off. But I thought of Eventide and knew that she would like to have you for a plaything, so I brought you up to her for a puppy dog."

Smith had said nothing up to this point, but his eyes were carefully taking stock of height and reach and build, and his mind dwelled on plans of escape—some method he might figure out to make his escape from the pit; to tangle man to man with the giant that towered above him like the Colossus of Rhodes, with his two legs astraddle one corner of the pit.

"If you were a man," Smith fairly shrieked, "you'd let me out of this pit so we could fight it out on even terms. Or else you'd drop down here yourself. The best man lives and comes out, eh? No. You're too yellow for that!"

The giant Schmidt went to cackling again, a horrid chuckle that sifted through the lush growth and rattled the fronds of the palms.

"Haw, haw, haw! That's good. The likes of you mouthing that. There ain't a gun on the island, me boy. If you want to fight me, you'd have to fight me with bare fists. And there's no man alive who has ever stood up before Hans Schmidt. Why I'd break you in two, then where'd you be—

dead, eh? That's what you want I know. But I am going to ease the death in slowly. What's the use of dying all at once? It's much more pleasant to die by inches—"

HE LEFT off there, with that bit of irony, and a sardonic grin spread over his bold features as he disappeared in the bush. Smith heard the heavy crunching footsteps as he ploughed through the tangled undergrowth, and listened to them intently until they faded away in the distance. Then he set to exploring the pit in which he was imprisoned like a bear in a trap. A spring seeped from a clay bed in one corner, but the four walls of the ravine were of sheer lava and almost as smooth as slate, with no possible chance of gaining a handhold to attempt escape by climbing the walls. And the thick viny stalks of the trailing arum, that had previously overhung the rim and extended far down in the pit, were lifted up now. Escape was absolutely impossible unless he had outside assistance. Smith realized that salient fact after his inspection.

There was only one thing for him to do, so he did it. Sat down and waited for something to happen—for Eventide to come again to the rim of the ravine. If she would only drop down some of those vines that rimmed the pit he would have an effective means of escape.

Chapter Four

PADDING FEET

NIGHT FELL with the suddenness of the tropics, just as though a dark blanket had been drawn over the opening of the ravine, and Smith still sat in silence waiting for something to happen. The bones and muscles of his lean body still ached, but the torment in his mind dispelled all sense of feeling and he didn't even notice it.

It was perhaps two, three hours afterward that he heard a noise above the rim of the ravine. He had been sort of half dozing and the sound startled him. He leaped erect and peered up into the darkness. Then came a soft voice, tuneful and vibrant.

"Herr Schmidt he is asleep, so I have brought you something to eat. Are you asleep?"

"Eventide?" Smith asked, still not entirely clear of wit. "Eventide, is that you?"

"Yes, Mister Man."

Smith's vision cleared now, and he saw something white on the rim of the ravine, something white and bulky with a fragrant, warm aroma that assailed his nostrils pleasantly.

"But how am I going to get it down to you without spoiling it?"

Smith's heart leaped in his throat when he prepared to answer. Of course she could lower it on the end of one of the trailing creepers.

"Just tie one end of a vine around it and drop it down in the pit."

And if he ever secured one end of that vine—tough and strong as muscle sinews—he would have means of escape.

"But no," she replied. "Herr Schmidt has told me not to do that."

Snark Smith's heart stopped pumping for a moment and he held his breath. It had seemed so easy, yet here were his first hopes dashed on the instant.

"Do you always do what he tells you?" he asked finally.

"Yes, always," she replied.

"Then go away and let me sleep!" Smith snapped back in sudden anger.

He didn't know why he had spoken that way, but the words came out, sharp and incisive, before he knew it. The girl reacted by dumping the white bundle over the side of the ravine, letting it splash down as it would.

"There!" she uttered and kicked at it with her foot. "Pick it up from the dirt and eat what you can. Goodby, Mister Man, I'm going away."

Smith's jaw dropped and he stood momentarily aghast. He heard the soft padding of feet on the rim of the crater—and a series of sounds that sounded like sobs. He cried out automatically. "Eventide! Eventide! Come back here!"

And for reasons that only women know, even if they are but native women, Eventide heeded the command, turned on her heels and crept back stealthily to the rim of the crater. First her glistening black head of hair appeared over the rim of the ravine. Then her eyes and finally her full face. And tears were streaming down it.

"I didn't mean it, Eventide," Smith said. "I'm sorry."

And as a matter of record it was the first time that Smith had ever acknowledged to any woman—native or white—that he felt sorry.

"You are too anxious," she replied. "If you but had patience. If you had waited maybe two or three days. The master he goes away then, flies away in the big airplane thing to trade bird of paradise skins on a distant island. For a long time he would leave us alone. But now you have spoiled all of that. I wanted to play with you, to touch you. But now? No! I hate you!"

Snark Smith crunched his teeth together madly. For a second time a haven of hope had been revealed to him only to be wiped out by his own damnable impatience.

"But no, Eventide," he pleaded, and his voice now held the pitch of plaintiveness. "I didn't mean it. I was crazy with fatigue and pain. I wasn't in my right mind. You are lovely—"

"Lovely—what is that?" she broke in.

The mad spell was broken and she sat down on the rim of the pit while Snark Smith tried to explain what he meant by "lovely." Slowly and cautiously he played with her now, sparred back and forth with meaningless words and phrases that meant a whole lot—and yet nothing—to anyone but a woman.

"And he's mean to you, isn't he?" Smith said. "He hits you and curses you, don't he?"

"Yes," Eventide answered.

AND SMITH was certain now that he was preparing the ground properly this time. The thorny creeper would yet be let down—before the moon had reached the zenith or the dawn came to proclaim the new day.

"But only when I am bad," she added, while Smith was gloating to himself. "Then, I deserve his curses and blows."

And again Snark Smith shook his head hopelessly. This sparring with words and ideas with a wild thing on a remote isle north of Guinea was driving him to distraction. In a moment of anger he picked up the bundle of food she had dropped him and heaved it back at her. It balanced on the rim of the pit for a second, then toppled back into the ravine. And with it came a mass of thorny creeper —a means of escape.

Snark Smith grasped it eagerly, as if he were afraid Eventide would pull it back before he did so. But no, she just stood on the rim of the ravine and laughed, soft rollicking peals of laughter.

Smith was up the thorny creeper like a monkey. He took no heed of ache or pain or scraggly thorn. A means of escape had been offered him and he took it before it, too, vanished

into thin air as had the others.

The moon was up now, fully, round and roseate like a yellow apple, immediately above their heads. And the beams, slanting down on the radiant feathers of the gorgeous garment Eventide wore, made a picture of exceeding beauty, even more amazing and scintillating under the light of the pale but waxing moon than under the bright rays of the blazing sun.

"Eventide," Smith said when he recovered his breath. "Show me this airplane you spoke of and we will flee to the ends of the earth. This Schmidt he is cruel to you, mean and brutal. You deserve better than that—"

"Show you, yes," she broke in and smiled warmly while her black eyes flashed spiritedly. "But flee—what is that?"

Snark Smith didn't have time to shake his head this time. For she was away with the speed of an antelope, tripping swiftly through the luxuriant grass. He followed her and came eventually to a great bamboo walled and thatched affair that was built upon a narrow strip of sandy beach, hard, white and dazzling in the moonlight.

"There," she pointed with her slim finger when they approached it. "There. It is in there. But I dare not go in with you. The Master forbids me to go near it when he is not along."

Snark Smith threaded his way across the white sand in the moonlight and presently came to the queer hangar that housed the airplane—if there was such a thing on the island. He was still doubtful in his own mind of its existence, for it seemed very improbable. Yet this queer building he was about to enter must have been built for some purpose. And then, too, the narrow strip of hard beach sand served ideally for a take-off and landing field.

He searched some time for a door and finally came to one around the corner of the hut. His heart was pumping wildly now and he held his breath while he entered. If there *was* an airplane inside that bamboo affair the fact would be almost too good to be true. Eventide stood outside on the sand while he tip-toed in.

"I will watch," she said. "And if the Master comes I will sing a little song."

The building inside was black as pitch and Smith felt his way along carefully until his eyes became accustomed to the darkness. Then when they did he noticed that along one side, thin rays of moonlight seeped through as they would through a shutter. He stole farther in and presently his outthrust hands encountered something hard and unyielding. His heart leaped and his breathing stopped momentarily. He rubbed the tips of his fingers across the rigid surface upon which his hand rested, and from his trembling lips came a wheezing gasp.

"My God! It *is* a plane!"

There was no mistaking that touch. He knew it too well. His fingers had rubbed across the doped linen surface of an airplane wing. He hurried forward now, still keeping his hand on the linen wing, and came presently to the outer wing strut. He gasped again.

"My Gosh! Metal!"

The plane must have been a modern one or else——

His attentions were suddenly distracted by a sound he heard outside, so he jumped back and listened. No more sounds came though, and he threaded forward again until he came to the fuselage. His eyes had become quite used to the darkness now and he could make out vaguely the dim outline of the plane.

And now that he had assured himself that there was really a plane in the hangar he became supremely confident. He looked around and saw that the moonlight seeped through on the side which the plane fronted.

"Hmm," he mumbled to himself. "That's fairly simple. This side of the building must open up."

He explored a bit with his hands and found that the front was yielding to the touch, not solid like the other walls. And that it appeared very much like the lateen sail on a Chinese junk.

"Cinch," he mumbled to himself again. "That's what it is—a lateen curtain that drops down and covers the front of the hangar when the plane is inside."

 HE TURNED and stalked back toward the door by which he had entered, walked through it out into the moonlight and along the front of the hangar, saw that it was just as he had figured. Rising hope was buoyant within him now and he whistled gaily as he threaded back to the door and found the rope that lifted the lateen front. He pulled on it huskily and the whole front of the building divided like a parting curtain in the theater.

The moonlight streaked in and flooded the whole interior of the hangar, clearly revealing the plane. And Smith gasped again. What he saw was like an apparition to him.

"Good God! A Fokker!"

He could scarcely believe his eyes and rushed forward to place his hands on it and feel of it again to make sure that it was real. Yes, it was. A wartime Fokker of the vintage of 1918 with camouflage still on it—and of all things, a twin set of Spandaus mounted on the nose.

And yes, the black Maltese Cross was still painted on the wings. Snark Smith made a dive for the fuselage around the wing tip. He was so excited now that his heart pumped like a trip hammer and he felt the warm blood flush on his cheeks.

But he drew up stark still and silent the second he rounded the wing tip and saw——

"Oh, no! It can't be," he gasped weakly and the strength seeped from his lanky limbs. "No, no! I'm crazy!"

Eventide approached now from the spot where she had been standing on the sand. Smith's dizzy, reeling movements had alarmed her. But Smith paid her no heed. He staggered weakly toward the cockpit with blurring eyes narrowed down and intent gaze centered on a painted insignia right below the pilot's seat—the crude representation of a black Devil squeezing a bleeding red heart.

Snark Smith's memory flashed back through the years on the instant—to a gray day on the Western Front almost fifteen years before.

"No, no, NO! It can't be!" he muttered crazily while foamy froth drooled from the corners of his open mouth. "I'm crazy! Crazy as a louse!"

Eventide approached nearer now, fear written in her wide open and staring eyes. She put her hand on Smith's elbow.

"What's the matter, Mister Man?" she asked plaintively.

But Snark Smith had no ears for her words. His fingers traced grimly the hazy outline of the painted insignia and he muttered and babbled unintelligible words and phrases mingled with blasphemy and profane oaths.

The vivid memory of that final day on the war front burned like an acid etching in the very lining of his soul. Here was the cause of his downfall and degradation on a remote reach of the Forgotten Islands north of Guinea. For months after, he had tried to make amends and explanations. But no one, not even his immediate superior, had lent a willing ear. Then followed Blois and dishonorable discharge. Now for fifteen years he had been trying to forget.

This was the selfsame plane he had encountered on that gray day on the western front. And now that he had put two and two together to make four, he knew that Hans Schmidt was the pilot who had been the cause of his downfall. He remembered now the leering, sneering scowl on that helmeted pilot's face. And he remembered the thick-set lips and massive features. Yes, that enemy pilot of fifteen years ago on the western front and Hans Schmidt were one and the same. And the plane Smith was standing by now was the very one he had duelled with in the long ago.

And an A1 pilot he had been up to that time, had a reputation that was as good as any other on the American Front. Then came that gray day and the duel with Hans Schmidt, to blast it all away in the twinkling of an eyelash. Smith remembered that now, remembered it clearly.

Schmidt had pounced down out of a cloud while he was on patrol with the C.O. on one of his infrequent flights over the front lines. The diving Hun in the Fokker had taken him unawares while he was exploring the terrain below, had got in a couple of Spandau bursts on his tail before he knew he was being attacked.

That was all right. That was fair in war, part of tactics and strategy.

But Smith in his Spad, by agile stick handling and manouvering, had wormed out of the death stream of fiery tracers. In the next split second he transposed positions with his attacker and got in firing position himself. One burst slithered away from his Vickers and tore through the Fokker's center wing section. And Smith was riding the Hun's tail now in a way that his adversary couldn't worm out. He needed but to edge the stick forward slightly to blast the Hun pilot's head off. And he did edge the stick forward, but just as he prepared to press his Bowdens and spray another burst, the Hun pilot rose in his seat and pointed to the breech of his Spandaus. A look of fear was in the Hun's eyes and his face was white. His gun seemed hopelessly jammed.

And Smith, because of some inner trait of character that would never allow him to take advantage of the underdog, released his grip on the Bowden triggers, allowed the Hun to win free. The Hun then showed his appreciation for Smith's mercy by wheeling up in an abrupt bank that lined the nose of his Fokker on the C.O.'s Spad. Then followed a burst from the Hun's guns that blasted Smith's C.O. from the skies. He went tumbling down, to crash in horrid death on the shell-cratered earth below.

And before Smith had time to think or act, a whole squadron of Fokkers clipped down from above and drove the remaining Spads back over their own lines.

The Flight Leader, rabid because of the loss of the C.O. while out on patrol with his Flight, preferred charges against Snark Smith, accused him of funking it when he had the enemy pilot who afterwards killed the C.O. dead in his sights. And Smith hadn't been able to refute the charges. His own actions had looked bad, and he knew it. Followed then disgrace and dishonorable discharge from the army.

For almost fifteen years he had been trying to forget.

Chapter Five

Retribution

 NOW ON a remote islet north of Guinea he had come face to face with his Nemesis — the heinous Hun who had played him

such a trick.

He fumbled his fingers over the insignia for some seconds, then of a sudden straightened erect and threw back his shoulders. The lambent pools of fire in his deep-set eyes leaped in eager flame. He stalked out of the hangar like a wild jaguar.

"Take me!" he blazed, and his voice had the tone of stern command. "Take me to this man you call the Master— Herr Schmidt——"

Eventide, her feathered robe flowing and black eyes staring wildly, jumped back. "But he will kill you," she said. "You will have to go back to the pit now. If you don't I will get whipped."

"Take me!" he repeated sternly.

And because of his overpowering will she did, tripping silently and swiftly back through the lush tropical growth that led to the clearing in the jungle.

Smith pounced up on the verandah close at her heels.

"Tell the yellow scut to come out here," he rasped. "Tell him the man he brought you for a puppy dog is going to kill him. After that we fly away to civilization."

Eventide slipped softly in the door and Smith heard her talking to Schmidt, trying to awaken him. He stood poised on the verandah with both fists doubled and lean jaw outthrust.

Finally there came sounds from inside and a lamp was lit. Smith sized up the length and breadth of the verandah by the light that streaked through the door, grimly took stock of his battle ground. Then loud guffaws of raucous laughter issued through the door.

"Haw, haw, haw! That skinny scum will kill me, huh?"

Then Smith heard heavy footsteps and he set himself solidly on his feet with legs apart, leaned one shoulder forward and drew back a tensed fist in readiness.

The giant Hans Schmidt came bounding through the door like a rogue elephant. His hideous yellow teeth were bared and profane phrases poured from his lips.

"I'm the guy you pulled a dirty trick on over the Marne fifteen years ago," Smith rasped at him as he charged. "I'm the guy you double-crossed with a fake plea for mercy because of jammed guns. And I'm going to kill you now. I give you fair warning beforehand."

The giant Schmidt hesitated for a moment, then a pale glow of recognition flashed in his eyes and he lowered his bull-like head and charged with both massive paws flailing.

Smith waited, tense and charged with that dynamic strength and will power that only supreme anger can foster. His drawn back fist was balled up, but that was only a bluff. He knew that he couldn't stand and trade blows with the giant before him. That hand would do its work when the opportunity showed. His extended shoulder was poised to take the brunt of the first charge, to slip the giant to one side and at the same time guide his fist over it.

Closer they came and the giant lashed out with his left as Smith figured he would, poked it straight out to prepare the way for his following right. Smith took it on the point of the shoulder and the ham-like fist slithered past his left ear. Like a flash Smith's right zipped forward and up. And his thumb was upthrust and rigid. The rigid thumb laid into the giant's armpit where the nerve ganglia from the vertebræ are closest to the surface. It was a trick he had learned in Japan.

The giant bellowed in pain and rage, and his left arm hung limp as a rag from his husky shoulder. And even before the bellow was out of his bull throat Smith brought the point of his right knee up hard to the groin. The giant Schmidt fell writhing to the floor and grasped his middle, moaned and groaned like a wounded bull.

Smith drew back his booted foot and prepared to finish the job, to bash the man's brains in until he died. He was helpless now and at his mercy. His debt had been paid at last.

But even as he drew back his foot for the first blow, Eventide, with the litheness and agility of a panther, leaped at him and sunk her teeth in the flesh of his forearm. He drew back, stared at her, then shook his arm and threw her off.

"What — what's the idea?" he grunted. "Don't he whip you? Beat you? Curse you? I'm giving him some of his own medicine."

But the look that flamed in her eyes now was one of seething hatred, and the way she pursed her lips when she answered was a horrid thing to see.

"But—but I, what you call it— love? Yes? I love him."

Smith stepped back and the native girl fell on the floor beside the giant Schmidt—her Master. She smoothed his massive brow and cooed sweet words in his ear.

"And me, what about me?" Smith managed finally to gasp. "Aren't you going with me?"

"No!" she hissed back and spit in his face. "I hate you!"

Smith put his hands on his hips and shook his head.

"Just a wild thing on a Forgotten Island north of Guinea," he muttered to himself as he backed off the verandah and stalked down the path that led to the hangar on the beach.

It was a matter of but half an hour or so, when he got the plane wheeled out on the beach and the motor started. The Fokker with its Mercedes engine was new to him, but Snark Smith was an A1 mechanic as well as a pilot. And he realized that Hans Schmidt must have been, too, for the plane and engine were in excellent shape. The gas tanks were filled to overflowing and it appeared that the ship was all set for flight. A leaf-wrapped bundle was stowed away behind the pilot's seat, but Smith paid no attention to it. What interested him most was the chart that hung alongside the throttle control.

He studied it for some moments in the light of the moon, then put it back in its place, gave gradual gun to the motor, and took off from the narrow strip of breach—with a song in his heart and a very definite idea about women.

Chapter Six

In Full Payment

 JAN VAN ZANDT was just opening the doors of his trading post store when Snark Smith strode down from a field that overlooked the harbor. A leaf-wrapped bundle was under one arm and his sun bronzed—if scarred—face was wreathed in smiles.

The fat half-caste's jaw dropped and he stared at Smith as if he were seeing a ghost.

"Vat? Vat? Ees eet you?"

"How much for the pelts of the Royal Cuckoo?" Smith asked and threw the leaf-wrapped bundle athwart the counter.

"No, no. You do not haff ze pelts of ze Royal Cuckoo. No white man has efer brought zem to me."

"Open the bundle," Smith said.

And Jan Van Zandt did. His beady eyes almost popped from his fat head and his drooping jowls trembled and shook when he gazed at the dazzling array of flaming feathered skins exposed before him—purple and gold—the colors of royalty.

"Where? Where did you find zem?" Van Zandt gasped.

"I asked you the price you will pay today," Smith replied coldly.

Jan Van Zandt made some hasty calculations with a pencil upon the counter top and stated a figure to Smith.

"Sold," said Smith. He took the pencil from Van Zandt and put down some names and amounts on a slip of paper he picked up from the floor. "And keep the cash and send it to these people," he added. "I am selling out and getting out of the business."

"But—but," the half-caste sputtered and tossed both his hands up in a Yiddish gesture. "Zat island where you haff found zem ees worth many fortunes——"

Smith cut him short with a cold stare.

"And I have come back with my head," he said as he went out the door.

"I don't sink you haff," Van Zandt piped after him.

Jan Van Zandt stood and whirled his dirty finger around the rim of his right ear as he watched Snark Smith's purloined plane being swallowed up by the blue haze that mantled the eastern horizon.

THE RED COSSACK

A Novel of
American Cavalrymen
and Red Russians
in Siberia

By

MALCOLM
WHEELER-NICHOLSON

Synopsis

Part One

 BORIS NAGOI, the Red Cossack, and his desperate band of mounted Bolsheviks have been running wild over the Siberian countryside, ruthlessly maiming and killing all men, women and children in their path.

Lieutenant Dick Ryan and his ser- geant, Miller, scouting the barren countryside alone and some hundreds of miles away from their American cavalry detachment, in search of the Red Cossack, encounter a band of roving cavalrymen and hide in the trees that border a dusty road while the detachment passes.

The troops pass and wheel their mounts in at the nearest village where they ruthlessly kill or maim almost all the inhabitants. Ryan and Miller ride into the village after the raid and learn from one of the survivors that the band was com- manded by the Red Cossack himself, and that they themselves had seen him pass, mounted at the head of his troops and swinging a bloody sabre over his head.

Angered because they had been balked, Ryan and Miller hastily organize the few remaining men in the village, and on horses that they have commandeered they take off in pursuit of the Red Cossack and his band. Each village that they reach adds more recruits to their ranks, and finally Ryan feels that his troop is strong enough to encounter the Bolshevik cavalry leader in combat. His band does meet up with and defeat a roving band of raiders, and several of the vanquished immediately join up with Ryan and his band. One of them is an officer and the other a former Cossack sergeant. They ride on with the augmented ranks, and Kardoff, the former Red officer, is accused of being a spy and traitor, but he proves his innocence satisfactorily to Ryan. The big sergeant proves out to be one of Ryan's best aides in organizing and drilling the unschooled recruits who join Ryan's little band to avenge the deaths of their loved ones at the hands of Boris Nagoi, the Red Cossack.

But all along the march to the headquarters of the Red Cossack, strange murders have taken place in the ranks of Ryan's band. Soldiers have been found with their throats cut from ear to ear, the same manner in which many of the villagers had been murdered by Boris Nagoi. Kardoff, the former Cossack officer is accused of the murders because of his many strange absences from the troop, but Ryan, despite Miller's warnings, is sure of his innocence and allows him to continue with the band.

Then while enroute to the Red Cossack's headquarters, a soldier comes back with an urgent message for the commander of the troop, Ryan. He is asked to rendezvous at a certain point alone and meet somebody who will be there. Ryan is busy at the moment, so Miller goes instead. He does not return to the troop at the appointed time, and Ryan, fearing foul play, goes in search of him. He finds his tracks in the woods and comes across the body of the soldier who delivered the message. The soldier's throat is slit from ear to ear in the same gruesome manner as many before have been killed. Then —GO ON WITH THE STORY BELOW.

Chapter Eleven

THE RED COSSACK SPEAKS

RYAN FOUND himself stretched prone at the edge of the forest and heard the sound of a struggle going on above him. Someone's foot came into violent contact with his shoulder, but he was still so dazed from the blow which had knocked him out that he could not tell what had happened. As his returning consciousness waxed keener the shouts and confusion around him died down. Suddenly he felt rude hands grasping his shoulders and he was quickly jerked up to his knees. Dim figures wavered about and in his head a thousand bells were clanging madly. He was so faint that he nearly fell as he struggled upright, but strong hands held him up while other hands bound his arms behind him. Then he was dragged forward towards the *stanitza*.

Dimly he could sense the presence of four or five men about him. Stumbling often, he was jerked forward until at last he saw the vast bulk of the gate towers of the *stanitza* looming above him. A sentry peered into his face. The gates were thrown open. He was jostled inside and soon found himself gazing down a street bordered on both sides by long, low, log buildings. There were Cossacks everywhere, and men in peasant garb formed in groups, drilling. As in a dream he felt himself being hustled along towards a building larger than the rest through the entrance of which came and went many Cossack officers and soldiers.

At last he found himself inside this building, facing an officer who glared at him from behind a heavy desk. It struck dimly on his consciousness that he had seen this face before. The cruel, hawk-like features and angry eyes he vaguely remembered. Some dim memory came to him of that Cossack *Essaoul* whom he had seen first in the little village, ordering the execution of the young peasant. Then it dawned upon him that he was gazing upon the Red Cossack himself, Boris Nagoi, whose bloodthirsty activities had nearly laid waste the countryside. The officer was speaking to him and he heard the voice coming as though from a great distance.

"Dog!" the voice was saying, "What have you to say for yourself before I have you torn to pieces?"

The tangled cobwebs began to clear from Ryan's head, a hot anger at this insult began to well up in him. He attempted to speak but only mumbling, inarticulate sounds came from his lips.

"Speak, dog!" The words came out hissingly and the Red Cossack leaned forward and slapped him across the face. The sharpness of the blow cleared his head as if by magic.

"What talk is this of dogs?" answered Ryan steadily. "Free my hands and I'll soon show you how to still the yapping of an ill-bred cur!"

The Red Cossack stared at him spellbound and speechless for a second and then sat back in his seat, a reflective look in his eyes. But Ryan's voice went on indignantly.

"It is such swine as you that disgrace the profession of arms! None but a low bred imposter, a clown dressed in officer's uniform would strike an unarmed man. Unloose my hands!"

The words had a peculiar effect on Boris Nagoi. He had been an officer and some recalling of the officer's code had returned to him. His face flushed as he rose from his chair.

"Softly, softly!" he cautioned. "Your point is well taken. In my anger at the losses you have caused me I forgot myself for a moment. I will remember it when your time comes to die and will assure you a fitting death. But in the meantime I require you to tell me if it was you that attacked my *stanitza* near Paulovna, if it was you that attacked my third *sotnia*, if it was you that caused my second *sotnia* to fire into and massacre the band of partisans?"

"It was me," Ryan responded. "What are you going to do about it?"

"So-o-o," returned the Red Cossack, and nodded to himself, his eyes enigmatic, "that remains to be seen. But first you will tell me how you recruited your men and armed them, and where are they hiding now?"

"First, I will do nothing of the kind," Ryan snapped, "but I will ask you what you have done with my sergeant?"

"Oh, your sergeant! Meeler, is it not? I have him of course, as I have three other Americans and as I will seize every American sent to me. It remains to be seen how the Americans will die under the lashes of the *nagaika*. But you have not answered my question. I await your reply." The Red Cossack inclined his head, cocked one ear forward.

"And I will not answer your question," Ryan retorted crisply, "I demand the immediate release of myself and these American soldiers. I demand safe conduct to the American lines. Further than that I will have no dealings with you."

The Red Cossack gazed at him shrewdly. Evidently this defiance and this fearlessness of the man before him was a thing to which he was unaccustomed and he had the strong man's respect for the fearless.

"It is senseless to talk of demands," he replied. "I hold you in my power. Do you realize that every breath you take is a gift from me? Do you realize that your life is in the hollow of my hand? Do you realize that I have only to raise my hand and your life is snuffed out like a candle flame?"

"Raise your hand then and be damned to you!" returned Ryan promptly.

The Red Cossack shook his head.

 "NO," HE SAID, "I will defer that. We are sensible men, you and I, and leaders. The rabble will follow where we direct. It is my idea that you could be very useful to me. My officers are little better than the men. I have need of your technical knowledge. I offer you a chance for your life if you will join me, bringing your men and adding them to my forces. What do you think of that?"

"I think it is ridiculous," returned Ryan flatly.

"So!" responded the Red Cossack gravely, "maybe its ridiculousness will be less apparent after a little reflection. I will give you an hour to think it over. At the end of that hour one of your American soldiers, your Sergeant Meeler, will be flogged to death. In another half hour the next one will be flogged to death and the next until at last your turn comes to meet the same fate. That is all!"

He rose and beckoned to the guards who led Ryan out of the hall and down the street to a long, low iron barred building, before which a sentry paced up and down. As he was led in through the doorway he thought he heard Sergeant Miller's voice, but could not be sure. The Cossacks tramped before and behind him, leading him down the corridor until they came to a cell, a narrow affair dimly lighted by one heavily barred window. Thrusting him inside they locked the door and clumped up the corridor again where he heard them open another cell.

It was Sergeant Miller that they took out of this cell, Sergeant Miller did not know what form of death he was going to face but he prepared to face it bravely in whatever form it came. Unaware of the close proximity of his lieutenant, the sergeant was led out of the prison and escorted to the headquarters building where the Red Cossack held court.

Ryan looked about his cell and tested the heavy door and the strongly barred window. They were both hopelessly strong as a quick survey convinced him. From the window he could look out upon the open place and could see a portion of grassy parade ground. In the center of it was a heavy upright stake at the foot of which lay the huddled body of a man, his back and shoulders cut to ribbons by the *nagiaka*.

Ryan studied this sight a moment. So this was the fate that they held in store for Sergeant Miller should the American lieutenant not agree to ally himself with the Red Cossack? It was not a pleasant thing to contemplate, this pulpy, bloody form lying at the foot of the stake; and Ryan turned away from the window with something like nausea rising within him. His head still felt heavy and dull from the blow he had received and he wondered what treachery had led him into this mess. But there was only an hour left in which to solve the question and he began to reason out some method of escaping.

Down the corridor he heard the rattle of tinware. By peering through the bars of his door he could see the jailer going back and forth about his duties of feeding the prisoners and bringing them water. Ryan's cot was a crude affair made of saplings on which ropes had been tied and interlaced back and forth to form a mattress. His wrists were still sore from the ropes with which he had been bound, bindings which had only been cut as he was shoved into the cell. A close survey told him he was not observed, so he worked away at one of the ropes on the bed. At last he had it untied. He immediately fastened an end of it to one of the bed legs, attaching the other end to a small iron ring sunk in the wall. The rope was now stretched across just inside the door and only three or four inches above the floor. This arranged, he went to the door and shook it, calling loudly for the jailer in a high, excited voice.

"Make haste, I am dying!" he shouted in mock agony. The jailer hurried forward. As he placed the key in the lock, Ryan crouched in the far corner of the cell, bending over and groaning loudly as though in dire pain. The door was flung open and the jailer hurried across the threshold.

Chapter Twelve

NADINA'S BEDROOM

 RYAN CONTINUED to writhe and groan as the jailer came towards him. Then the man's foot collided with the rope stretched taut across the floor. It flung him forward on to his face. In that second Ryan struck savagely. Ryan whisked the man's revolver from his hand. Then he quickly gagged the unconscious jailer, listening meanwhile to the other footsteps hurrying along the passage. In a second he was out of the door, in time to face two Cossack sentries, their rifles at the trail. He leaped at the first, striking him fair and square on the point of his bearded chin. The man staggered backwards with a grunt, and fell into the man behind him. Ryan reached forward with the butt of his revolver and struck the second man heavily on the side of the head. He collapsed like a stricken animal. There seemed no one else in the corridor so Ryan hurried to the door, stood in the shadow and peered out. The sentry was still pacing back and forth along the length of the building. Evidently his attention had not been caught by the commotion inside. Two more Cossack soldiers sat nearby playing with a greasy deck of cards.

If Ryan were to get out of this place at all, he had to get out quickly. So he turned and ran again down the corridor where the two men he had knocked out lay still unconscious. He stooped over one and hastily ripped off the coat, then he put it on over his own, thereafter taking the man's black fur cap and putting it on his head. Next he seized the Cossack's rifle. Thus costumed he walked quietly to the door and shambled out.

The two Cossacks playing cards did not even look up as he passed. The sentry was walking the other way, his back to him.

Without increasing his shambling gait Ryan moved along towards the other corner of the building expecting any second to hear a shout or a challenge behind him. He had nearly reached the corner when the tramp of feet sounded in his ears and a Cossack officer and eight or ten men marched up to the doorway he had just left. Discovery was now only a matter of seconds and he rounded the corner of the building just as a shout went up from behind him.

Directly in front of him lay the parade ground with the stake and the body of the man who had been killed under the blows of the *nagiaka*. To cross that parade ground was out of the question, there were too many chances of discovery. To his left extended another building, longer and larger than the first and he walked rapidly in rear of it, moving towards the center of the camp. There was an open space and beyond that a small log house of five or six rooms and an upper floor. The yelling behind him had increased in volume and he could now hear the sound of running feet. He turned into an open door and found himself in a kitchen. The fire was going in the stove and water was boiling for tea but there was no one there.

The only sign of life was a powerfully built hunting dog which rose from under a table and wagged his tail in friendly fashion. Through a doorway in the opposite side he heard someone approaching the kitchen from the front part of the house and looked about for a means of escape. It was evidently a woman as he judged by the step and he feared that she might scream when she saw him standing there. Outside on the parade ground there was running and shouting and the Cossacks were pouring out of their barracks. A bugle blew from somewhere and he heard sharp commands as men assembled in ranks. The hunt was on without any doubt. The door opposite him opened and a young girl, whom he judged could not be more than eighteen or nineteen years, repressed a faint scream as she stood there, her hand raised to her throat in fright.

"I MEAN no harm," he said in Russian, "but I am in danger. Please do not betray me."

The girl continued to stare at him in fright, one hand placed on the portal behind her for support.

"Who—who are you?" she gasped.

"I am an American officer. My life is in danger. Help me, I beg of you!" He glanced behind him apprehensively and closed the outer door for hurrying footsteps sounded along the rear of the building. The girl, whom he took time to notice, was not a peasant girl but evidently the daughter of some officer, suddenly made up her mind. Womanly pity and perhaps, something attractive about this tall American had evidently decided her, for she let her hand drop from her throat and beckoned him to follow. Someone was knocking on the outer door and it swung open just as he passed into a small hallway that led to the front of the house. A steep stairway led up here to the upper floor. He heard voices in front, a heavy masculine voice which sounded familiar somehow and a quieter, feminine voice. Cautioning him to be silent, the girl ran nimbly up the stairway and he followed after, unconsciously admiring the trim grace of her and the lightness of her step. They arrived in an upper hallway from which four room doors opened. Into the nearest of these she led him, and a little flushed and breathless she was as she bade him remain there. Without another word she slipped out and closed the door behind her.

After looking about him he became immediately certain that it was into her own room that she had led him. For the trim single bed, the bureau covered with a few toilet articles, and some dresses hung against the wall, showed it to be the room of a young girl. While listening intently he heard the rumble of voices coming from below, so he stepped to the open window which looked out upon the next house. Little could be seen, but he heard parties of men moving about the *stanitza*, knocking loudly at doors and searching everywhere. From below stairs came the rumble of voices and he heard the girl's voice replying to questions. His heart almost stopped when he heard the tramp of feet coming up the staircase and he wondered, after all, if she had betrayed him. He slung his gaze over the room hastily and saw a small clothes closet in which were hung more dresses and a fur coat. He placed himself quickly behind these. The footsteps paused outside the door. It was opened slowly and the girl herself stepped backward into the room.

"You see," she said, "there is no one here. This is my room."

Ryan could hear the shuffle of feet followed by an awkward silence and he knew without seeing that his pursuers were gazing within the room. Evidently their scrutiny satisfied them for they made no effort to enter. The door was closed and the footsteps moved along to the next rooms. In a few minutes there was the tramp of feet going down the stairs again and the house became quiet. Not daring to move yet, Ryan listened to the excitement from outside, the yells and shouts of the men seeking for him and the tramp of many searching parties. Above the sound he heard the stentorian voice of the Red Cossack cursing out his men for their failure. Downstairs a door slammed in the front of the house and the heavy voice of the Red Cossack shouted through the place. There was a stir and movement below and then the voice stilled.

Minute after minute dragged by while Ryan listened for more sounds of the pursuit. It seemed to have drawn off into other parts of the camp. Again a door slammed downstairs and he heard the angry notes of the Red Cossack's voice as he shouted commands and curses in the street outside. Wondering what the Red Cossack was doing in this house he waited tense and breathless for new developments.

He had not long to wait until he heard a light step on the staircase which creaked under the weight of some person coming up from below. It was a cautious step and he could not tell whether it was friend or enemy but resolved to take no chances. He still had the revolver and the rifle he had taken from the Cossacks. Quietly he examined the revolver, and found it a heavy old fashioned weapon, loaded with six cartridges. The footsteps halted outside his door. The door swung open quietly and closed again. From his hiding place he could not see who had entered and did not dare disclose himself until he was certain whether it was friend or foe. Whoever it was approached his hiding place. A timid voice whispered.

"It is I, Nadina," came the whisper and he stepped out from his hiding place to look into the eyes of the young girl.

"Oh, it is terrible," she said. "They seek for you everywhere. The watches are doubled at the gates and extra sentinels put around all the walls with instructions to capture you, dead or alive. You must remain here and what shall I do?" She wrung her hands. "My father will be so angry."

"You have been wonderfully kind," Ryan gravely whispered, "but I have no desire to cause you trouble. I will leave immediately. . . ."

"No! no! no!" she shook her head emphatically and glanced at the door behind her. "You cannot leave! You will be killed instantly. Perhaps, after night, when it is dark, but not now. Never. It is of my father that I am afraid and of his anger."

"Who is your father?" asked Ryan.

"He is the *Essaoul* Saltikoff and the

second in command here," she answered.

"He is, of course, friendly with the Red Cossack?" Ryan asked.

The girl nodded slowly, lacing and interlacing her fingers.

"Yes and no," she replied. "He fears the Red Cossack. That terrible brute has him completely in his power." The girl's eyes flashed with indignation.

"You dislike the Red Cossack?"

"I loathe him," she said very bitterly, "and tomorrow I must marry him!"

"Marry him!" Ryan's voice expressed his surprise. "How—why—?"

"It is because my father fears him and it is to save my father's life."

Ryan digested this information in silence. But his musings were suddenly interrupted. A heavy step sounded in the hallway. There came a knock at the door.

Chapter Thirteen

A VOICE IN THE DARKNESS

 THE GIRL'S face turned white. Cautioning her to be silent Ryan stepped backward again into the shelter of the small closet.

"Who is it?" her voice quavered.

"It is me," rumbled a deep masculine voice and the door was flung open.

"Oh," Ryan heard the girl reply, "it is you, father. What do you wish?"

"I have just come from Boris Nagoi. He has given me fifteen minutes to find the escaped American. If I do not find him I am to be degraded and shot! The prisoner was last seen going in this house. Tell me Nadina, where are you hiding him? My life hangs in the balance!"

Ryan heard something like a gasp of dismay from the girl and then a silence, a silence which was broken at last by the father's voice.

"Time is flying, Nadina," the voice of her father rumbled through the small room.

Ryan was doing some swift thinking. The situation had reached an impasse. No man worthy of his salt could ask this girl to risk herself and her father. He drew in a deep breath and started to push aside the curtain when her voice again fell on his ears and he paused.

"Father, I don't know where he is," she said in a low voice. Ryan thrilled at the loyalty of her but his mind was made up. Pushing the curtain aside, he stepped out into the room. The girl gazed at him in consternation but his eyes were fixed on the man standing there, a tall, grey haired officer in a sweeping, wine-colored Cossack coat, with the silver and ivory cartridge cases across the chest and a curved, jewel handled sword slung at his belt. The eyes of the old Cossack officer regarded him gravely and without surprise.

"I am the man whom you seek," said Ryan. "And I have no desire to bring any trouble on this house. I will give myself up to the Red Cossack. Here are my weapons." He handed over his revolver and rifle.

The older officer clicked his heels together and bowed.

"That is generous of you," he stated. "I regret exceedingly that my chief sees fit to treat you so harshly."

Ryan glanced at the girl and found her eyes fixed on him inscrutibly, her face was pale and her hands were tightly clenched. Somehow he knew that she was close to the verge of tears and fighting hard for self-control. To avoid any scene he bowed gravely to her.

"You have been more than kind," he said, "I am trying to repay your goodness of heart in the only way possible to me." Then turning to her father he added, "if you are ready we will go."

Behind him he heard something like a stifled sob and then the measured footsteps of the old officer following. The two men went out the door. The Russian closed it softly behind him, and together they descended the stairs.

They came out at last in the street. A patrol of Cossacks spied them and a shout went up. The outcry was carried from group to group, and men came running from all directions. By the time they had reached the porch of the headquarters building the street was jammed with a crowd of Cossacks, pressing close to glimpse the escaped American for whom the search had been carried on.

As he stood waiting there on the porch, Ryan saw that a new band of partisans had arrived, nearly two hundred roughly clad men, armed with a variety of weapons including everything from Russian army rifles to old fashioned shot guns. Their leader was a pompous and throaty Commissar, dew-lapped like an ox, who strode back and forth importantly marshalling his forces. It came over Ryan that an overwhelming force was being concentrated here to march against the Americans, for, as nearly as he could estimate, there must be nearly a thousand Cossacks and Bolsheviki partisans in and around the *stanitza*. He thought of those small detachments of American soldiers thinly scattered along the line of the railway and his heart sank as he realized his helplessness to warn them.

Minute after minute passed and still he stood there, Nadina's father, the old Cossack officer at his side. Soon there came three Cossack soldiers armed with rifles, who fell in before and behind him. Their leader said something in a low tone to Saltikoff, Nadina's father, and mumbling an apology he hurried into the building leaving Ryan standing there under guard. The slow minutes dragged along. Cossack officers, Bolshevist Commissars, orderlies and messengers came and went. The headquarters building boiled with activity and it was plain to be seen that some movement was contemplated. After a few minutes the Cossack officer, Saltikoff returned, his face troubled.

"My chief refuses to see you," he said. "He has ordered that you be confined, that you and the other Americans be executed at daybreak!"

Ryan received this news without any trace of emotion.

"I am sorry," said Saltikoff and gave some orders to the Cossack soldiers. Then he bowed to Ryan as the soldiers shouldered their rifles and motioned to their prisoner to move out and march down the steps.

 HIS CAPTORS, however, did not lead him to the building where he had formerly been imprisoned but marched along past, the line of barracks until they came at last to a heavy square log building, rising up for two stories. A sentry marched around this building. The lower room was a sort of a guard room with an arms rack and several beds, upon which sat five or six Cossacks. A lieutenant came from a smaller room in the rear and received the prisoner.

Ryan was led up a narrow stairway to the second floor and placed in a small room at the corner of the building. After searching him, his captors went out, slamming the heavy door behind them and dropping a stout wooden bar into place on the outside.

The American officer wasted no time in studying his prison cell, but it took very little time to convince him of the hopelessness of trying to escape. The door was heavy and solid. The one window of the cell-like room was closed with three heavy wooden bars sunk deeply into the stout framework. Nothing but an axe could have loosened those bars. The room was furnished with a wooden cot, upon which was some musty straw and some thin cotton blankets.

Some two hours passed after he had entered the *stanitza* when night fell. It was dark on the roadway below the cell, but a faint reflection of light from the guard room glinted from the sentry's bayonet as he passed and repassed.

Ryan paced the floor of his cell until he grew tired and then sat on the edge of his cot, trying to figure out some plan of escape. The situation looked pretty hopeless. What had happened to his troop of men back there in the woods he did not know. He tried to reason out who it was that had dealt him the treacherous blow while he waited at the edge of the forest, and he could only conclude that it must have been the young Cossack *khorunji* whom he had befriended. He cursed himself for a fool for ever having trusted the fellow, and, as he recalled his many suspicious actions, he wondered how he could have been so blind. But that did not help matters now. The slow minutes that passed were remorselessly ticking away his life, for he was certain now that the Red Cossack would waste no more time upon him, but would have him executed at daylight as he had promised. He half wondered what had become of Sergeant Miller, but reasoned later that the Red Cossack had deferred his execution until tomorrow morning, and, that probably all the American prisoners would be executed together. From what he had seen of the excitement around headquarters, Boris

Nagoi was making ready to move out with his entire force to attack the Americans along the railway.

He found it impossible to sleep and after awhile rose and went to the window and listened to the various noises of the camp as they floated up to him. Directly below him the sentry walked back and forth. As he stood there idly watching the gleam of the man's bayonet as it passed and repassed the light from the guard room, he noticed a shadow flitting along the road. It came to a halt near the corner of the building and the sentry challenged. A feminine voice answered and Ryan became immediately alert when he recognized Nadina's soft voice. The sentry had relaxed and was leaning nonchalantly against the log wall below, talking to the girl. Her voice carried up to him clearly. She was talking gaily to the man who was replying in kind. But as Ryan listened he found something inexplicable in her words. It came over him suddenly that they were meant for his ears and he leaned forward, and listened intently to the conversation below.

Chapter Fourteen

THE DEATH WATCH

THE GAY quick tones of her voice floated up as she flirted with the sentry.

"Feodor Stepanovitch," she addressed him. "They must have a very important prisoner here if they put you on guard!"

Ryan heard the man's reply given in obviously pleased and flattered tones and heard him say somthing about the *American officer.*

"Oh, *that* one," replied the girl in

well simulated surprise. "But he is very dangerous! No wonder they put a brave man like you to guard him. Aren't you afraid that he will escape again?"

The sentry's voice rumbled again in boasting note as he swore that no prisoner could ever escape from him.

"And the poor man is up there," she asked and looked up at the window curiously. Ryan could see her upturned face, a blur of white in the darkness. Taking his handkerchief from his pocket he waved it once or twice through the bars.

"It is such a strong prison," she went on, "like the old tower in which they imprisoned the princess. Do you remember that old story, Feodor Stepanovitch? It was about the princess with the long and golden hair." Then she went on to tell the story of Rapunzell. "Rapunzell, Rapunzell let down your golden hair," she quoted, "Do you remember that? It is very lonely for you, poor Feodor Stepanovitch," she commisserated.

The sentry, flattered and delighted, twisted his mustaches and admitted that it was very lonely.

"And for me as well," said the girl. "There is no one in my house. Perhaps you will let me stay and talk to you, Feodor Stepanovitch?"

Ryan heard the man mumbling something which he could not understand, but the girl's clear voice soon enlightened him.

"You go off duty for two hours Feodor Stepanovitch? That is too bad. But I will come again and we will talk for I am very lonely."

There was a tramp of feet as the new sentry came to relieve the man on guard and Nadina disappeared into the shadows. Ryan heard her voice caressingly repeat the words, "in two hours I will return," and thrilled as he realized that it was to him she spoke. The man below swaggered back to the guard room, and twisted his mustaches vainly, highly

pleased with himself. Ryan sat again on the edge of his cot. The reference to the Rapunzell story could only mean one thing. She was asking him to lower a cord of some sort whereby she might send a saw or a weapon. He walked about his cell looking for something remotely resembling a piece of string but could find nothing. At last he came to the thin cotton blankets on his bed and his face lit up.

In a second he jerked off the topmost blanket and commenced to tear it into strips. In a few minutes he made himself a rope long enough to reach to the ground, and strong enough, if need be, to support his own weight. After testing it out, he coiled it in readiness by the window and paced the floor of his cell waiting for the two long hours to pass.

It must have been close to midnight, he estimated, when the guard was again changed below. A few minutes later he heard Nadina's voice again, talking to the delighted Feodor Stepanovitch who was all set for a pleasant flirtation.

Peering down through the window Ryan dimly made out the form of the girl, close to the wall below. She was engaged in animated conversation with Feodor whose back was towards the window.

Moving quietly, Ryan carefully dropped his blanket rope, sliding it out between the bars. The girl's keen eye must have seen it for she shifted about so as to have it behind her back. So dark was it that Ryan could not see what she was doing, but he felt the rope moving under his fingers as though something were being tied to it. Below there was a faint exclamation.

"No, no, Feodor Stepanovitch, you go too fast." He heard her say breathlessly, and heard the sounds of a faint struggle underneath as the soldier attempted to take the goods the gods provided. The faint scuffling went on below and Ryan took advantage of it to haul in his rope. There was something heavy at the end of it, which scraped and bumped on the face of the logs as he drew it up. But the amorous soldier was too intent on his own affairs to hear and at last the object, whatever it was, was just outside the bars.

Ryan reached forward and seized it, found it to be a short handled axe. He pulled it through the bars then stopped suddenly and listened.

There was a tramp of feet coming up the stairway outside and someone began to fumble with the bar on the door. Ryan whirled and began to work swiftly.

As the bar was removed from outside the door he untied the rope, bundled it up, leaped across the room, shoved the rope and axe under his remaining blanket, then sat down upon the bed, just as the door opened.

 THE JAILER entered, a revolver in one hand and a pan of food in the other. Behind him stood two Cossacks, carrying rifles with fixed bayonets. Certainly they were taking no chances on this dangerous prisoner. The jailer, a huge, red bearded man, advanced cautiously into the cell room, staring about him by the light of a lantern, held by one of the Cossacks at the door.

"None of your tricks now," he growled. "I have orders to shoot you down like a dog if you but raise a finger." Saying this he came farther into the room and advanced towards the bed where Ryan sat. It was evidently the man's intention to put the platter of food on the bed. The Cossack carrying the lantern came into the cell a few steps. Fearing every second that the hiding place of his axe and rope might be discovered, Ryan looked indifferently at the jailer, trying his best to show no sign of anxiety.

"But, my little pigeon," rumbled the jailer, "you are due to be cooked this time. Boris Nagoi will not wait for daylight to have you polished off. He sends for you in half an hour, you and your soldiers. Even now the executioner is making ready. He has commanded that you be watched until the guard comes for you. So, eat this, for it is your last meal on earth, and God have mercy on your soul!"

Ryan heard this news without a flicker of worry betraying itself upon his features, yet, his last hope of escape went crashing down. In half an hour—thirty minutes—he was to be led out and during those thirty minutes the guard would stand watch over him. Escape now seemed hopeless.

The jailer backed away after leaving the platter of food on the bed. It was a deep metal platter, containing steaming hot *borsch*, the inevitable Russian beet soup. With the jailer went one of the Cossack soldiers. The other lounged in the doorway which was left open. The lantern was left outside in the corridor and shone dimly in the room.

The sentry, a stupid looking Cossack, glared belligerently at the American seated on the bed. The footsteps of the retiring jailer and the other guard died down as they went down stairs. There was a burst of conversation as the door into the guard room below was opened, which quickly died as the door was shut again. The sentry in the doorway carried his rifle under his right arm, its muzzle and bayonet pointing into the room. The Russian and Ryan stared at each other. The Cossack hitched his shoulders about and then began to scratch with his free hand.

Ryan listened for sounds outside, but could hear nothing for the moment. Then he heard Nadina laughing and joking with the sentry. This somehow had the effect of cheering him up and he studied the sentry reflectively. It was plain to be seen that the Cossack had orders to shoot and to shoot to kill, for as he arose, the fellow raised his rifle threateningly, only to lower it again as Ryan stretched and yawned. Minute after minute passed while he waited for the Cossack to relax his vigilance, but the fellow continued to watch him alertly.

The odor of the steaming hot *borsch* assailed Ryan's nostrils and he picked it up and began to sip from the side of the bowl. As he placed it to his lips he noticed that the Cossack had turned his head slightly to listen to some sound outside. The door at the foot of the stairway had opened again and there was the steady clump of many feet ascending the steps.

This was undoubtedly the squad of soldiers coming to take him to the executioner. The footsteps mounted higher and higher. When Ryan figured that they must be half way up the steps, the sentry brought his rifle up and placed its butt on the floor.

Chapter Fifteen

THE EXECUTION CELLAR

SERGEANT MILLER sat in his cell in the main prison, waiting for the minutes to go by until he should be called again for the last time.

Like an old soldier he had grumbled at being led out once before and marched to the headquarters. Here he had stood around under guard for nearly three-quarters of an hour only to be sent back again to his cell. From

his guards he had gathered that Lieutenant Ryan was also a prisoner and that he had escaped. This news had given him a momentary hope, but this hope was soon dashed when his guards informed him that the American officer had been recaptured. Following up this statement was the announcement that all of the Americans were to be executed at dawn.

But now even that reprieve had been shortened for a later announcement informed him that he and his fellow Americans were to be executed in half an hour. The half hour was nearly up. He sat on the edge of his bunk resignedly and waited for the coming of the guard.

He had not long to wait. Even as he listened he heard the steady clump of men marching to command and heard a detachment of Cossacks halt outside the prison. There was an interchange of question and answer, then the sound of doors opening farther down the corridor. Those would be the other Americans, whom he had not seen as yet, but, whose voices he had heard. There was the clang of opening and shutting doors, the tramp of feet and the sound of men coming to his cell. He arose, his shoulders drooping slightly. It was a pretty tough break. If only the lieutenant had escaped there might be some hope, but with his officer a prisoner as well, and the nearest Americans fully forty miles away there was no chance.

A lantern flashed into his cell and he saw its light glinting from the bayonets of the guard—five or six Cossacks. The door was flung open and an officer beckoned him to come out.

Once outside the Cossack guard fell in before and behind him and he was marched through the doorway and out to the roadway where in the light of lanterns he saw two other American soldiers. They raised their heads as he came out.

"Hello Sergeant," said one, the taller of the two. "It looks like they're going to give us the works."

"A short life and a merry one," said the other, a freckled faced, red headed private, "That's what we get for goin' A. W. O. L. tryin' to find us a shot of hootch somewhere."

"What outfit are you guys from?" Sergeant Miller asked.

The taller started to reply when a Cossack officer struck him across the mouth with his open hand.

"You orey-eyed son-of-a-son-of-a," growled the tall soldier.

Before the Cossack officer knew what had happened the soldier drove his fist full into the face of the Russian and knocked him backward into a heap. The officer, cursing furiously, untangled himself from his sabre and spurs, drew his sword and rushed on the American. For a second things looked bad for the prisoner, but another officer, an older one, came into the circle of lantern light and shouted to him to desist. The first officer obeyed sullenly, and returned his sabre to its scabbard as the little column of guards and prisoners was set in motion.

Sergeant Miller looked about him for Ryan but could see no sign of him. Another prisoner was brought from the cells, this man a Russian. He could not have been more than twenty-five or twenty-six. His teeth chattered with fright as he was prodded along by his captors.

"Come on buddy, buck up and be a man," said one of the American soldiers.

"Yeah!" added the other, "take your medicine and say nothin' to nobody. It'll soon be over."

But the poor devil of a Russian, even if he understood them, which he very probably didn't, continued to tremble and shake so that he had to be half carried along by the Cossack guard. Their way led them towards headquarters, but instead of entering by the front they were led around to the side to a cellar entrance. Going down a few steps they found themselves in an underground basement room. Here they were halted.

Sergeant Miller looked about him, and saw another door that led out on the far side of the room. By this door stood a mean looking Cossack with a pock marked face. He was loading a revolver. As Sergeant Miller watched, the man slipped through the doorway into some deeper part of the cellar. Miller remembered now a favorite method of execution used by the Bolsheviki and saw in a flash what was intended. For rather than waste a volley on a prisoner about to be executed they sent the poor devil through an underground corridor, in which was stationed a man with a pistol, who blew out the back of the victim's head as he passed by.

Minute after minute passed as they stood there, prisoners and guards, until finally an officer came down the steps and glanced at his watch. The Cossack guards came to attention as he entered and the silence in the cellar became oppressive. The Cossack officer, an exceedingly sallow-faced man with burning eyes, glanced again and again at his watch and strided about impatiently. The officer grew more and more impatient. Finally he called one of the Cossack guard and gave him an order in a low tone. The man saluted and hurried up the staircase.

 SERGEANT MILLER gazed about him, studying the heavy, brutal faces of his guards— shaggy, bearded men with huge black fur hats, each of them armed with rifle and sword, with the bayonets gleaming dull red in the dim light of the lanterns.

The cellar was filled with cobwebs and the sergeant found himself idly wondering over the fact that those insignificant insects, the s p i d e r s, would be busily spinning their webs fifteen or twenty minutes hence, just as though several lives had not been snuffed out in their immediate vicinity.

Grotesque shadows leaped and wavered on the walls of the cellar as men moved the lanterns about. The two other Americans stood near him. When glancing at them Miller found a little thrill of pride go coursing through him, for they showed so little fear in the face of certain death. The poor devil of a Russian who was wild eyed and staring, was leaning weakly against the wall, with a look of unutterable horror on his face. The Cossack officer glanced about him impatiently.

Finally he snapped shut the lid of his watch and barked forth a command, pointed at the Russian prisoner at the same time. Two Cossacks jumped to the side of the poor devil and swiftly bound his hands behind him. The man shrieked and sagged. Oblivious to his terror they finished their task and hauled him to his feet.

What followed was an unpleasant thing to watch, for the poor devil shrieked like a woman and grovelled at the feet of his captors. Once he broke away from them and pleaded with the officer who eyed him incuriously as some scientist might eye an insect that feebly struggled as he was about to impale it.

But the outcry of the wretched man availed him nothing but more abuse. The two burly Cossack guards heaved him to his feet and half dragged, half carried him towards that small door, a veritable portal of death. Once arrived in front of it they shoved him inside, one of them with fixed bayonet stabbed him in the seat of the pants as he tottered into the gloom.

A tense silence fell over the cellar.

Miller found himself listening in a detached sort of way as though he were watching some scene in the theatre. The slow and dragging footsteps of the Russian could be heard as he tottered forward into the darkness of the passageway. Then the footsteps ceased and Miller could visualize the man crouching against the wall, with his arms over his head in a futile attempt to fend off the death that awaited him so inexorably. One minute after another dragged by and still there was no sound. The officer looked up impatiently and made a quick stride towards the doorway. The guards stirred and muttered uneasily. Miller heard one of the Americans near him grumble to himself:

"I wish to hell they'd get it over with!"

At that second there came a single muffled shot. It was followed in a few seconds by a dull thud as of a sack of grain heaved into a corner. A sigh went up from the guards and prisoners in the cellar. Some of the Cossacks crossed themselves in the Russian fashion.

The officer glanced at his watch again and looked up the staircase for the return of his messenger. Again he snapped his watch shut and barked out a command, this time pointing to Sergeant Miller. Two Cossacks, one carrying a cord to bind his hands, started for Miller.

Chapter Sixteen

AN INTERRUPTED EXECUTION

 LIEUTENANT RYAN, with the bowl of hot *borsch* raised to his lips, held it suspended there as the heavy, fateful, tread

of booted feet advanced up the stairway to the corridor outside his room. The sentry had lowered the butt of his rifle to the ground and stood with his face half averted, listening to the approaching guard.

Ryan glanced at the window. His roving gaze took in the lump on the bed which marked the hiding place of his axe and rope. In another few seconds the guards would be upon him and all hope of escape would be lost. There was one desperate chance, a chance that he must seize instantly.

He raised the steaming bowl of *borsch* above his head and flung the contents full in the face of the sentry. Blinded for a second the man staggered backward. Ryan was on him like a tiger. With one terrific blow of his fist he completed the downfall of the sentry, who fell into the hall as his rifle clattered to the floor.

Grasping this, Ryan raised it just as the guard reached the top of the stairs and began to advance along the hall. Twisting the unfamiliar bolt, Ryan assured himself that the rifle was loaded. Then he stepped out into the hall and fired point blank into the first of the advancing guards.

The roar of the explosion filled the little hallway. The lantern of the leading man dropped to the ground and sputtered out. A terrified yell went up from the men in the darkness. Ryan fired another shot into them at random and there was a hasty rush to the staircase, men falling over themselves in the darkness to get out of the way.

There was a vast commotion below stairs and much shouting. Ryan did not waste a second. He leaped for the bed with his rifle in the left hand, seized the axe in his right and sped to the window.

The blade was razor sharp and cut easily into the heavy wooden bar. The first bar was chopped out and

he threw the piece into the room. The clamor and shouting downstairs still continued but he thought he heard cautious footsteps in the hallway.

Ceasing his labors for a moment, he hurried again to the door and fired two shots towards the head of the staircase. He had acted well, for again there was a rush of feet and the thud of a falling body. In the temporary respite thus gained he hurried back to his window and attacked the second bar. A few strokes broke it away from its base and he chopped at the top part, listening between blows for a renewal of the attack.

Outside, the alarm must have been given for he heard a yell go up from the camp and a bugle blew somewhere. Undeterred by this he continued his chopping until the second bar came away in his hands.

There was now room for him to squeeze through, so working very swiftly he tied the rope to the third bar and dropped it out of the window. There seemed to be no one below, but again he heard a sound in the hallway and decided to protect his rear before trying to go through the window.

This time he fired two shots and emptied his gun. But again he scored a hit. And again he heard the quick retreat of his attackers. Taking advantage of this lull he hurried to the window and glanced out before starting to make his escape. As he looked down the sentry came around the corner of the building and stood beneath, a black shadow with a faint gleam of light showing from his bayonet tip.

Behind him he heard the creak of the stairs and the slow and cautious approach of many men. In front of him was the open window with the sentry waiting below. He had his choice of two evils.

He could hear the scrape and creak

of bodies now at the top of the stairs. Picking up his rifle from where he had leaned it against the wall he hurried to the window with it. Here he raised it, butt foremost, knowing full well that the sentinel below could not see him.

Then he leaned forward and crashed the heavy rifle down into the darkness with all the strength he could muster. The butt smashed into the face of the man below, who dropped as though he had been shot. Then flinging his axe out of the window, Ryan raised himself and shoved his feet through the opening.

As he balanced there for a second on the window sill, the roar of a revolver crashed behind him, and a bullet spattered into the wall not three inches above his head.

Grasping the rope with both hands he flung himself down. Half way down he let go and landed on his feet with a jar, not two inches from the prone body of the sentry.

A rifle cracked above his head but the bullet thudded into the sentry instead. Ryan leaped across the roadway into the shadow of a building just as men began to pour out of the guard room.

"Thank God you are here!" a voice breathed out of the darkness. Nadina grasped his hand and ran ahead of him, keeping in the shadows of the building. The whole camp was in an uproar. Lights flashed here and there. Several Cossacks went by them in the darkness. Ryan noticed that Nadina was leading him towards the gate.

HE CAME to a sudden stop in the shadow of a barracks.

"Where is my sergeant?" he asked.

"Oh, there is no time for that. I am afraid you are too late. I saw him marched to the execution cellars many, many minutes ago."

"Where are those cellars?" Ryan asked.

"Under Nagoi's headquarters," she breathed. Without another word he turned, still retaining the grasp of her hand and hurried back towards the center of the camp.

Dressed as he was, in Cossack coat, it was easy to pass through the excited and running gangs of men they met, so he slowed down and walked very sedately with Nadina at his side. As they moved towards the headquarters building she took a revolver from her blouse and pressed it into his hand.

The feel of cold steel in his hands brought him renewed courage and he strode past the headquarters, where seven or eight horses were tethered, then around the corner where Nadina led him to the entrance to the cellar. After cautioning her to remain above stairs he started down the steps.

Halfway down the steps he saw the guards. Two more downward steps and he saw the interior of the cellar. His startled eyes took in the sight of Sergeant Miller with two Cossack guards about to bind his hands behind him.

"Attention!" Ryan shouted. His voice reverberated through the cellar.

"The first man that moves dies. Throw up your hands!"

The startled inmates of the cellar turned towards him like one man. The Cossacks stared open-mouthed at this apparition of the American with his deadly cold eyes and the deadly gleam of that revolver which seemed pointed at each one of them. Sergeant Miller was the first to break the spell. He very calmly slugged the nearest guard.

"Holy smoke!" shouted the tall soldier, and followed his example with another guard. The sallow-faced officer in the middle of the cellar was the first Russian to recover his presence of mind. His hand dropped to his pistol holster and he turned, snarling at the intruder. It was the last gesture he ever made for Ryan drilled him neatly through the chest with one emphatic slug of his revolver.

"Get that fellow's pistol, Sergeant Miller! Grab a couple of rifles you two!" he pointed to the soldiers, "Get up here. Make it snappy."

The words were scarcely out of his mouth before the three Americans came surging up the stairway.

"Get five horses in front of that house! Put the girl outside there on one of them! Bring me one! I'll hold this gang until you are in the saddle!"

The three brushed by him without a word. Ryan stood there, his revolver ver carelessly resting on his left arm as he stood sideways on the staircase, watching the Russians and listening for the return of his men and their horses. It seemed an eternity before he heard the trample of horses' hooves behind him, but it was actually only one or two minutes. Then backing up the staircase, he closed the heavy door of the cellar and dropped the bar into place over it, after which he leaped for the saddled horse awaiting him. Scarcely waiting to put foot into stirrup he led the little group through the darkness towards the main gate.

Chapter Seventeen

ALLIES

AS THEY galloped through the darkness behind the row of barracks they heard yells coming from the building they had just left and lights flashed through the *stanitza*.

"We'll make for the main gate," said Ryan to Nadina, who galloped quietly beside him.

As they neared the gate a squad of horsemen came out of a side road in front of them and made for the same place. Ryan kept up an easy gallop behind them, keeping some fifty or seventy-five yards in the rear.

"They have strict orders to watch for you at the gates!" cautioned Nadina.

"So much the better," returned Ryan briefly and loosened his revolver from his belt.

He swept up to the gates just as the sentinel on duty was preparing to close them again.

"Out of my way, dog!" Ryan shouted. "You have just let the Americans escape through here! Send back the word that we are pursuing!"

The startled sentry did as he was ordered, not even looking up in the gloom. Men began to tumble out of the guard house at the gate just as Ryan and Nadina, followed by the three soldiers, galloped through. Behind them all was noise and confusion. The *stanitza* buzzed like a hornet's nest. Before them was the calm and quiet of the forest.

Ryan followed the main road and headed for that point where he had withdrawn his troop into the forest. The five riders soon crossed the open space and were galloping along in the gloom of the woods.

As they swept around a turn there was a shout and a flash of steel.

Ryan drew his horse down on its haunches. The man in the rear jammed into him, so sudden was his halt. He felt rather than saw a solid block of horsemen in front of him, filling the roadway. The point of a sword came out of the darkness and was thrust against his chest.

"Who and what are you?" asked a voice.

It was the voice of the Cossack *khorunji*, Kardoff; the man whom he had befriended—the man whom he thought was responsible for his capture.

"It is me, the American officer,"

"Thank God for that! I was on my way to atempt your rescue."

"But—why—I thought—" Ryan stuttered, nonplussed.

"You thought I was a traitor," returned Kardoff simply, "but I was not. I killed the real traitor—"

"That is splendid," interrupted Ryan. "Is the entire troop here? It is? Splendid! I want to go back and get the Red Cossack!"

He turned his horse about and a subdued cheer went up from the men behind him. He gave the order to march after telling Nadina to wait at the edge of the woods. She obeyed dutifully enough and he put his troop at a gallop.

They swept up to the gate with a clatter and rattle. Kardoff boldly demanded admittance. The gates were opened without question and the *sotnia* of horsemen, lance pennons streaming, surged up the main street of the *stanitza*. They drew up in front of headquarters.

Dismounting swiftly, Ryan called a squad of his men and strode into the building. He swept in and came to the far end where he kicked open a door and found himself face to face with Boris Nagoi, the Red Cossack.

"You're coming with me," Ryan rasped. "Oh, no you don't!" He leaped forward just as the Red Cossack reached for his revolver. There was the thud of fist against flesh, a startled grunt from Nagoi. A surge of men from behind Ryan seized the startled Cossack chieftain and bound him, stifled his outcries.

Swiftly and silently they hustled him back to the horses and threw him across the saddle. As Ryan started out two of his men brought in to him a tall and familiar figure. It was Saltikoff, Nadina's father.

"You are now in command," said Ryan. "The Red Cossack is finished.

Report to me at the railroad with your forces. And you must promise to cooperate with the Americans. I am taking Nadina with me."

Saltikoff turned pale.

"You will not harm her?" he asked anxiously.

"Certainly I will not harm her," he retorted brusquely. "It happens that I love her." And with that he was out and into the saddle.

It was not until his troop was some five *versts* beyond the place that they had halted in the forest that he lifted Nadina tenderly down from the saddle.

Kardoff came up to me.

"Come with me," he said, and led Ryan down the column to where the Red Cossack lay across the saddle. But there was something limp and shapeless about the form of the man. Closer view showed that his throat had been cut from ear to ear.

"Who did this thing? Who has been doing these murders? Who is the traitor who knocked me unconscious?" demanded Ryan.

"It is easily explained," Kardoff shrugged his shoulders. "Your man, Ivan, the non-commissioned officer, whom you trusted was a spy of the Red Cossack's. There were other spies in the troop. Ivan did not meet his fate until after the others were killed. He was the one who struck you from behind. He lived exactly ten minutes after that."

"But who killed or executed all these men? Who cut all these throats?"

Again Kardoff shrugged his shoulders.

"Someone who had your interests at heart," he replied cryptically, and walked away without further word.

And thus it was that the Red Cossack passed out on the eve of his wedding, and thus it was that this section of the Ussuri Cossacks under their sub Ataman, Saltikoff, became firm allies of the Americans.

Eastward Ho!

The Reader's Own Department

Conducted by the Editor

This is the fifth issue of FAR EAST Adventure Stories to reach your hands. And each successive issue from the first has shown an increased circulation, but even so, we have not enough readers yet.

FAR EAST Adventure Stories is one of the most costly magazines in the men's fiction field and our production cost is as high as many established magazines that have been before the public for a decade or so. The authors who appear regularly every month in FAR EAST Adventure Stories are among the highest paid authors in America, and the artists likewise. Because of our efforts to give the reader absolutely the best men's magazine that it is possible to produce, we are entering the new year with a substantial deficit staring us in the face, and cannot continue for many more months unless we secure the whole-hearted cooperation of every present reader of the magazine.

If each reader who likes the present and past issues of the magazine will take it upon himself to see that at least one, or possibly more, of his friends and acquaintances purchase a copy from the newsstands, this deficit will be wiped out in a single month and you will be assured of having the pleasure afforded in the reading of FAR EAST Adventure Stories continue throughout the year.

We ask you individually, as readers who have enjoyed the magazine as it has been presented to you, to do this. If each one of you who enjoy the book, assume this request as a personal responsibility, noth-ing, not even the falling stock market and the unemployment situation, will prevent us from carrying on.

JOHN SOLOMON

With this issue we are beginning a new serial by H. Bedford-Jones. GOLD OF ISHMAEL is this famous writer's latest complete book-length novel. And the editors of FAR EAST Adventures Stories consider themselves very fortunate in being able to present this engrossing novel in serial form to the reading public.

John Solomon, the inimitable Cockney who is the hero of this story, is one of America's most famous fiction characters. For over twenty years his exploits throughout the world have furnished amusement and entertainment to millions of readers.

This latest story, GOLD OF ISHMAEL, finds John Solomon involved in altering the destiny of the Moorish countries on the south shores of the Mediterranean. His method of doing so furnishes material for one of the most interesting novels that has ever run in serial form in any magazine in America.

As this serial will later appear in book form, after it has run in FAR EAST Adventure Stories, this is another reason why you readers who are interested in having FAR EAST Adventure Stories come to you once a month regularly, should prevail upon your friends and acquaintances to buy copies of the current issue from the newsstands.

And from now on this famous character, John Solomon, will first appear ex-
clusively in the pages of FAR EAST Adventure Stories. Mr. H. Bedford-Jones, John
Solomon's creator, has   supreme faith in
the future of FAR EAST Adventure
Stories, or he would never have allowed us
to begin this John Solomon serial. If the
present readers have as much faith as the
author, this will be but the beginning of
many such serials in which John Solomon
shapes and alters the destinies of many
countries in the Far and Near East.

SERGEANT SMITH VISITS US AGAIN

Ever so often Sergeant Herbert E.
Smith comes in from Governor's Island to
call on us, and we immediately break out
the box of five cents cigars and get Smith
started on spinning yarns. Smith writes
a pretty good tale and we asked him,
among other things, what his methods were.

"Well," he said, and used five good
matches in getting our five cent cigar to
functioning. "The 'Old Timer' who spins
my yarns is a real character, although his
name is not Harvey Long. I don't really
write these stories I sell you. I just listen
to this 'Old Timer' spin his stuff and I
take it down in shorthand on my cuff.
When I get back to the office I pound
it off on the typewriter and that's the
story. I get the checks and cash them,
and the 'Old Timer' is lucky if he gets
more than three or four treats out of it,
but then, it is my contention that anybody
can write a story but it takes a good man to
sell one, so I think we are about even,
because the 'Old Timer' would never stir
off his ankles long enough to call on editors or pound typewriters."

Smith's story sounded good, but I told
him, "That's all well and good, but even
so, you've got to know something about
the subject on which you are writing. You
can't get it all second handed."

"Maybe so," he came back, "but service
men who have pulled a tour of tropical
service with the 31st Infantry in the Islands
usually know a little about soldiering in
the Far East.

"Soldering in the Philippines is great
stuff and I hope to go back for another
tour in and about Manila some day. I have
had two tours out there already in addi-

tion to seeing a bit of action in Polar
Bear Land with the A. E. F. Siberia, that
expedition about which so little has ever
been told. I have also seen quite a bit
of China and was a member of the picked
platoon of doughboys which was rushed
from Manila to Yokohoma in September,
1923, to the relief of the Japanese victims
of the big tidal wave and fire.

"The East wears an inscrutable mask.
That is its most potent appeal for we
Yanks, I reckon. I believe it is about the
only country left where a white man can
find adventure without looking for it."

"All well and good," I said to him.
"But you haven't told me yet what our
readers would like to know. Give me a
little personal stuff. How old are you
and how many wives have you, etc.?"

"Personal stuff, huh," he came back
and fell to chewing the cigar now. "Well,
I'm twenty-nine, still a Regular and proud
of it. Also a confirmed pipe smoker."
Smith tossed the cigar in the cuspidor.
"Am fond of a pot of beer now and then,
also football, baseball and ice hockey. And
I worship at the short story shrine of O.
Henry. I have been knocking out fiction
yarns but a short time myself and am still
in the struggling author stage, as I reckon
your readers have discovered. As hobbies,
well, put down: firearms, camplife, horses,
dogs, and the call of the East—which you
probably know is 'Boy, another round!'—
for there ain't no Eighteenth Amendment
out there."

The Sergeant left before I could check up
on his matrimonial affiliations, but I'll try
to get him to spin that yarn next time.

NEW AUTHOR'S CORNER

This month we publish the third of our
new author's yarns, THE MAN FROM
SUVA, by Tom Camden.

This department has worked out as we
thought it would, proving to be one of the
most interesting features in our magazine.
And even though these authors are new
in the business of writing stories, many
of the readers have written in and stated
that they enjoyed the new author's yarn
as well as any other in the book. Mr. Tom
Camden, the author of THE MAN FROM
SUVA, is the first of these new authors
who has received any instructions in short
story writing. He is a student at the

Palmer Institute of Authorship in Hollywood, California.

Judging from the story he has turned in to us, we will admit that they do a good job of instructing out there in the village where the movies are made, but if Tom Camden wants to hit us again he will have to go into competition with all the well-known writers who fill our pages now, for he is no longer eligible for the New Author's Corner. I am writing this here as sort of a challenge to Tom to try us again just to see what he can do in open competition with such writers as H. Bedford-Jones, Theodore Roscoe, J. Allan Dunn, Malcolm Wheeler Nicholson and others who have been writing stories for years.

ONE ON THE BUTTON

Editor FAR EAST:
Dear Sir:
Have just gone through you third issue and have found the address of your office. Missed out on the previous number. You ask for criticisms. First, I'd say you've got some good material mingled with some awful slush like RED RUNNING WATERS and THE LAST OF THE GUGUS. As for D'Arcy's spasm, it's just punk, but I judge that Ace Williams served in the Islands so long ago that his memory of affairs is a bit mazy. He should be more careful for some of us old timers are familiar with his period, locale, and military technique.

J. Allan Dunn at times is brilliant and in his POACHERS OF PIRATU has done well. Roscoe, whom I know, averages high enough in his FANGS OF ASIA. As for "Tubby" Burk's PHANTOM SAMPAN I okeyed that, but others I know don't like it. Why, I don't know. The rest of the contents seem good.

As for make-up—well, you know how it looks. Not so hot. But I'm mighty glad somebody has the guts to start a FAR EAST book in the face of all the maudlin Westerns. Gosh, how I hate Westerns! Except, of course, the really big stuff.

And boy—you need fillers. And a department. Your book looks bare as is. And now, who the hell am I.

Just an old stiff of fifty who put in twenty-five hectic years in the Far East. Military Intelligence and Customs Secret Service. Also a prospector, explorer, trader, sailor—Gawd knows what—but all the time a newspaper man. Don't get excited. I'm a bum fictionist, although I have peddled a few yarns here and there. Expert on tropical stuff, East and West Indies, firearms, etc. Have been in the States lately. But last April I heard a steamer whistle and I shoved off.

Yeah, the old stuff. Cuba, Haiti, Santo Domingo (during cyclone), Porto Rico and the Virgins. Color features BOSTON SUNDAY POST, travel articles NEW YORK TRIBUNE, etc. Bunch o' West Indian fillers to ADVENTURE and ARGOSY. Now Senor, can you use fillers of various lengths or adventure fact articles, and if so what do you pay—and when? Drop me a line if you think it's worth while. Expect to blow into New York before many moons if publishers checks come through as hoped for, but right now would like to slum you up. Far East is my meat. I breathe it—love it. Some day I'll go east of Suez to croak.

Yours,
C. A. FREEMAN,
St. Thomas,
Virgin Islands.

This fellow burned us a little, but we bought an article from him that will appear in an early issue. If any of you readers see where he has missed out on anything— I'll be tickled to death to throw the bombshell at him—just to make it fifty-fifty.

IT ISN'T IMPOSSIBLE

Dear Sir:
An entire issue by H. Bedford-Jones! What do I think of it. I don't think, I know, it would be impossible but if you can do it, boy what a hit. It should go over big. I'd gladly pay fifty cents or more for a copy, and I ain't the only one.

Here's hoping and wishing you a world of success.

A. MOHR,
Chicago, Ill.
P. S.—Your authors sure are great. Jones, Burks and Roscoe are favorites of mine.

FROM AN INVALID

Gentlemen:
The November issue is the first number of your FAR EAST magazine to fall into my appreciative hands. I am a shut-in, have been bed-fast from arthritis for ten years. Was all for the wide open spaces, too. So, your kind of stories come the nearest to making me forget the pains. Of all the magazines I take, Adventure holds first place, and Short Stories second, and now, FAR EAST is claiming third. Can you supply me with the back numbers, or how many? As I understand it there would only be the September and October numbers.

Kindly oblige,
Very sincerely,
L. M. RODABAUGH,
Los Angeles, Calif.

WANTS A STORY OF THE TROGLYDYTES

Gentlemen:
Much too short was H. Bedford-Jones' account of the semi-human beings who live in the dark on the desert as described in

Chapter One of SATAN'S WELL. A story about them would be mighty interesting written in his own way. SATAN'S WELL was a great yarn. FAR EAST Adventure Stories should soon become the "best seller."

Sincerely,
GEO. C. MACK,
New York City.

FROM THE HEAD OF A FAMILY

My dear Mr. Bamber:

I like your magazine very much, except the verses. Those pages might be used for short stories.

I bought this first copy because of seeing the name of H. Bedford-Jones, whom I started reading way back befo'-de-war in the Blue Book. Do you recollect his Far Eastern stories of the cockney Englishman Solomon?

Theodore Roscoe I also know well and delight to read. I read every single story—simply great.

An entire issue of Bedford-Jones would be good stirring reading, of course, but I am sure we readers would like all the different good writers you can find.

We have Western story magazines galore and we out West here know all about that "ridin'-ropin'" idea and the nearest we get to the Far East in Sax-Rohmer.

This family of young men and myself hope you will continue with FAR EAST Adventure Stories.

By the way, why don't you print your address in a prominent spot in the magazine? I had to ring up the Central News Agency here to get the correct address—

great oversight.

Best wishes and hopes for a successful future.

Very sincerely,
MRS. E. B. PRETTYMAN,
Los Angeles, Calif.

FROM A YOUNG BOOSTER

Dear Mr. Bamber:

Who says your magazine is not the best on the newsstand; let me at them. I have read three issues of the FAR EAST magazine and all the stories are *great*. The only thing I don't like about your magazine is it's not a weekly.

I am a fellow of eighteen who craves action and someday hope to see the Far East.

Yours truly,
HARLAN HUTCHINSON.
Uvalde, Texas.

LAST MONTH'S GUESSING CONTEST

Last month we started a little fun by having the readers guess which one of the stories in our January issue was written by a woman. We have had hundreds of answers so far, and only one of them has been correct. There are still two prizes left and the contest will be held over for another month until winners are announced.

WALLACE R. BAMBER.

I LIKE STORIES BY THE FOLLOWING AUTHORS:

. . . .
. . . .
. . . .
. . . .
. . . .

Name . . . .
Address . . . .

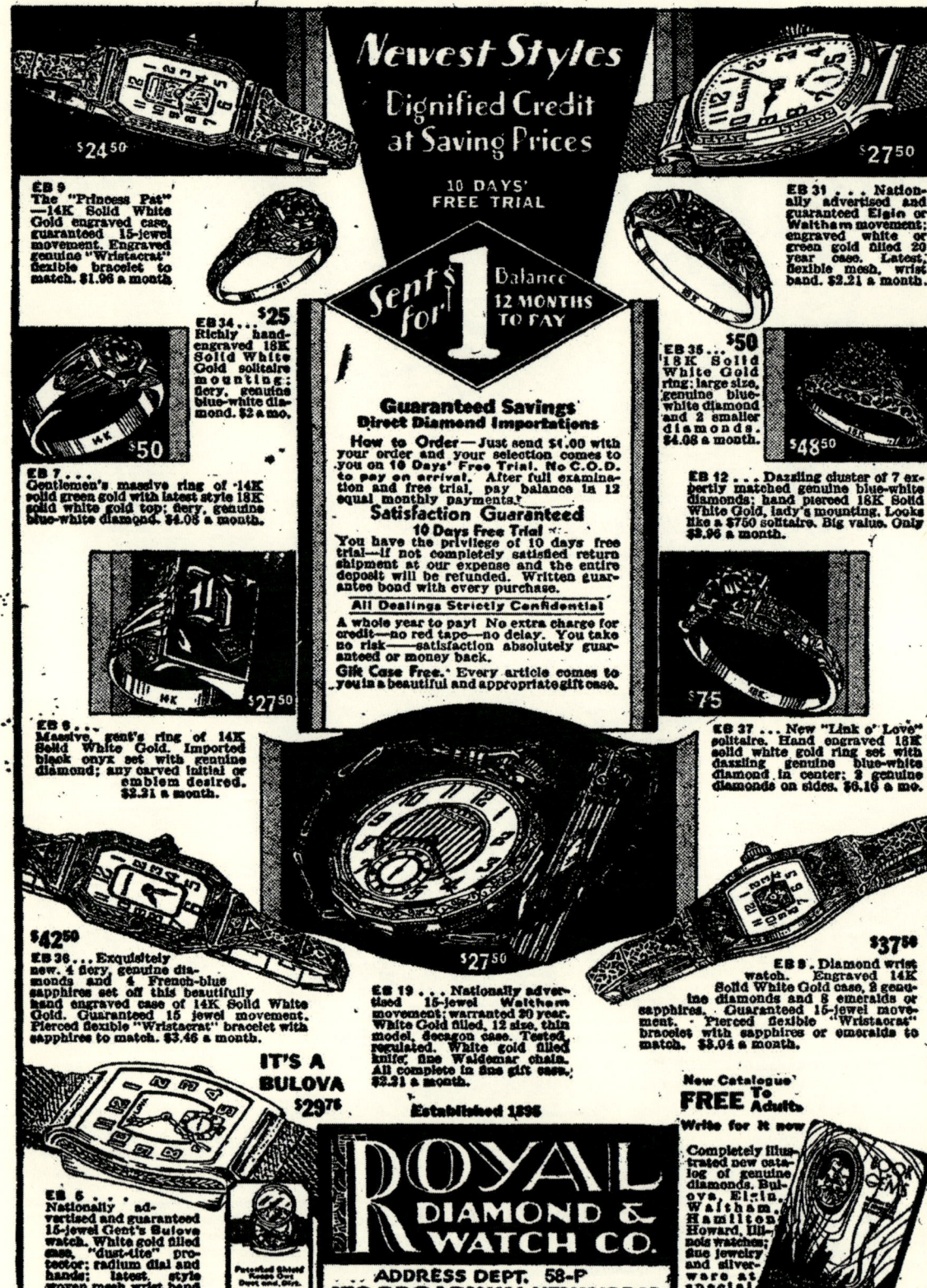